EXPOSE

BOOK 8 BEYOND THE THAW

TAMAR SLOAN
HEIDI CATHERINE

SEQUEL HOUSE

LUCA

*L*uca struggles as he fights the layers of darkness that don't seem willing to let him go. He grapples for consciousness, some part of him knowing it's important he do so.

There's danger…

Something he needs to remember.

Mercy.

Luca listens for her, only to find nothing. He draws in a deep breath, and his lungs fill with little but the scent of dust and smoke.

Sweet Terra, he's in the Round House!

He shoves himself up off the dirt as reality hits him like a slap. They were trying to destroy the sap, but the statue of Ronan was knocked over.

Then Corbin was there, with Raiden. And Grace.

I'm sorry. Had to leave you. I hope you find me one day. My name is Grace.

He told her what he learned before someone knocked him unconscious.

Looking around, Luca blinks furiously, trying to bring his

surroundings into focus. They swim and smudge, a haze of shadows and smoke. Finally, he makes out a form.

Grace.

His mother.

The Commander.

She's standing by the statue, which is once again upright. Her hands are clasped tightly, her spine ramrod straight. Her gaze doesn't leave him, as if she's been watching him the whole time he was out.

Luca pushes himself to a sitting position, then leans back against the bench seat lining the wall. "Where are Mercy and the others?" he croaks. It doesn't matter who Grace is, he needs to know they're safe.

Grace seems to be barely breathing. "I had a feeling that would be the first thing you'd ask. You weren't raised in the Outlands, obviously."

"Where are they?" Luca growls, wanting to press his hands to his pounding head but not willing to show any weakness.

"Not dead, if that's what you're worried about. They're being held in a hut nearby."

So, Grace wanted to talk to him. Alone.

She takes a small step forward. "Tell me how you came to be here."

Although the words are a demand, Luca swears he hears Grace's voice tremble. His gut clenches, feeling like it's suddenly full of rocks. She's not asking about their boat trip.

Or the one before when they first arrived as Seekers.

"I was found as a baby in Fairbanks by a woman who established a colony for misfits and orphans." Luca never questioned that he fit right in. "She raised me."

Grace doesn't twitch a muscle, although it's obvious she's listening intently.

"When I was five, others came from Askala. I went back with them." Luca watches her closely. "They became my family."

Kian and Nova loved him unconditionally. They were the parents he'd never allowed himself to dream of. People like him didn't have parents like that, siblings like Sam and Seb...everything they could ever have wished for.

Leaving them was the stupidest decision he ever made.

Grace nods infinitesimally. "I see."

Luca frowns. "That's all you have to say? I see?"

"There's nothing else to say," she snaps.

Luca struggles to stand, only his head whirls the moment he moves. He collapses onto the bench behind him, nausea weaving its way up his throat. "Why?" he half-whispers as he looks up and pins her with his gaze. "Why did you leave me?"

Grace's arms wrap around her middle, looking like she's trying not to double over. "I didn't. I'm not your mother, Luca."

Luca's about to speak but she holds up her hand.

"I was six years old when you were born. Grace isn't the name I was born with."

"But Raiden and Charity—"

"Are Corbin's children." Her arms tighten around her waist. "Your mother died a long time ago."

For some reason, her voice cracks on the final statement.

Silent and still as he tries to process this, Luca watches Grace in the gloom. She doesn't flinch, doesn't look away. In fact, her chin lifts an inch, the pale light gliding over her smooth skin.

She's telling the truth.

Luca doesn't know if he's elated or devastated. Learning that his mother's name was Grace had thrown his world upside down. But at least the note said she was sorry. That she wanted him to find her. Even if he'd thought Grace was the Commander's wife at the time.

But his mother is dead. He always suspected she was, but hearing the words makes it final. All he feels is...hollow.

In fact, he's not sure whether losing the tenuous link to the woman standing before him hurts more. Knowing he could be her son had given him hope they could stop the invasion of Askala...

But Grace isn't his mother. Nor is she the Commander's wife.

She *is* the Commander.

Pushing up to his feet, Luca pretends his surroundings aren't spinning. He needs to stay focused. He needs to get as many answers as he can. And Grace is still holding back information. "You knew her, didn't you? You knew my mother."

Grace's lashes flicker. "She told me you were dead."

The words slash at Luca's heart so viciously that he involuntarily gasps. "Who—"

But she waves a dismissive hand. "That was my old life. I have more important things to focus on."

The greatest threat Askala has ever seen.

"Because you're the Commander."

Grace lifts her chin. "Yes. I united the Outlands." She glares at him fiercely. "Against our common enemy."

Luca's hands clench. "What you're doing is wrong. Too many people are going to lose their lives."

"Hundreds already have," Grace snaps. "Probably thousands. And Askala has done nothing to help every starving, desperate soul!"

"Askala's shores were never closed to you." Askala was Luca's saving grace. Without it, his trajectory would've been very different. He blinks. His trajectory could've been Grace's. "All you had to do is come in peace."

"Peace," Grace hisses, like the word is dirty. "Do you know what my childhood was like? Desperate. Starving. Violent. I've lost more than you can ever imagine. Sacrificed more than I believed was possible."

Luca extends a hand. "I know. I grew up with that. I saw it when I returned—"

4

"Askala is the reward. For all of us."

Sweet Terra. Grace's face is full of conviction. At that moment, Luca's glad she's not his mother. And yet, how can they ever change her mind now?

He straightens, suddenly wanting to be with Mercy. "What do you plan to do with us now?"

Grace looks away. "Returning here was foolish. I'm expected to kill you."

Whatever link Luca has to Grace has stopped that. "But you haven't."

Jaw tense, she glares at him again. "Your lives no longer matter, dead or alive. You won't stop what's coming to Askala." She glances at the fire in the center and Luca realizes what she means.

The sap is gone.

No doubt on its way to the Outlands so they can complete the boats.

"Take me to the others," Luca says quietly. He needs Mercy.

He needs hope.

"That was my intention, once I clarified two things."

That Luca is the closest he's ever been to finding his mother but has still failed to do so.

That the attack on Askala is only a matter of time.

Another failure on his part.

Grace turns to the door and raps on it sharply. It opens immediately, one of the goons sticking his head in to peer around the hut. Seeing Luca on the other side, he steps back, allowing Grace to leave.

Seeing the man's protectiveness—the assumption that Grace couldn't look after herself—makes Luca realize she must've made some ruthless decisions to become the Commander. A female at the helm of the Outlanders isn't something any of them expected. It's why the Seekers automatically assumed Corbin, with his bully personality, was the leader.

Grace is far more unpredictable and unknown that Corbin ever will be. Which makes her infinitely more dangerous to Askala.

Luca follows her out, tense and ready as he steps through the door. The last time he left the Round House, he was almost knocked unconscious. Just as he suspected, there are men on either side of the door, waiting to attack the moment Grace gives the word. The two men growl deep in their throats. They're unhappy that Luca's still breathing, let alone moving.

But Grace ignores them. She walks ahead, not bothering to check whether Luca's following her. It's a given, really. Grace's presence is the only thing keeping him alive right now.

She doesn't go far, stopping outside a hut close to the center of the village. They're making sure the prisoners are well guarded. Luca grits his teeth. They're making it impossible to escape.

Grace stops by the door and turns to him. "You try to leave, you die."

"We stay, we die," Luca points out to her.

Something shifts in her eyes and she looks away. "Like I said, you shouldn't have come back."

Two more guards stand outside the door of the hut, although Luca can't hear anything inside. Please let Mercy and the others be okay.

Corbin appears by Grace's side, his face twisted in a ferocious scowl. "You didn't kill him."

Grace stiffens. "I told you I wasn't planning on doing that. These prisoners are to be kept alive." She settles a cool gaze on Luca. "For now."

Anger is vibrating through Corbin's body. "They're better off dead."

Luca's muscles coil, recognizing the truth in Corbin's words. To his right, the two men by the hut lean forward, shifting their center of gravity. They're ready to remove the threat from their midst.

Grace spins to face him, her own fury now pulsing. "Leave us."

Corbin's nostrils flare as he draws in a sharp breath. The whole time the Seekers were here, he pretended he was the Commander—this is the first time he's had to be submissive. The pretense is over.

Grace doesn't waver, no doubt knowing she needs to prove her dominance in front of Luca, and possibly everyone else. Power is everything in the Outlands.

Her head dips. "Now, Corbin."

Hands clenched and spine as straight as a spear, Corbin spins on his heel and stalks away.

Grace turns back to Luca, her face cold in a way he hasn't seen before. "I want you out of my sight."

Luca eyes the door, knowing he's going to have to pass through the two guards, and wondering whether the men are going to want to remind him of what they're capable of. At the same time, he needs to see Mercy and the others are okay.

Moving toward his prison, Luca stops, knowing he has to try one more time. "You could still stop this. It's not too late."

When Grace suddenly steps in close, his first instinct is to retreat, but Luca holds his ground. With her beautiful face close to his, he sees that she is, indeed, younger than they'd assumed. If the Seekers had looked closely enough, they would've realized she's too young to be Raiden and Charity's mother.

"My reward isn't Askala," she whispers harshly, her arms lifting as she prepares to shove him through the door. "My reward is to finally be with the man I love."

HAWK

*H*awk and his father leave their hut, closing the door quietly so as not to wake Hawk's sisters. Their relationship has shifted since he returned from the Newlands. It's like a mutual respect has sprouted where a distance between them once thrived.

They take the path to Askala's freshwater lake and silence wraps itself around them like a well-worn blanket.

Hawk remains quiet, knowing his dad will feel the need to talk before he does.

"Your mom's happy to have you home." His father puts a hand on Hawk's back. "So am I."

Hawk nods. "Thanks. It's good to be home."

"Looks like Sam's happy to have you back, too." His father smirks.

"Well, she was the one who came to get me," Hawk points out.

"I'm glad you two seem to have finally figured things out. Not everyone's lucky enough to find someone to love them like that." His father lets his hand fall. "I knew as soon as I met your mom that she was special."

"It's surprising you knew how to love," says Hawk. "I mean, I saw what it was like out there. How men treat women with such contempt. I never understood before what it was like for you growing up."

His father shakes his head. "Having Wren for a twin taught me a thing or two. If I ever disrespected her, she was sure to let me know."

Hawk clears his throat as he tries to find the words for what he wants to say. To tell his father how much he means to him. "Dad, I—"

"It's okay, son." His large hand returns to Hawk's back, but this time it's more of a thump. "I know. You don't need to say it."

"I'm proud of you, Dad," Hawk says, not prepared to be silenced.

"Far out, Hawk!" His father blinks his moist eyes. "You're making me emotional here. I'm the one who's proud of you."

They look at each other and grin. And as the path opens out to the lake, Hawk realizes this is the first time he's really felt properly like the son of Phoenix. They'd always looked similar, apart from Hawk's mop of curls, but now it seems their hearts are in alignment, too.

It's early morning, which means the lake is quiet with just a gentle whisper of breeze sending a ripple across the surface.

Hawk's father pulls off his shirt, then slips out of his trousers and runs into the water buck naked, letting out a loud whoop as he plunges under the depths.

But as Hawk is about to lift his own shirt, he remembers there's something he hasn't told his father about just yet. That they look more alike than he realizes…

He draws in a deep breath and removes his clothes. His dad was going to see his inked chest sooner or later. Maybe it's better to get it over with now.

Wading out into the water, Hawk pauses when it laps at his waist and waits.

His father turns, his eyes wide when he takes in the black lines streaking across the upper half of Hawk's body. Markings so similar to the ones his father was branded with when he was young. Except in his case, it was by choice.

"What did you do?" his father asks, walking closer, his jaw falling open.

"I didn't do it." Hawk holds still so his dad can look.

"Who then?" His father runs a fingertip down one of the lines.

"The Commander," Hawk explains. "I was passed out at the time. I woke up to find…this."

"He wanted to make you one of them," his father says, blinking away his shock.

"He wanted me to fight in his Tournaments." Hawk breaks away and dives into the water, wishing he could wash the markings from his skin along with the morning's sweat.

When he comes back up to the surface, his dad is still standing in the same spot, running his hands through his cropped orange hair, mulling over what he just discovered.

"The Commander saw potential in you," his father says, letting his hands fall.

"Yeah, the potential to kill me." Hawk shakes his longer hair, sending droplets of water flying.

"He hoped you'd become one of them," his father insists. "He'd never have marked you otherwise."

Hawk winces. "I'll never become one of them. You didn't see what they did to Gust."

"I know how brutal they can be." His father leaves the water and walks back to his pile of clothes.

Hawk dives under the depths once more, enjoying the cool feeling on his skin.

Knowing that lingering is a luxury they don't have right now with a ship needing to be built, he emerges and gets dressed.

"There you are!" Wren bursts from the tree line and plants her hands on her hips.

"Lucky you didn't arrive a few minutes earlier," Hawk's dad laughs.

Wren rolls her eyes. "You're my brother. He's my nephew. Trust me, it's nothing I haven't seen before."

Sam steps out from behind Wren, her cheeks flushed. "Just for the record, I haven't seen it."

Hawk almost chokes on his next breath as he adjusts his shirt, avoiding Sam's gaze.

"What are you two doing up so early?" Hawk's dad asks. "And what can I do for you?"

"Actually." Sam lifts her head. "It's Hawk we were looking for."

"Oh." Hawk's dad looks a little crestfallen but quickly recovers as he nods at Hawk.

"Charity won't talk," says Wren. "She won't say a single word. We thought maybe Hawk would have more luck."

"Me?" Hawk looks around, wondering if there's another Hawk in Askala he hasn't heard of. "I've barely met the girl."

"Yeah, but you know her mom," says Sam. "You were the only one of us who Grace actually liked. She might talk to you if you tell her that."

"And what do you want her to say exactly?" he asks, not liking this idea any more now that he has an explanation.

"We want to know why." Wren shakes her head. "Who put her up to this? We need answers. That girl slept in my own daughter's bed under my own roof."

Hawk's dad clears his throat. "You'd be better to find out what you can about the invasion. Everything we're doing is based on a bunch of guesses right now."

Wren nods. "That too."

"And you really think she'll talk to me?" Hawk asks.

"Well, she's not talking to anyone else," Sam huffs. "Believe me, I tried. We all have."

Hawk smiles at the thought of Sam trying to extract information out of anyone. Diplomacy is not exactly her forte. Except when it comes to him. One smile and he'd tell her anything she wants to know. Sam's his greatest weakness.

"I'll give it a go," he says.

Sam rewards him with a smile, and he melts on the inside. They haven't had a chance to be alone since they returned from the Newlands and it's making him anxious. He just wants to hold her close so he can breathe in everything that is Sam.

"What are you waiting for?" Wren taps a foot.

"What?" Hawk startles. "You mean, now?"

"I mean five minutes ago." His aunt grins.

He holds up his palms. "Okay, okay! I'm going. But no promises."

"I'll take him." Sam loops a hand in his arm and drags him down the path like he doesn't know the way. But he's not complaining. Because now he has that stolen moment he was just dreaming about.

As they step into the forest, they're alone, with only the ancient mangrove pines beside the path to watch over them.

Hawk pulls Sam to a stop and reaches for her hands.

"Not now, Hawk," she says, unable to hide her smile. "We're in a hurry."

"A kiss would really settle my mind for this crazy mission you're sending me on." He steps forward until she's pressed up against him. "Do it for Askala."

Sam's smile morphs into a laugh and she lets go of one of his hands to slap him playfully on the chest. "Well, you've got me there. If it's for Askala I can't really say n—"

Hawk swoops down, unable to wait another second to feel his lips against Sam's.

"You're so beautiful," he murmurs between kisses as he

threads his fingers through her hair. With his stomach contracting in pure bliss, he lets out a soft moan, wanting nothing more than to do this all day.

Every. Day.

"Hawk," Sam pulls back slightly. "I don't think this is settling your mind."

He smiles, leaning forward, knowing this has to come to an end for now.

"You're right," he says, peppering her lips with small gentle kisses. "I'm feeling particularly unsettled. Know anything we can do about that?"

Sam steps back, shaking her head. "This is important!"

"You're important," he shoots back, unperturbed.

"Okay, just one more kiss." Sam steps up on her toes and kisses him with a burst of passion that tells him she's enjoying this just as much as he is. If only they had more time alone...

"Hawk," she says, her voice breathless. "I love you."

"I love you, too." He breaks away. "But you're right... Now's not the time."

She nods. "We need to focus."

He throws up his hands. "Look, I'm settled now. I'm focused."

"We'll see about that." She leads him further down the path while he turns over potential conversations with Charity in his mind. She's hardly going to talk to him. But at least if he tries then he's not letting Sam down.

They arrive at the hut Zali used to live in before Charity killed her, which makes it a kind of ironic place to keep her prisoner. But it's not like Askala has a lot of other options. Apparently, the old ship, Oasis, had a prison they called the brig. One of those would come in handy right about now.

Dex is on guard. It makes sense he'd be in on this crazy plan that Sam and Wren cooked up.

"I wasn't sure you'd agree to this," says Dex, nodding at Hawk.

"You know how much I love talking to people." Hawk winks. "I couldn't resist the chance."

Dex smiles. "Yep, times are tough when we're sending you in for a job like this."

"I don't mind. Besides..." Hawk tilts his head toward Sam. "I didn't have a lot of choice."

Dex smiles knowingly. "Get used to that."

"I'm not making you do this." Sam crosses her arms. "You agreed to it."

"I was joking." Hawk puts a hand on her shoulder. "Let's get this over with."

Dex slides back the bar that's holding the door closed and cautiously opens it.

"Want me to come in with you?" Dex asks.

Hawk shakes his head.

"We'll be right out here," says Sam, a tinge of fear in her eyes. Is she scared Charity will hurt him? He's twice the girl's size!

"Don't come in unless I call for you," says Hawk, giving Sam a quick kiss on the cheek. "Love you."

He steps inside. It's dark and he blinks as he waits for his sight to adjust. It's a small hut of only one room and has been emptied of all Zali's belongings. There's not so much as even a bed in here, evidence of how much Charity is trusted. Or respected.

He sees her in the far corner sitting with her knees pulled up to her chest. She's looking directly at him, watching his every move.

Stepping a bit closer, he tries to read the expression on her face. It's hard to believe this young girl is a murderer. She killed at least a dozen people with the deadly nightshade, including Sam's little brother. Seb was one of the nicest kids Hawk ever met. He had enough struggles as it was without having his life snuffed out like that. And she tried to kill Sam...

Resisting the urge to throttle her, Hawk reminds himself he has a job to do. Or at least a job he needs to try to do.

He sits on the floor a few feet away from Charity and pulls up his own legs, mirroring her position.

And he stares right back, not saying a word.

She shifts her weight slightly, the only sign she's not entirely comfortable with the situation, which is exactly what he wants.

Hawk's used to this reaction when he resists doing the one thing most people seem to find so necessary—fill the air with words. He could sit here in silence all day if he needed to. He's had years of practice.

There's the mutter of chatter coming from outside the hut. The sound of wind brushing through the roofing material. The occasional birdsong. It's quite peaceful.

Time passes. Then more time ticks by. Hawk never moves his eyes from Charity, knowing he needs her to talk first.

He has no way of telling without the sun, but they must sit there for an hour or more.

"What do you want?" she eventually asks. Her voice is terse. Reproachful. Confused.

He smiles at her but doesn't answer. It seems his strategy has worked. Because according to Sam, Charity just said more to him in that one sentence than she's said to anyone else.

"So, you're just going to sit there looking at me all day?" she asks. "Would you like me to sing you a song?"

He shakes his head, hoping she'll continue.

"You must want something." She tucks her knees up tighter to her chest and glares at him.

He waits another minute for her frustration to grow, then clears his throat.

"Do you do everything your father tells you?" he asks.

Charity rolls her eyes. "You think poisoning those people was his idea?"

Hawk shrugs, wondering why anyone would want to take credit for such a heinous act. "Was it?"

"I have a brain of my own," she snaps. "I could see what needed to be done. And I wasn't afraid to do it." She pulls back her shoulders and her eyes shine with pride. She's telling the truth. Hawk's certain of it. And he's not at all sure if this makes her crimes better or worse. Is a killer acting on her own instincts more dangerous than one acting on orders she might not fully understand?

"Seb was just a little boy." His voice breaks under the strain.

"I had a little brother once," she says. "He starved to death, just like most people's little brothers in the Outlands. Growing up isn't an expectation out there. Not like it is here."

He raises a brow. "You killed Seb to even a score?"

She shakes her head firmly. "I killed him to prove a point. Why should you have so much when we have so little?"

"We wanted to share it with you." Hawk dares to shuffle a little closer. "We wanted to show you how to care for the land so that it cares for you. We wanted you to have a better life."

"That's not true." Charity's glare returns. "You're selfish. All of you. But not for long. Soon you'll all be dead."

Fear winds its way through Hawk's gut as he realizes just how important his job is here. Either the Outlanders are planning something big, or Charity has already set something in motion to do the job for them. The only way to find out is to keep her talking. It seems Sam and Wren knew what they were doing when they asked him to come here.

"What else have you done that we don't know about?" he asks, hoping she hasn't somehow managed to poison their water supply. Now that he thinks of it, his stomach is a little queasy since his swim with his father. Or is that just nerves?

Charity smiles proudly. "Let's just say I've left gifts all over this stinking island. Except you won't know about them until it's too late."

Hawk knows the first thing he needs to do when he leaves this hut is to tell the leaders to dispose of all their food supplies in the kitchens. They can't risk it. Precautions are going to have to be taken. It looks like there are going to be some lean times ahead.

Charity sits forward. "All I was doing was getting a head start on what's to come. Soon Askala will be in far less selfish hands."

Hawk swallows, afraid to say anything in case she clams up again. He's already gotten her to say a whole lot more than she has to anyone else.

"Your father was trying to marry you to a man in the Outlands," he says, cautiously. "Just like your mom was sold to your father. And you're calling us selfish?"

"Is that what she told you?" Charity laughs softly as she shakes her head.

Hawk nods. "She told me a lot of things."

"And you believed her?" Charity asks. "That's interesting. And gullible."

Hawk feels the balance of power tipping and decides to wait for her to talk again. He's possibly already said too much.

"She wasn't sold to my father." Charity rolls her eyes. "If anything, it was the other way around."

Hawk is a little stunned by this. Grace had told him that story in confidence, and he'd believed her. She was the only person he'd come to trust in the Newlands, apart from Alyx. But either Grace had made it all up, or Charity is lying to him now. Which just goes to show that the smartest move now is not to trust anybody.

"And what about you?" he asks. "Did you come here to escape being sold to the Outlands?"

Charity openly laughs at this. "My father would never do

that to me. I was sent here as a spy. I thought that was obvious by now."

Hawk ignores the smug tone to her voice. "But your mom told us—"

"My mom, as you call her, is a liar," says Charity.

"She's not your mom?" Hawk dares to ask, wondering if he really knows Grace at all.

"She's not Raiden's either. Our mom died giving birth to the little brother I told you about," she says. "I bet women don't die having babies in Askala."

"They do sometimes," says Hawk, trying to fit some of these puzzle pieces together.

Charity leaps to her feet and Hawk tenses, reminding himself that she's more dangerous than she looks.

"I wasn't going to talk to anyone." She twists her face into a grimace. "I think I've said enough."

He shakes his head. "I think you've only just started."

Charity draws her fingers across her lips. She's done talking. If he wants to get more out of her, he'll have to come back another day.

"I'll have some food and water sent into you." Hawk stands and brushes off his trousers. "Because despite what you think, we're not selfish here. We'll share what we have with you. That's more than your people would do for someone who betrayed them."

"Just make sure it's not the broccoli," she says. "Or maybe I left your present with the crickets. I forget now. Actually, it could have been the dried turmeric... no, I think it's the parsley you should be careful of."

"I thought you were done talking?" He tilts his head, wondering if bringing her a plate of food is one way to find out if it's safe for the rest of them to eat.

She frowns at him and he has to stop himself from feeling sorry for her. Was she born this evil or is she just a product of her upbringing? It's impossible to separate the two to figure it out. And maybe it doesn't matter. She is the person she is.

And she killed Seb.

"Dex!" Hawk calls, walking backward to the door, not foolish enough to turn his back on Charity for even a moment. They already learned what happens when she's underestimated. "We're done here."

The door flies open immediately and Hawk steps out and turns to face the small crowd of people waiting for him. But the only face his eyes search for isn't there. The face that he's carried with him in his mind since he was a small boy. The only face that seems to matter right now.

"Sam went to the infirmary," says Wren.

He nods his understanding. Sam has important work to do. Just like he did when he spoke to Charity.

How can his success feel so much like a failure? He got Charity to talk, only now he has questions he didn't even know he had to ask.

Sam's brother was killed in cold blood. And now according to Charity, the rest of them will be joining him soon.

"Over my dead body," he mutters, feeling the truth in these words. He'll die saving Askala if he has to.

It's time to clear out the kitchens and help his father finish the boat.

And the first person he's going to load on it will be Sam.

SAM

"She's asking for you."

Sam looks up to find Avis standing in the doorway of the small office in the infirmary. She puts down the jar she was holding as she glances at the bowl in front of her. The antidote is almost finished. It took some searching, but she found the Calabar bean—the vital ingredient— tucked at the back of the highest shelves, understandably because it's such a dangerous plant.

Then she ground them up and steeped the powder in water. Sam's about to add the final ingredient and it will be complete. Ready to be disseminated among the patients poisoned by Charity.

But her mother's awake. And if she's asking for Sam, then Sam's not going to say no.

Closing the door behind her, Sam follows Avis through the infirmary. They had to bring in extra cots, then makeshift mattresses for the floor. Although they managed to stop Charity's devastation, so much damage had already been done.

Sam reaches her mother, noting Aarov in the cot next to her.

He's sleeping deeply, his breathing shallow and thready. He needs the antidote, and soon.

Her mother's eyes flicker open as Sam approaches and the shadow of a smile spreads across her face. "Sam," she whispers.

Sam falls to her knees beside the bed, her chest hollow and aching. Her mother's so sick, the deadly nightshade poison having wreaked havoc on her body. But she's been strong. Resilient. Had nothing but faith in Sam the whole way through.

Her mother's smile grows. "Is it finished?"

"Almost," Sam assures. "There weren't many Calabar beans, but there'll be enough."

"Yes, they're hard to find."

And dangerous to harvest. Deep in the forest, the plant climbs its way through the branches of only the oldest and tallest mangrove pines. It's the only way the plant can ensure it reaches the top, seeking out the essential sunshine it needs to grow.

"And it's highly poisonous," Sam points out.

She's explained to her mother that Calabar beans contain physostigmine, an alkaloid that interferes with the metabolism of tropane—the devastating poison in deadly nightshade. Except Calabar beans can be poisonous themselves. The right dose will save a life. A dose and a half will kill.

"Yes," her mother wheezes. "I'm sure you've got the calculations right."

Sam hopes so. They don't have a choice but to find out, really. Without it, every person in the infirmary will die.

"Sam, I just wanted you to know..." Her mother swallows, the process slow and pained. "I knew you could do it. I knew you'd find the cure."

Sam grips her mother's hand, tears pricking her eyes. "Only because—"

"No, don't say it was luck or chance. It was because you

didn't give up. It's because you used your strengths and gifts to help others."

The pride in her mother's soft gaze leaves Sam mute. She nods, unsure what to say.

"Wait till I tell your father," her mother teases gently. "Our daughter was speechless."

Sam nods again, glad her mother realizes how much her words mean to her.

Her mother tries to sit up a little, only to collapse back down and Sam hides her frown. She needs the antidote. "What else must be done?" she wheezes.

"It's almost complete. I've added reishi mushroom, and now it's just the turmeric."

"Good thinking, daughter. It's a powerful anti-inflammatory."

Sam flushes, knowing her mother's quoting her. Sam noticed her tendency to share information with whoever's in her vicinity. "It won't be long before we can give everyone their first dose."

Small amounts, repeated doses. That's what they decided would be best. The compromised bodies of those poisoned by the *Belladonna* can have time to assimilate it, whilst those caring for them can monitor the effects.

Her mother relaxes into the bed, seemingly content that everything will be okay. Her eyes flutter shut and Sam's about to move away when they fly open again. "How's Hawk?"

"He's recovering well from the Newlands," Sam assures, wondering where that came from. "He's okay."

But Sam's mother's gaze holds her and doesn't let go. "And?"

Realizing what her astute mother is asking, Sam stills. "He's everything, Mom."

Her mother's smile is soft and gentle as she squeezes Sam's hand. "I know."

"I just didn't see it at first."

"But you did. With time."

Thank Terra Hawk was patient.

Her mother's hand relaxes as her eyes close again. "Just like you did with the cure."

Sam doesn't bother correcting her mother by pointing out it's an antidote, not a cure, because a moment later her shallow breathing evens out. Extricating her hand, Sam rises. It's time to finish making it.

Avis is moving around the infirmary, Thea and Rose helping as they offer water and broth to those who are awake, anxiously checking on those who are not after they lost another Askalan this morning. Sam's determined that no one else will join them in the ocean's ceremony.

Back in the infirmary office, Sam closes the door, hoping she won't be interrupted. She picks up the small jar of turmeric, glad she doesn't have to measure this out as carefully as she did the Calabar bean. A few spoonfuls should do it. Picking up the wooden spoon, Sam tips out the first one. The turmeric wasn't where Sam expected it to be, having been shoved on a shelf below the usual spot. But luckily, it's bright orange coloring had made it easy to find.

There's the sound of raised voices in the infirmary and Sam pauses. Aarov must be awake again, possibly hallucinating. Knowing she's probably better off not helping with that, she measures a second spoonful of turmeric.

Sam's about to add it when the door bursts open, sending her heart shooting to her throat. Hawk stands in the doorway, breathing hard. "Thank Terra," he puffs. "You haven't finished making the cure, yet."

"The antidote," Sam points out. They don't know if it'll be the cure they're all hoping for, yet. "What's wrong? I was about to add the final ingredient—turmeric."

Hawk's face pales. "Turmeric!"

"Well, yes. The bioactive compounds are not only a powerful anti-inflammatory, it's a potent antioxidant—"

Hawk leaps forward, clasping the hand that's holding the jar. "You can't!" He looks down, taking in the orange tinge of liquid in the bowl and his shoulders droop. "I'm too late."

Sam frowns. "What's going on, Hawk?"

"I spoke to Charity. She claims she's poisoned our food and herbs."

Horror crashes through Sam. She never doubted that Charity would talk to Hawk, but that's the last thing she expected Charity to confess. "She what?"

Hawk releases Sam's hand, his face desolate with the truth. "She said she left little gifts all over Askala, then hinted they might be in the broccoli, or the crickets." Hawk swallows. "Or the turmeric."

"And the jar of turmeric wasn't where it's supposed to be," Sam whispers.

Hawk's eyes widen. "Sweet Terra."

Feeling lightheaded as she tries to understand the implications, Sam blinks. She looks to the bowl of life-saving liquid she just prepared. "But that means..."

In another ten minutes she would've given this to her mother. To every other person in the infirmary. To anyone who developed symptoms as the poison wreaked the last of its havoc on Askala's population.

Hawk engulfs Sam in a hug, and she clings to him. "I know," he murmurs. "We told the kitchens they need to destroy any reserves we have, but then I thought about you and the cure."

"Antidote," Sam says automatically. Pulling back, Sam frowns. "She could be lying."

"She could be, but we can't take the risk."

Turning back to her antidote, Sam knows Hawk's right. Charity's proven how far she'll go to hurt Askala—she's killed without impunity. Children, elderly, as many people as she could...

Sam flops onto the stool behind her. "But that means..."

They no longer have an antidote. Food. Any way to feed and care for their people, let alone heal those who are sick. Sam's throat tightens as her eyes prick with moisture. Even from her prison in Zali's hut, Charity is still destroying Askala.

Hawk slips an arm around her shoulder and Sam leans into him. She breathes in his scent and his strength, trying not to think of how much longer her mother has left.

"Your father and a few others have already gone out searching for food," says Hawk. "And we have the pteropods. We might even be able to use some stuff from the garden if we thoroughly wash it."

But no antidote.

Sam shoots to her feet as she turns to Hawk. "The Calabar beans! I just used the only supplies we had!"

Hawk pales. Sam was so excited when she read about the plant's ability to neutralize the effects of deadly nightshade, she ran straight to him, wanting to share the news. He knows there's no chance of saving the others without it.

"Plus, who knows whether Charity interfered with any of the other ingredients," Sam adds.

"Sam?" They both spin around to find Avis in the doorway, her hands clasped tightly.

Sam freezes. Her mother...

"It's Aarov," Avis chokes. "He's gone."

Sam looks beyond Avis and into the infirmary. Rose is bending over Aarov's still form, lifting the sheet to cover his face. Her face is crumpled with the weight of another death.

Grief punches Sam in the gut and she's not surprised to find Hawk beside her as she turns away. Burying her face in his chest, she holds onto him tightly.

Aarov is dead.

It's only a matter of time before her mother is next.

"I'll make sure he's taken care of," Avis murmurs before walking away.

Sam looks up at Hawk, suddenly realizing their roles as Seekers never ended, despite their return to Askala.

His handsome face settles into determined lines, probably coming to the same conclusion. "We need to go get more. We need to find the ingredients."

Sam nods. "The turmeric is in the garden, and we use the root, so it should be fine. I know where we can find reishi mushroom." She presses her hands to Hawk's chest, gaining strength from the steady heartbeat she feels beneath her palm. "The Calabar beans won't be so easy."

"We'll do what needs to be done," Hawk states resolutely.

Hope flickers to life in Sam's chest. "It's a day's trek away. Beyond the cliffs."

"We need to get going, then."

Releasing her, Hawk picks up the bowl and walks to the window. Sam winces as he tips the compromised antidote out, knowing it needs to be done, but flinching at its loss, nonetheless.

Hours of work, that will take countless more just so she can repeat the process.

Hawk returns to her. "We'll only tell our parents we're going. We don't want to worry the colony any more than they already are."

Sam nods. The trek will be dangerous.

The climb to the top of the mangrove pine to harvest the bean pods will be even more dangerous.

There's no guarantee they'll be able to do this.

And yet, they have no choice.

Sam takes Hawk's hand, glad they're facing this together. "We're Seekers. We can do this."

Hawk presses a quick kiss against her lips, and she tastes the kaleidoscope of emotions that mirror her own.

Fear. Hope.

The knowledge they can't fail.

Wishing there was time to find the other emotions she's discovered in Hawk's kisses—love, passion, heat—Sam pulls away.

They need to get going.

Askala is depending on them to succeed.

MERCY

*M*ercy launches herself forward as Luca is thrown into the hut, trying to break his fall. He lands in her lap and she lets out a whimper as she leans over and covers his beautiful face with kisses.

"I thought they killed you." Her eyes well with tears. "I honestly thought you were dead."

"Still here," he says. "Still breathing. Although, they have this hut surrounded, so I'm not sure for how long."

The relief is immense. It floods every cell of Mercy's body as she dares to believe that somehow Luca has come out of this alive.

"Luca!" Tarquin scurries over and wraps her arms around him.

Even Alyx looks relieved from her position at the rear of the hut. She's barely said a word since they were imprisoned here.

But that's not important now because Luca is alive. Mercy had been certain there was no way they'd let him live, no matter what kind of hallucination he was having when he'd told Grace she was his mother. He must have read that note all wrong.

Grace might be older than Luca, but she's not nearly old enough to be his mom.

"How many of them did you kill?" asks Tarquin. "Or did you just kick them all in the nuts?"

"I didn't hurt anyone," says Luca, extracting himself from Tarquin's clutches. "Sometimes it's just as important to know when not to fight."

"Bo-ring." Tarquin crosses her arms.

"Don't be rude," Alyx scolds.

"Are you three okay?" Luca squints at them in the dim light.

Mercy turns her face, not wanting him to see the cut on her lip from when Corbin slapped her. But Luca never misses anything, and he reaches for her, pulling her face gently toward him so he can inspect the damage.

"I'm fine," she whispers. "Honestly, it's nothing."

"Why do you think Grace is your mother?" Alyx asks, sitting forward and finding her voice. "I can't work it out."

"I don't," he says. "Well, not anymore. I had a note telling me my mother's name is Grace. But Grace told me that's not her birth name. That she was only six when I was born."

Mercy tries not to roll her eyes. Are men really that hopeless at deducing a woman's age? She could have told him that and saved him a whole lot of trouble. Although, there's no mistaking that Grace had reacted quite strongly when Luca had handed her that note.

"Grace was the name she took as the Commander," says Alyx, nodding. "So, what she's saying actually makes some kind of sense."

"Hang on." Mercy turns to Alyx. "You knew she was the Commander, and you didn't tell us?"

"It was better you didn't know." Alyx holds out her palms. "She'd only have killed you if you found out before she wanted you to."

"I think Grace named herself after my mother." Luca sits up, wrapping one arm around Mercy and letting Tarquin snuggle in on his other side. "She asked me a lot of questions about how I grew up. She had to have known her."

Mercy puts a hand on Luca's chest, wishing she could draw the pain out of him. It seems the mystery of his mother is one that might never be solved. Just when they think they have it figured out, something else gets in the way.

"When can we get out of here?" Tarquin asks on a yawn. "Are they going to let us out soon?"

"Tarquin, they might never let us out," says Alyx, her voice laced with fear.

"Never, as in ever?" Tarquin wriggles away from Luca and stands up, planting her hands on her hips. "Well, that's not going to happen."

"We don't have a choice, Tarquin," Mercy says as gently as she can.

"Luca says we always have a choice," Tarquin insists. "We can't just sit here and starve to death, can we?"

Mercy raises her eyebrows at Luca. "I think we created a monster."

"She's always been like that." Alyx frowns.

"Of course." Mercy shoots her an apologetic look, her heart breaking at how Alyx must feel to see her sister switching loyalties like this.

"I have an idea." Alyx reaches into her pocket and gets out a piece of paper. "Hawk told me if I need help I should send him this note."

Mercy takes the small slip of paper from Alyx and studies it closely, wondering what she's missing. There are no words on it at all.

"It's a child's drawing of a boat," she says, handing it to Luca.

"I drew it." Alyx pulls back her shoulders. "I can't read or write."

"Oh." Mercy flushes. "I'm so sorry." She's never met anyone

who couldn't read before, but it makes sense that Alyx would never have had the opportunity to learn.

"Hawk will know what the drawing means," says Alyx.

"When did he return to Askala?" asks Luca, giving the note back to Alyx.

"Not long ago." Alyx clutches the note tightly. "He tried to make the best of it here without you. Gust did, too."

"You didn't tell us how he died," says Mercy, not sure she actually wants to know. But it seems too important a detail to gloss over. Gust was a Seeker and even though Mercy knew there was a chance that one of them might die when they set out for the Newlands, that's three of them now including Siena and Nikita. Gust deserves some respect.

"He was killed in a Tournament. It was pretty brutal." Alyx looks to the floor. "Hawk knew he was next, so he came to me for help. We attracted a raven using my necklace and sent a note to Askala. A boat came to get him."

"Why didn't you go with him?" asks Mercy, relieved that at least Hawk is okay.

Alyx nods her head toward Tarquin. "I wanted to be here in case she came back."

Now it's Tarquin's turn to look sheepish. "You gave up your chance to get out of here for...me?"

Alyx nods. "Of course, I did. You're my sister."

Tarquin makes a whimpering noise, goes immediately to Alyx and plonks herself down in her lap, wrapping her arms around her neck. Alyx holds her tightly, pressing her cheek to the top of Tarquin's head.

"I came back," says Tarquin, talking as if she's the adult. "I'm right here."

"Which is exactly the problem." Luca starts feeling his way around the edges of the small hut, looking for a weakness. "We need to get out of here. Grace might not want us dead, but the moment she takes her eyes off us, Corbin will kill us."

"Let me help." Mercy gets to her feet and presses her palms against the wall, checking for any loose boards.

Tarquin climbs off Alyx's lap. "You're doing it all wrong. Those boards have been sealed tight. I watched the men build these huts. You'll never get out that way."

Mercy's shoulders slump. "What do we do then? Dig our way out?"

"The ground is too hard." Tarquin shakes her head as she points up. "But the roof is thatched. It's the weakest part. We can easily make a small hole."

"She's right." Luca stops still and looks up. "Good thinking, Tarquin."

"We need to be smart about this," says Mercy, not as convinced as Alyx and Luca seem to be that this is such a good idea. "We're surrounded. They'll see us escaping. Unless we wait for night."

"We're not going to escape, silly," says Tarquin.

Mercy frowns at Tarquin's cheek.

"We're going to attract a raven," says Luca in a far kinder tone than his young shadow.

"Oh." Mercy does feel a little silly now.

"It's doubtful those oafs will notice a bird land on the roof," he says. "We'll send Alyx's note to Hawk. If he comes with a few of Askala's strongest we might just be able to get out of here."

Mercy sits down on the dirt floor and sighs. This plan is flimsy at best. But without some help from someone outside this hut, they really don't have much chance. It's worth a shot, no matter how terrible a plan it is.

"Climb on my shoulders," says Luca, squatting down in front of Tarquin. "I can't reach the roof and there's nothing to stand on."

Tarquin scrambles up Luca's back, balancing her feet on his shoulders with the kind of dexterity only a child seems to possess.

Luca stands to his full height and Tarquin gets busy separating some of the dried branches that make up the thatched roof.

Light filters through the hut, casting rays of hope across their despair. Mercy lets her eyes trail down Luca's lean frame, marveling at how toned he is despite the lack of food he's eaten recently. His chest is so firm, and his arms look so strong as he holds onto Tarquin's ankles, keeping her safe.

It really isn't fair of him to look so damn hot when there's not a thing she can do about it right now. Will she ever get the chance again to feel his bare skin underneath her fingertips? Because she wouldn't mind...

"Pass me the necklace, Alyx!" Tarquin calls down when she's managed to make a hole the size of her head.

Alyx slips a chain from around her neck and Mercy's eyes widen at the blue stone that's hanging from the end. Even in this dim room it's catching the light. That thing must have been worth a fortune in the old world.

"Is that a blue diamond?" Mercy asks, impressed to see one so large.

Alyx shrugs. "I have no idea. It was a gift."

Mercy nods, realizing it's possible this was Alyx's payment for selling Luca out. In which case this sparkling stone is covered in Luca's blood. Suddenly, it doesn't look so impressive.

"Position it so it glints in the sun," Luca instructs as Tarquin takes the stone from Alyx and reaches up again. "Then cover the hole over."

"But then we can't see if a bird flies down," says Tarquin as she fiddles with the branches.

"Do it quickly," says Luca. "Hurry!"

Mercy frowns, wondering what the rush is, until she hears someone at the door. Her heart pounds as she goes to it, preparing to make some kind of distraction for whoever opens it.

It flies open just as Tarquin's managed to shift most of the thatch back in place and Corbin fills the doorway, light spilling in behind him and making Mercy squint.

"Let us out," says Mercy, gripping the front of Corbin's shirt and forcing his eyes to her, knowing Tarquin won't need more than a few seconds to slide back down to the floor. "You can't keep us locked in here without food or water."

"Stupid woman," Corbin mutters as he shoves her aside. "Can't you see what I have here for you?"

As Mercy steadies herself, she looks down to see he's holding a bucket filled with dirty water. She then dares to look at Tarquin to see her standing innocently by Luca's side. Her cheeks are pink but there's no other sign that only moments ago she was standing on someone's shoulders putting a diamond once worth more than this entire island through the thatch in the roof.

Corbin puts down the bucket, not seeming to care that some of it sloshes out onto the floor. If that's the only water they're going to get to drink, then every drop will count whether it's dirty or not. Not that Mercy should expect Corbin to care.

"Consider yourselves lucky." Corbin looks at each of them with a sneer. "If it were up to me, I'd kill you all. I still might..."

"Thanks for the water," says Alyx from her corner of the hut. "We appreciate it."

Corbin seems to find this amusing. "You do like your gifts, don't you?"

Alyx doesn't reply and Mercy has to physically bite her tongue to stop herself saying anything. There's no point talking to someone like Corbin. Grace is the one they need to speak to if they have any hope of getting out of here.

With one last smirk, Corbin leaves and secures the door.

"That was way too close," says Tarquin, wiping sweat from her forehead in a dramatic gesture.

"Who's for a drink?" asks Luca, peering into the bucket.

"I think we wait until we're a little more desperate," says Mercy, cringing. "Who knows what parasites are in there."

"You sound like Sam now," he smiles.

"No, if I were Sam, I'd have told you exactly what kind of parasite might be in there, including their first name, last name, and the name of their great-great grandfather's aunt." Mercy smiles back, missing Sam with a sharp pang in her chest as she hopes her cousin is okay.

"True." Luca steps back from the bucket. "And I agree about the water."

"I want to check for a raven." Tarquin tugs on Luca's shirt. "I think I heard something."

"It's too soon," says Luca. "You just put the necklace up there."

"I hear it," Tarquin insists, tugging harder.

"Careful, I need this shirt!" says Luca, squatting down.

Mercy begs to differ. A shirt really is unnecessary when it comes to Luca.

Tarquin climbs back onto Luca's shoulders and he lifts her up to the roof.

Mercy goes to the door, deciding she might need to remove her own shirt if Corbin bursts back in. They'd been very lucky last time. He won't be so easily distracted again.

She cringes at the thought.

Tarquin pulls the thatch apart and peers outside.

"I told you," she hisses down to them. "There's a raven."

"You're joking." Alyx gets to her feet and cranes her neck, trying to see.

Mercy isn't quite sure just how dehydrated Tarquin is, but if she's hallucinating like that then perhaps it's time to drink the dirty water after all. Surely, a raven hasn't arrived so soon?

But before Mercy can say anything, Tarquin throws a giant black bird into the hut.

"Sweet Terra!" Mercy gasps as she covers her head.

The raven flaps its wings, circling the small hut, squawking. Corbin's men will hear this for sure. This really was a very bad idea.

Worst. Plan. Ever.

Quick as a flash, Tarquin starts singing at the top of her lungs. "Squawk goes the raven! Squawk, squawk, squawk! It sings all day, and it sings all night. Squawk, squawk, squawk!"

Alyx quickly joins in the off-key singing while Luca tries desperately to catch the bird and Mercy stands in utter shock, hoping that when Corbin kills them, he'll make it quick.

There's a bashing at the door and Mercy feels it vibrate through her shaking legs.

"Keep it down in there!" a man shouts.

"Squawk, squawk, squawk!" Tarquin and Alyx sing, just as Luca plucks the bird out of the air and brings it to his chest, holding the sharp beak closed.

"You can stop singing," he says, keeping a tight grip on the raven. "We'll just give it time to calm down. I can feel the poor thing's heart beating."

Alyx gets her note from her pocket and tears a string of cloth from her shirt, tying the paper to the bird's leg while it's being held still.

Mercy shakes her head, unable to believe that this plan has gotten so far already.

"More good thinking with the singing," Luca says to Tarquin with a wink. "You really have been very helpful today."

"That's because I'm going to be the Peregrine when I grow up." Tarquin grins at him.

"Hey, I thought you were going to be the Falcon." His face fills with mock horror.

Tarquin waves her hands. "I'm a girl, silly."

Mercy laughs quietly. "I think you're already a Peregrine."

"Truly?" Tarquin's face lights up.

"Truly," Mercy and Luca say in unison. There really is no

stopping this little girl. She's twice as smart and half as timid as Mercy was at her age.

Luca loosens his grip on the bird and cautiously sets it down on the floor. "We'll let him recover a little before we send him back out."

Tarquin brings the bucket closer. "I think he's thirsty. Can we spare some water?"

"Just a little bit," Luca says. "As a thank you."

The bird struts around the bucket two times before it dips its beak into the liquid and throws back its head.

"He's very thirsty," says Tarquin, watching closely. "Can I go next? I'm thirsty, too."

"Of course, you can." Alyx pats Tarquin on the head.

The bird takes another drink. When it seems to have had enough, it fluffs out its feathers, struts toward Mercy and looks at her, tilting its head.

"Yeah, yeah," she says, smiling. "I was the one who thought you were a bad idea."

"Yay!" says Tarquin, taking the bucket. "My turn!"

Mercy reaches out a hand to stroke the raven's head, admiring how beautiful it is at such close distance, when the bird opens its beak wide as if in a silent scream. It shudders violently for a couple of seconds, then falls over on its side, perfectly still and very obviously dead.

"No!" Mercy catapults herself across the hut and knocks the bucket from Tarquin's hands, sending water spilling across the floor.

Tarquin's face crumples as she bursts into tears. "Mercy," she sobs. "I'm so thirsty."

"Look." Mercy points at the dead bird, noticing that the note tied to its foot is completely sodden. "It was a trick. Corbin poisoned the water."

Luca curses as he inspects the dead raven, while Alyx goes to Tarquin and comforts her.

Silence hangs in the stifling air of the hut as Mercy takes in how close they just came to losing Tarquin. The muffled sound of men laughing outside the timber walls reminds her how many people out there want them dead. Corbin must be rubbing his hands together as he imagines them all lying on the floor just as dead as that poor raven.

"This bird saved our lives," says Luca, moving it to a dark corner of the hut.

"It did," Mercy agrees, deciding that attracting a raven to their hut was actually the best idea ever. Or perhaps the luckiest.

"We need to be more careful," Luca says, going to Mercy and slipping his arms around her. She molds herself into his chest, drawing in the feeling of being so close to him, even if he is wearing that annoying shirt.

What little hope they had, has faded. Maybe they'd have been better to have drunk the water and been done with it.

Because with the hut surrounded and no chance of Hawk coming to save them, they're all as good as dead.

LUCA

*T*hey're trapped.

Luca glances at the dead raven lying in the shadowy corner of the hut, then quickly glances away. If any of them had even a mouthful of the water, that would be them.

Mercy tightens her arms around his waist. "We need a plan," she says quietly.

Alyx is sitting on the opposite side of the hut, her legs tucked into her chest. Tarquin is sitting next to her, looking like the worried older sibling she isn't.

A plan.

A plan would give them hope. Some shred of faith that there's a possibility the four of them will get out of this alive.

Except Luca can't think of a thing. They're trapped in a hut. Surrounded. Their one, desperate attempt to get help was killed by poison meant for them. The truth is Corbin's going to try to find a way to finish them while Grace figures out what she's going to do next.

She won't let them go. She can't. The Commander must be strong and ruthless at all times.

Plus, she's planning an invasion of Askala. No matter what

Luca's link is to her, it can't compare to the salvation Askala represents.

"Luca?" Mercy asks.

But Luca can't look her in the eye. He's never felt like he's failed her more. "Yeah, we really do need a plan."

Tarquin shoots to her feet. "We need to fight them. Get back to the boat. And get the hell out of here."

Luca's lips thin. He's already thought of that. If he were on his own, there's a slim chance Tarquin's suggestion could've worked. But there are three others with him, all with limited fighting experience.

Someone would be hurt. Killed.

Maybe all of them.

Luca shakes his head. "Too risky, Tarquin. That sort of desperate move is exactly what Corbin and his men will be watching for."

And he'll be waiting to slaughter them, then claim self-defense to his Commander.

Tarquin crosses her arms with a huff. "Then what?"

Damn good question.

"We could try to slip out at night," Mercy suggests, keeping her voice down.

Also what Corbin will be waiting for. "From what I can tell, there are at least three men near the front door, and four others around the hut."

"Oh." She looks away and Luca's gut clenches. She's coming to the same realization he is.

Their options are limited. With even less chance of success.

Alyx sighs. "Or we could just accept our fate."

Luca's hands clench into fists. "Not a great plan either," he growls.

Tarquin sits beside Alyx again, patting her knee. "Luca will think of something, you'll see."

Alyx doesn't even look up from the spot of dirt she's focused on. She's not willing to burst Tarquin's bubble, but she's also well aware that only her sister believes in the Falcon's invincibility.

Luca's about to pace when there's a rattle at the door. Whatever bar is across it is being lifted.

Someone's coming in.

In a blink, Luca finds himself flanked by three females. Mercy's by his side, Tarquin on his other. Alyx is right behind her, hands on Tarquin's shoulders, no doubt ready to push her out of the way.

Luca's struck by both their strength and their vulnerability. Women lack power in the Newlands. They're seen as weak. As prey.

And yet, these three aren't backing down. They're willing to fight for what they love.

The door opens and Grace steps through, quickly closing it behind her. She straightens as she scans the hut. Her gaze flickers over Mercy and the others, almost dismissing them, before falling on Luca. And staying there.

"I don't have much time, so I'm going to make my offer and leave. There'll be no negotiations or compromises. It's a yes or no."

An offer. For some reason, the word has dread blooming in Luca's gut, rather than hope. He looks at Grace, waiting.

She lifts her chin, her gaze holding his, unwavering. "Join us and you'll be spared."

"Never!" Mercy spits. "You want to take, no matter the cost."

But Grace ignores her, still staring at Luca. Trying to tell him something.

Luca's breath disintegrates. "The offer is only for me," he says grimly.

"Yes." Grace doesn't acknowledge the gasps that explode around Luca. "We have no use for the others."

"No."

Luca says the word flatly. With no hesitation. He glares at Grace, letting her know exactly how disgusting her offer is.

Grace shakes her head, as if that was the response she was expecting. "Don't be a fool, Luca. You wouldn't be expected to fight. This is your chance."

To live.

At the cost of Mercy. And Tarquin. And Alyx.

Luca's about to shout the next denial when a hand presses on his arm. He looks down to find Mercy biting her lip. "Maybe you should..." she whispers. She looks up, her gaze heavy. "You'd have a chance, Luca."

He hopes she means he'd have a chance to rescue them. To make sure they all get out of this with their hearts still beating.

Luca takes her hand and squeezes it before turning back to Grace. He has to bite his response out through gritted teeth. "Hell. No."

Disappointment floods Grace's eyes. "Very well."

Without a backward glance, she's gone.

Alyx returns to her place against the wall. "You should've gone."

Mercy folds into him, her arms anchoring around his waist. Luca pulls her in tight, breathing in his reason for living. For all he knows, the order could've been to butcher Mercy and the others the moment he stepped through the door.

"I'm glad you didn't go." She sighs. "And I wish you did."

"I love you, too," her murmurs in her hair.

Tarquin kicks the empty bucket on her way to flopping down beside her sister. "Well, we'd better find a way out of here. I'm hungry. And thirsty."

Luca draws Mercy to their stretch of wall to sit down. His own mouth feels as dry as the Outlands. His stomach is rebelling against the feeling of being hungry again.

And no matter what comes through the door, they can't eat or drink it.

Mercy tucks into his side. "Maybe have a rest, Tarquin. We'll think of something."

For once, Tarquin does as she's told. She lays down and puts her head in Alyx's lap. Several minutes later her even breathing fills the hut.

No one speaks, everyone knowing there's little to say. Until one of them can think up a way out of here, they're best off conserving their energy.

Except Luca has run out of ideas.

Hours pass and the sliver of light around the door slowly disappears, Luca progressively becomes more and more wired. Darkness is just the sort of cover Corbin would be waiting for. There's no way he's going to let the four of them still be alive by morning.

And Luca's not sure Grace is likely to stop him.

Mercy shuffles so her lips are against his ear. "No regrets, Luca," she whispers.

His chest tightens painfully. Mercy knows. She knows he's thinking he should never have brought her here.

Mercy turns his head so he's facing her, their lips only inches apart. "Because of you, I got to try. I'm proud of that. Of us." Her hands tighten. "No regrets."

Sweet Terra, this woman has no idea what her words mean to him. He presses his lips against hers. Briefly. Fiercely. "Well, I do have one or two…"

Mercy's eyes glint with the same passion Luca just wove into his words. "Once wasn't really enough, was it?"

"Nope. It really wasn't."

"Then we'd better find a way out of here, Falcon," Mercy breathes.

Hope tingles along Luca's skin, powered by the beautiful girl who's holding him with little more than the desire and love he can feel throbbing between them.

But before Luca can see if that hope stands a chance of gaining life, the door rattles again.

The four of them shoot to their feet, Tarquin dashing to Mercy's side even before she's fully awake.

On high alert, Luca braces himself. Grace wouldn't come back to make her offer a second time.

The lumbering form of one of Corbin's men enters, shutting the door behind him. He sneers as he finds the four of them standing on the other side of the hut. "Dying of thirst is a whole lot slower than dying of poisoning, you know."

No one answers. If the man was here to check whether they're still alive, then he has his answer.

The man takes another step in. "Corbin wanted me to let you know your boat made great firewood."

He throws a shard of timber onto the ground between them. As long as Luca's forearm, it's covered in sap. Undeniably, it's a piece of their boat.

Alyx lets out a low moan, but it's enough for the goon to hear it. His face lights up with satisfaction. "You guys figured out how this is gonna end, yet?"

Mercy takes a small step forward. "With greed and selfishness losing."

Despite their desperate situation, Mercy hasn't given up hope that Askala will prevail.

The man's dark eyes flare, and Luca goes to grab Mercy but he's too late. The man leaps forward and clamps onto her arm, jerking her toward him. Mercy stumbles and a second later she finds herself pinned, her back to his front, his arm clamped across her throat. Luca freezes as her eyes widen with terror.

"Might as well have us some fun before you're all dead," the man growls against her ear.

Luca's heart thunders out a denial. Mercy's been attacked before, and she won't be willing to be in the same vulnerable position again. She'll fight.

And this man will kill her the moment she puts up a struggle.

He takes a step back, taking Mercy with him as he uses her like a shield. "I'll bring her back," he says with a slimy smile. "I promise."

Luca knows if this guy gets Mercy out the door, he'll never see her alive again.

The goon must see something in Luca's eye because his face hardens. "You come at me and I'll snap her neck."

Helpless rage surges through Luca, burning so hot it makes it hard to think. But this is the time he needs to think hardest. Mercy's life is on the line.

He steps back and sees the man's eyes flash suspiciously.

Luca shakes his head in defeat. "You know what?" He shoves Alyx at him. "Why don't you take her, too? Make it worth your while."

Tarquin cries out as Alyx throws Luca a panicked look. The goon recovers quickly, reaching with his other arm and grabbing Alyx.

"Smart," the man sneers at Luca. "This could buy you some time."

Alyx's face goes blank as she stands passively beside her captor. She's accepted her fate. Probably believes she deserves this.

"Come like a good girl and no one gets hurt," he murmurs to Mercy.

Mercy ignores him, her gaze locked onto Luca. She's wanting some clue as to what he's planning.

He crosses his arms, ignoring her as he keeps his gaze on the man. "Hurry up will you. This isn't nice for anyone."

With Mercy pulled against half his body with an arm across her neck, yanking Alyx by the wrist even though she's following submissively, the man takes a step back. He smacks his lips. "Tonight is gonna be a good night."

Knowing the window of opportunity is small, Luca moves.

He vaults forward and snatches the fragment of wood that was thrown to the ground. In one swift movement, Luca spins, generating the momentum he's going to need. In the split second before Luca releases what is now a weapon, he holds his breath.

He focuses everything he has on getting this right. He can't afford to sacrifice accuracy for speed. The fragment needs to be moving fast enough to impale his target, but his aim has to be true. A few inches either side and Mercy or Alyx will be his victim.

"Hey—"

The goon is abruptly cut off as the makeshift dagger lodges in his chest. His eyes widen and his mouth falls open.

But there's no chance to cry out. Blood gushes over his bottom lip like a flooded dam was just breached. The man's final movement is a blink before his body crumples to the ground. Mercy and Alyx leap away, leaving him to fall face first. His body hits the ground, no doubt jamming the wooden stake further into his chest.

Mercy's in Luca's arms before he has a chance to draw in a breath. Tarquin rushes forward, slipping in between them so she can wrap her arms around Luca.

"Yeah! Go the Falcon!" she crows.

Luca shakes his head. "Death isn't to be celebrated."

But Alyx nudges the man's body with her toe, her lip curled in disgust. "You didn't see what Raggid did to Gust."

Luca looks away, noting the pool of blood that's forming under the man. Although he doesn't regret what he had to do, he can't bring himself to celebrate it.

Mercy looks up at him. "What now?"

Luca stills as he realizes the ramifications of what just happened. Sweet Terra. He just killed one of Corbin's men. A dead bird in the corner of the hut was a risk, but there's no way they can hide a dead man when the others come looking for Raggid.

Which means they no longer have a choice.

Luca looks from Mercy to Alyx. "Next time the door opens, we run."

Mercy's face settles into determined lines. Luca watches as she finds the strength and courage that allowed her to become the Peregrine. "And we fight," she states flatly.

Tarquin juts out her skinny chest. "Damn straight, we will!"

Alyx holds out her arms. "Tarquin, come here."

Tarquin does as she's told and Alyx scoops her into her arms. The little girl's face scrunches with confusion but she doesn't pull back, allowing Alyx to hold her tightly.

She doesn't realize her sister believes these will be their last hours alive.

When the door begins to open once again, Luca curses. There was no time to get the makeshift weapon out of Raggid's chest, the only thing they'll have to protect themselves. No time to tell Mercy and Alyx the plan—he goes first, takes down as many as he can. They run.

No time to tell Mercy one last time that she's right. There are no regrets.

When Raiden steps through, Luca tenses. Corbin's son is the last person they need in here right now.

The door closes and Raiden's about to take a step when he sees something is obstructing his path.

Raggid. Dead Raggid.

Raiden looks back up, raising an eyebrow. "I see."

Luca's balanced on the balls of his feet, ready to take this weasel down. Two out of the way are two less he'll have to fight on the other side of the door. One shout from Raiden and it's the last thing he'll ever say.

But Raiden looks unperturbed. He steps to the side as if being this close to Raggid is distasteful. "My mother sent me."

Alyx pulls Tarquin in closer to her. "Don't trust a word that comes out of his mouth."

Raiden flicks a disgusted look her way. "I wouldn't exactly trust you with my secrets."

Alyx blanches. Everyone in the room knows Raiden's referring to her betrayal of Luca.

"As I was saying," Raiden continues. "I have a proposal."

Luca waits, his center of gravity slowly shifting forward. Grace is about to find out he hasn't changed his mind.

"The real Commander has had enough. You've been nothing but trouble," Raiden's voice hardens, but he quickly modulates his tone. "There's a boat on the beach. I'll collect you at midnight and take you there. We leave here and never come back."

"We?" Mercy asks.

"I sneak you out, you take me with you. I want to be a part of this as much as Charity did."

"There's no reason we should trust you," Luca points out. "This could be a trap."

Raiden glances down at his dead comrade. "I won't tell anyone about Raggid. I'll say he took a woman out into the forest. No one will come looking for him."

Conscious this is the lifeline they were looking for—a tenuous one, but a lifeline nonetheless—Luca nods curtly. "Fine," he says, although he knows this decision is anything but that. "You sneak us out, we'll take you to Askala."

Raiden's lips curl up in a slow smile. "Looking forward to it."

Spinning on his heel, he leaves the hut.

"You know it's a trap," Alyx hisses.

And yet it's all they have, right now.

"We'll wait and see," says Luca. "If no one comes, then Raiden has covered up that one of his father's men is dead."

They remain in a line facing the door. Mercy's hand grips Luca's tightly as they watch and wait. Her breathing remains shallow and tense. She knows their chance of getting out of this alive depends on someone as slimy as Raiden.

Minutes pass. Then an hour. And another.

But there are no shouts of outrage. No calls for vengeance. No one bursts through the door, calling Raggid's name.

Raiden told them the truth. Corbin's men don't know Raggid is dead.

Which means at midnight, they'll be following Raiden out of here.

HAWK

*H*awk follows Sam deeper into the forest, each step leading them further away from the colony. Which means they're more alone now than they've been since everything shifted between them.

This beautiful girl with the flecks of gold in her hair is no longer his *best friend*.

She's his everything.

Perhaps she always has been, because he can't disentangle a single moment of his life from her. Even his memories of when she wasn't present still have her woven in every detail as he'd been carrying her in his heart.

Sam keeps her sharp gaze pointed skyward as she searches the top of the mangrove pines for a sign of the trailing leaves of the Calabar bean. So many lives depend on them finding it, including Sam's own mother. Nova looked so weak the last time Hawk had seen her. He's really not sure how long she can hold on, whether they find the beans or not.

But Nova's tough. And Sam is determined. There's still hope.

"Do you want to know something funny?" Sam asks, pausing

to smile at Hawk, despite how tired she must be from the last hours spent trekking.

"Sure." Hawk slips the water flask from the strap around his shoulder and holds it out for Sam, wanting to make sure she stays hydrated.

"*Physostigma venenosum* has another name," she says, taking the water.

"Yes, Calabar beans." Hawk winks. "Raiden broke my ribs, not my memory."

Sam has to try not to spit at the water as she laughs. "No, I mean another name."

Hawk takes the flask and has a small sip of water while he waits for her to enlighten him.

"It's sometimes called the Ordeal bean," she says, grinning.

"Perfect." Hawk chuckles as he seals the flask.

"Except let's hope when we find it, it's what ends this whole ordeal." Sam rests her forehead on his chest and slips her hands around his waist. "What if we never find it, Hawk?"

"Hey." Hawk tilts her face up to him. "That's not like you. We're going to find some, no matter how much of an *ordeal* it turns out to be."

She nods as if trying to convince herself and Hawk leans down to kiss the tip of her nose.

"Come on," he says. "We still have a few hours of daylight left. Let's make the most of it."

They continue to pick their way through the trees, squinting into the canopy to be certain they don't walk right past the very thing they're looking for.

"You know, Charity could just used our supply of Calabar beans instead of the deadly nightshade," says Sam. "They're far more toxic. She could have wiped all of us out with just that small supply we had in the infirmary."

"Lucky for us she didn't know about it." Hawk pauses to study a vine before deciding it's just a regular liana.

"Maybe we tipped it out for nothing," says Sam, looking at the vine and seeming to come to the same conclusion as Hawk as she walks on. "Nobody ever saw her in the infirmary."

"You know we couldn't take the risk," he reminds her. "This is the safest option."

Sam murmurs her agreement, but Hawk's attention is diverted by the sound of a breaking branch. He takes a slingshot from his pocket and spins around.

"Sam!" he hisses. "I heard something."

She stops and turns, scanning the trees.

He slides a rock into the band of the slingshot and pulls it back, ready to fire. Wren taught him how to use this thing as a kid. His skills are a bit rusty, but thankfully he'd joined in on a couple of the lessons she's been giving the colony on the beach. Maybe he should have concentrated harder. He hadn't expected to need to use one so soon.

Despite standing completely still for a few minutes, the sound doesn't come again.

"Maybe I imagined it," Hawk whispers.

Sam shrugs, although she remains on high alert. "I can't hear anything."

"Stay a bit closer to me," he says, not willing to put the slingshot away just yet. It's true he's felt a little jumpy since returning from the Newlands, but he was certain he heard a branch snap. It could have just been one falling from a tree, however, there's no way he's going to take that risk. He needs to be sure it wasn't something else. What he's not sure about is if he'd prefer it to be human or animal. Perhaps that depends on which animal. Or which human…

He's about to walk on when Sam points a shaking finger to the ground.

Hawk looks down to see a large footprint in the dirt.

"Polar grizzly." Sam keeps her voice low, but it doesn't stop the pounding that's started up in his chest. There's a reason

Askala has fences around their colony, and it's to keep these ferocious predators out.

Hawk indicates to the tree behind Sam, telling her to start climbing. They both know that bears can climb trees but being at a higher level still somehow feels like an advantage. It's better than being charged at by a hungry beast four times their size. And if they're quiet enough, maybe the grizzly won't realize and will walk right on by.

Sam turns to the tree and with Hawk's help, she hoists herself into the lower branches.

"Come on," she hisses down when he doesn't follow. The problem is that he has to put down the slingshot to start climbing. Which could be a deadly mistake. So, instead, he holds the weapon up for Sam to take.

Her eyes widen and she shakes her head. Even though she's been attending Wren's lessons, she isn't exactly what anyone would describe as a crack shot. In typical adorable Sam style, she puts in too much technique and not enough intuition. But he trusts her. If his life depended on it, he's sure she could find her mark.

He waves the slingshot at her more urgently and she reluctantly takes it. Even though their lives are potentially in danger, he can't help but smile at the concentration on her face as she positions the stone in the band and pulls it back. She's biting down on her lower lip and he just wants to scurry right up to her and kiss away all her worries.

But first, he has to make sure they're safe.

Thinking he hears another sound, Hawk wastes no time hauling himself up the lower part of the tree.

"Go up higher," he tells Sam, who tucks the slingshot into the back of her trousers and climbs up to a wide branch.

He follows and sits beside her, putting one arm around her shoulders and steadying himself with the other. Letting out a sigh, he decides he'd be happy to live in this bear-free tree forever. Other than the sound of the wind in the trees, the forest is completely silent and there's a cool breeze caressing them. No sound of mindless chatter from the colony. No sound of Corbin and his men trying to kill them. No sound of anyone crying after losing a family member as part of Charity's evil plan. If it weren't for the potentially lethal animal stalking them from below, it's like heaven up here.

"I can feel your heart pounding," she says.

"Shh," he tells her, as he glances down at the forest floor. "Why can't we hear any birds?"

"Oh." She grips his thigh as she leans over to help him look.

Her hold tightens as they see a matted clump of mottled fur move past a bush.

Hawk holds his breath. They were right to be cautious. There's only one beast with fur like that and it's exactly what he'd feared it might be.

Their only hope is that the polar grizzly hasn't seen them.

The bear steps out from behind the shrub, its nose to the ground as it sniffs at their footsteps. It's a huge beast, skinny like all the grizzlies out here but with an enormous frame. Hawk doesn't need to see the size of its teeth from here to know just how big they are. Or how strong its jaw is. It could crack their skulls in a single bite.

Hawk holds out his hand to Sam for the slingshot.

The bear is following their scent, which means it will only be a matter of moments before it figures out where they are. He needs to line up his first shot and hope it's good enough.

They've all heard the story of how Wren maimed a polar grizzly with a slingshot during her Proving by shooting a stone in each of its eyes. Which means this is possible. Nova later killed that grizzly with a spear. They can do this. It's not all over just yet.

Sam hands him the slingshot slowly, being careful not to drop any part of it and Hawk takes it from her.

He passes his small bag of stones to Sam so she can hand them to him as he needs them and readies the weapon in just the way Wren taught him. The bear is almost at the base of the tree, which means this show is about to get started any moment now.

Trying to steady his hands, he lines up his shot for the bear's head, hoping his aim will be accurate enough to hit it directly in the eye. If he can blind the beast like Wren did, they have a chance.

A loud clap of thunder sounds overhead, and Hawk almost falls out of the tree in shock. Instead, he watches with wide eyes and his breath held as the stone from his slingshot slips from his fingertips and sails down to the ground as if in slow motion. He hadn't even seen the lightning to warn him first.

The bear, who must be accustomed to Askala's sudden storms, barely reacts. The rock lands in front of its enormous paws and the beast lowers its nose to sniff at it. Hawk's scent must be all over that thing.

Sam quickly removes another rock from the pouch, although doesn't hand it to Hawk as he expects. She throws it down, aiming so it lands a few feet in front of the first rock. The bear takes a few steps away from the tree to inspect the rock.

Genius! Sam sure is a whole lot more than the prettiest face he's ever seen.

Hawk nods encouragingly at her, and she does it again, this time throwing the next rock a little further.

Then as if Mother Nature wants in on this plan, rain pours from the sky in a sudden burst. A flash of lightning heralds the arrival of an even louder clap of thunder.

This is the kind of rain that Hawk and Sam used to run from as children, with Mercy squealing and laughing as she skipped along behind them. But there's no running this time. There's only rejoicing in the hope that if this downpour lasts long enough, it will wash away their scent from the ground.

Clearly deciding it's in no need of a shower today, the bear lopes away. Although, Hawk knows this doesn't mean it won't be back. They need to be very careful here.

Sam grins at Hawk from beside him and together they climb higher into the tree, wanting more distance between them and any creature with a set of teeth to rival a leatherskin.

Moving carefully so they don't slip, Sam finds a space where a thick branch from the tree has grown into another branch from the tree beside it, creating a kind of flat bed with a narrow gap in the middle. It's wide enough for one person. Or two, if they stay close…

They crawl onto the branch where it's a little more sheltered and Sam nestles into Hawk's chest. He leans back on the trunk and stretches out his legs. Yep, he could definitely live in this tree. He may choose to never get down.

"That was lucky," says Sam, daring to speak with the sound of the rain masking her words from traveling too far.

Hawk smiles. "Lucky? Or unlucky to see the grizzly in the first place?"

"Definitely lucky." She snuggles in closer and he holds her tight, aware his heart is still beating fast, although now it's for reasons that have nothing to do with fear.

"This is called inosculation," says Sam.

Hawk nods even though he has no idea what she's talking about.

"Also known as a marriage tree," she says. "Inosculation usually only occurs with the same species but sometimes if two trees grow close enough together, different species can merge."

Hawk swallows, drawing far too many parallels between what's happening with these trees and what's happening right now between him and Sam. Two people who couldn't be more different yet have grown so close that they've come to feel like two halves of the one being.

Hawk raises a hand to Sam's face, trailing his fingertips over her cool skin.

"Are you warm enough?" he asks.

She nods. "The atmospheric temperature during a storm is—"

He leans forward and kisses away the rest of whatever scientific fact she was about to enlighten him with.

Expecting her to be hesitant, he's surprised when she returns his kiss with a hunger that rivals the bear they only just managed to escape from.

And he's not complaining.

"Sam," he breathes as his hand moves from her face to the curve of her back. Her damp shirt is clinging to her gentle curves and he longs to remove it so he can feel more of her than he's ever felt before.

As if they really are two halves of the same person and she can read his mind, she sits up and peels off her shirt, only breaking their kiss for a moment so the fabric can pass over her head.

His palms graze across her back, and the feel of her is everything he ever imagined and so much more. She's so soft, so feminine.

So. Sam.

Their kisses grow in urgency and he pulls her onto his lap. If they're not careful, they're going to fall right out of this tree. But he can't think of a more perfect place to experience the merging of two souls.

A marriage tree. So much better than the dare tree...

"Hawk." Sam pulls back to look at him, one hand cupping each side of his face. "We could have died today. We could still die tomorrow. But right now, we're alive, and I want to be close to you."

Surely, she's not asking his permission?

As a Seeker, he learned the value in talking. In knowing

when to use his words and how. But right now, instead of talking, he removes his shirt and wraps his arms around the only girl he'll ever love.

He's hers. Yesterday. Today. And tomorrow.

His heart belongs to Sam. He's told her this before.

Now it's time to show her.

SAM

*S*am draws back from a kiss that possibly just altered her DNA with its blazing passion. She's not only lost the ability to speak. She's lost the ability to breathe.

Hawk is gazing up at her, rain slicking down his handsome face, his eyes full of heat and promise, love and tenderness. His lips are parted. Waiting.

Undeniably wanting more.

They're dozens of feet off the ground. The rain is making not only their skin slick, but the bark and leaves beneath them. Who knows, if the bear is hungry enough, it could come back.

But they're in a marriage tree.

And this is Hawk. The only one who's ever made her feel like every cell in her body just melted and detonated all at once.

Sam slides closer, pulling in a sharp breath as his arms tighten, pressing their wet, bare chests together so close they both gasp. They seek each other out with their mouths, the heat growing exponentially. Sam doesn't know how steam isn't rising between them.

A moan lifts to the branches above, and Sam thinks it's hers, but she's not sure. Either way, the heated sound only fans the flames.

The chemistry between them explodes.

Clothes melt away. No matter how close they get, it doesn't seem close enough.

There's no shyness. Not with Hawk. Her hands explore him. Spear into his hair. Glory in the way his breath trembles with each stroke of her fingers.

Impatient, curious, and burning with desire, Sam straddles him. Their bodies join in a way they never have before. And yet, has never felt so right.

So...

Sam doesn't even try to finish that sentence. There are no words.

These minutes don't need any.

They keep their movements to a minimum. In part, because they're high up in a marriage tree. In part, because neither of them wants to release the tight hold they have on each other.

And when they reach new heights, they're there together. Soaring. Groaning. Finding something they discovered existed between them but have just learned exactly how breath-taking it is.

More minutes pass with no words. Just gasping lungs trying to find oxygen. Lips trying to communicate all the love and wonder they feel.

Sam pulls back an inch, finally finding one. The single word that has always captured it all. "Hawk," she breathes.

"Always," he whispers against her lips. "Always, Sam."

The rain and sweat starts to cool against her skin so she snuggles, letting out a sigh of contentment. Hawk's arms wrap around her, his chin resting atop her head. Sam listens to his heartbeat, his life-force.

And hers. Because her life is forever entwined with Hawk's. Just like her heart is.

Sam blinks away the rain collecting on her eyelashes, wanting to remember every atom of this moment. The feel of the corded muscles beneath her palms, of the warm skin pressed against hers. The scent of pine and rain and Hawk.

The sight of the mangrove pine needles, a deep, pure emerald, glistening with diamond beads of water. The misty ground far below them. The fragile tendrils of a vine weaving through them high up to her left.

Sam startles. A vine?

"What is it?" Hawk asks, concerned. "Is the bear back?"

But Sam isn't looking down. She squints, focusing past the rain at the light-green, veiny leaves tangled further above. "Calabar beans," she whispers.

Hawk straightens. "What? Where?"

Sam smiles so wide it almost hurts. She points at where she's looking. "There! Hawk, we found some Calabar beans!"

He follows where she's pointing, his arms still wrapped around her. His eyes widen. "Are you sure?"

Just when Sam didn't think she could be any happier, she discovers there's still room for more joy in her brimming body. "I'm sure. Pinnately trifoliate leaves, seed pods about one inch long with rounded ends, roughish but a little polished."

Hawk grins, pulling her in for a hard, quick kiss. "It's lucky we hung around, then."

Sam giggles, but then sobers. They're going to have to leave now, and she wants him to know. "I'm glad we did."

Hawk's smile is blinding, like she just gave him a precious gift. "Me, too."

They dress quickly, Sam sneaking glances at Hawk's rain-slicked body, only to find he's doing the same to her. They smile at each other, cheeks pinking, but not looking away, either. Sam hopes Hawk's wondering when they can do this again, too.

Hawk pulls on his shirt, covering the chest Sam wished she'd spent more time discovering. Maybe one day she could take her time, name each of the muscle groups. Hawk certainly has an impressive set of pectorals. And she could trace his oblique muscles, the transverse abdominals, and the V-shaped line below...the inguinal crease...who knew it could be so fascinating! So...touchable.

But Hawk's already looking toward the vine a few feet further up the mangrove pine. "You wait here. I'll go get them."

Sam nods, not bothering to object. She's accepted her skills aren't in strength or coordination. It was only the panic and fear that got her this high in the tree in the first place. "Be careful."

Hawk winks, the playful gesture making her heart flutter. "I have a lifetime of kisses to look forward to."

"Kisses." Sam agrees with a nod. Then she smiles cheekily. "And more."

Hawk looks surprised for a brief second, and she can't blame him. This is a side to herself even she didn't know existed. But he quickly recovers, winking again. "Also looking forward to that."

Turning back to study the tree, Hawk plots his climb. He may be strong, but he's also muscular and heavy. That means needing strong foot and hand holds. Reaching up, he grips a sturdy branch, tests it, then hauls himself up. He's just reached the second one when the rain increases in intensity, muttering a low growl of thunder high above them as if Mother Nature is trying to hurry them.

Sam chews on her lip. She doesn't want to distract Hawk. Being so high is precarious in itself. Climbing further up when it's raining is bordering on downright dangerous.

Hawk continues his steady ascent, Sam holding her breath the whole time. Rain falls in her eyes, each time feeling like a tiny needle, but she ignores it. It's totally irrational, but keeping her gaze on Hawk feels like she's helping him somehow.

Hawk finally reaches the first of the pods dangling among the branches. He stretches and snaps them off, slipping the precious haul into his pocket. Although she's relieved, Sam doesn't relax. Each pod contains two to three seeds. They're going to need a few more.

"There aren't many here," Hawk calls down.

That's because Calabar beans are dying off this time of year, having finished their cycle of shooting for the treetops, flowering, forming seed pods, and dying. Another two weeks and finding them would be next to impossible.

Sam swallows. "We'll need five or six pods." At least the beans are highly poisonous, meaning they won't need basketfuls of them. "Don't put your hands near your face."

Sam thinks he rolls his eyes, but she can't tell. Her sight is too blurred by rain.

Hawk looks around and he must spot some more, because he shuffles a little to the right. Extending his arm, he reaches out to another branch, this one higher up. Sam sees the pods— big thick ones that no doubt contain good sized beans. They dangle down, quivering in the wind and rain. Hawk shuffles a few more steps and Sam has to cup her hand over her mouth. Too far out and the branch will no longer hold his weight.

Surely Hawk will know when he should stop…

There's another rumble of thunder and Sam's eyes widen. It didn't hide the sound of wood creaking and splintering. The branch Hawk's standing on is about to snap.

Hawk freezes, his hand still extended. He stares at the pods that are only inches from his hand. Sam can practically read his mind—"If I could just…"

Sam sucks in a breath so she can scream at him that it's not worth it. They can't save Askala if they're not alive.

But lightning streaks through the sky, filling it with bright light and roaring thunder. Sam blinks, squints, is blinded for precious seconds, but she never takes her gaze off Hawk.

It means she sees the gust of wind that pushes Hawk's curls

back from his face. It plasters his clothes against his body. And presses the pods straight into his waiting palm.

"Got them!" he shouts triumphantly.

Sam's breath whooshes out with relief. "That will do," she calls up to him. "Come back down, now."

"But I only have four. You said we needed—"

"We can make it work. Those pods look big."

Lightning cracks again and the dark clouds suddenly feel lower. More ominous. It's going to be dangerous climbing back down the saturated tree.

Even in the gloom and rain, Sam can see Hawk's frown. Then he looks up again. "Just a couple more."

"But—"

The next flash of lightning is immediately followed by thunder, cutting off any objection Sam was about to voice. Hawk shuffles closer to the trunk again and reaches up. His hand grips the bough above him, but the moment he tries to haul himself up, his fingers slip.

Hawk drops, his foot slipping, too. Sam slaps her hand across her mouth again, cutting off the scream that just escaped. Hawk quickly wraps his arms around the trunk, anchoring himself. For long moments, he doesn't move. Sam doesn't move.

As the storm continues to rage.

A lifetime passes and Hawk releases the trunk. But instead of coming down, he looks back up, his jaw set. And then he's climbing again. Slowly. Determinedly.

Sam's lungs ache for air, but she can't breathe. Her whole body is frozen as she watches Hawk pull himself up to the next sodden, slippery branch.

The Calabar bean pod is closer than she realized, because he's barely balanced when he reaches out and grabs it beside the trunk.

He holds it down to show her. "One more!" Hawk calls triumphantly.

"That's enough, Hawk! We can make the antidote with what we have!"

Hawk looks like he's considering objecting, but Mother Nature opens the floodgates above. Water rushes over Sam's face and she loses sight of Hawk.

"Hawk!" But all that greets her is the sounds of the waterfall they're now in. "Hawk!"

"Don't move, Sam! I'm almost there."

Sam clutches the trunk as she waits, her hair and clothes plastered to her body. Long moments later, Hawk appears in front of her, smiling. Sam's never seen anything more beautiful in her life.

Hawk digs into his pocket and pulls out the pods to show her. "We did it, Sam. We can make the cure."

"The antidote," Sam responds automatically. She looks down at the pods in wonder, water pooling in Hawk's palm. "But yes, we did."

Askala will be strong enough to defend itself.

Hawk tucks them back into his pocket. He glances up at the deluge then down at the ground far below. "Maybe we should wait until this eases up a bit."

But Sam shakes her head. "The sooner we get back, the sooner people can have the antidote." She shoves her sodden hair out of her face as she pushes down her fear. "We'll just take it slow."

Hawk's lips thin even as he nods. Just because she's right, doesn't mean he likes it. "I'll go first."

Sam swallows as she watches him descend to the branch below. Water is weaving intricate rivers down the bark of the trunk. Everything is slippery and wet. The ground seems so far away.

But Askala needs the antidote. Her mother needs it. It means Sam's determined to reach the forest floor in one piece.

Carefully, she clambers down, relief coursing through her as

Hawk's arms wrap around her. Thunder rumbles. Lightning strikes. The rain is heavy and punishing.

One down. Right now, she doesn't want to know how many there are to go. She's going to take this treacherous climb one slippery branch at a time.

There's another rumble and they both freeze as they realize this sound is different. Quieter. And coming from below.

A part of her not wanting to, Sam looks down. Hawk gasps as he registers what Sam does.

The polar grizzly is back.

The massive beast shakes, water droplets spraying outward from its patchwork fur. It rears onto its back legs, letting out a roar that rivals the thunder.

Sweet Terra, and it's angry.

The bear doesn't drop after its violent bellow is finished. Instead, it wraps its powerful arms around the trunk and looks up. Directly at them.

Sam's knees go weak. It knows they're up here.

Fear clamps around her chest, making it hard to breathe. "Come on," Hawk shouts, still holding onto Sam with one hand as he starts to climb with the other.

She scrambles after him, soft bark crumbling beneath her hands and jamming under her nails. She slips, but Hawk only tightens his hold, and they quickly make it back to the branch they just left.

Below, the polar grizzly wraps around the trunk, digging its claws in. It leaps and shimmies, making its way up.

Sam's panting as she watches. She looks up. There are only a handful of branches that will be able to take their weight. It's only minutes before the grizzly reaches them.

Hawk must realize the same thing, because he presses her against the trunk then places himself in front of her. "Maybe I can knock it down," he mutters grimly.

The bear roars again, as if it heard Hawk and has accepted

the challenge. It releases its hold, leaps, and clamps on again. Over and over, it repeats the process. Release. Leap. Grip.

Each time, coming closer and closer.

Now, Sam can make out its dark eyes, alive with the anticipation of its next meal. She can see its claws, as long and as sharp as a knife, gouge into the tree as the bear holds its weight.

Those paws are what will swipe at Hawk. As he tries to kick at it, its claws will slice him open. He'll be shredded in one blow. Even if he doesn't fall, the smell of blood will have the bear in a frenzy.

And Sam's not strong enough to help him. Save him.

How can her brains help them now?

The flash of something wooden tucked in the back of Hawk's pants has her stilling. An idea she can't believe she's considering, comes to life.

She grips Hawk's shoulders. "Use your slingshot!"

He doesn't take his gaze off the bear as he shakes his head. "I have nothing to throw at it."

"The beans," Sam shouts hoarsely. "You need to get them in its mouth."

Hawk blinks. Sam's talking about poisoning the bear. As long as it works quickly enough, it could save them.

But if they do this, they could lose any chance of creating the antidote.

He looks over his shoulder. "But…"

Sam presses a hand to his wet cheek. "I know I should be sorry, but I'll always choose you, Hawk."

Which makes her selfish. More of an Outlander than she ever thought possible.

And yet, it still feels right. She knows deep down Hawk would make the same decision for her.

Sam also knows this is the Askala she wants to fight for. One where the parts are just as important as the whole.

Hawk's answer is to yank the pods out of his pocket and pass them to Sam. "You peel, I'll slingshot."

Hawk turns around, bracing himself, and Sam feels the tension corded through his muscles. The bear's close. They don't have much time.

The grizzly vaults again, the biggest leap so far and Sam instinctively gasps. But as the bear grips the trunk, it slides down the slick bark, claws gouging deep into the tree. It stops a couple of feet lower than it started, roaring its frustration.

But it's the respite they needed. That could save their lives.

Sam passes him the first few beans and Hawk draws the slingshot back and aims.

The first one sails right past the bear. The second hits a branch and spins crazily into the rain. Sam passes Hawk two more, throwing away the husks of the two pods they've now consumed.

Hawk pulls in a deep breath and steadies himself. He draws back and aims at the bear, rain streaming down his taut arms. He releases the slingshot and the bean flings down, spearing between two branches and hitting the polar grizzly in the eye.

It bellows, shaking its head. It leaps another foot up the tree, thick pelt rippling.

So far, all they've done is make it angrier. Sam draws in a sharp breath. But the bear had its mouth wide open.

"Do that again, Hawk! Hit it in the face, then get one in its mouth!"

He nods once before taking aim again. Each time, the bear is closer and closer. Although that makes the furious predator easier to hit, it also means they're closer to becoming prey.

Hawk aims and releases. The first bean hits the bear in the forehead, eliciting another roar. The second bullet follows the first in quick succession, sailing straight into the bear's mouth.

"Yes!" Sam exclaims.

The bear's eyes flash open in shock. It pauses, throat working as it shakes its head.

"It swallowed it!" Hawk says, sounding as surprised as he is excited.

There's a flash of lightning, an immediate clap of thunder as Sam and Hawk wait, breaths held, bodies still. Calabar bean poison works fast. It's a highly efficient defense mechanism that the plant has evolved. The sooner its poison can take out a hungry animal, the fewer beans it will consume.

The bear moves and Sam gasps. It's not slipping, not losing its grip on the trunk. It's continuing its trajectory.

Toward them.

Frantically, Sam peels the next batch of beans. "We need to repeat the process. Make it roar, get a bean in its mouth."

Hawk nods resolutely.

He releases two more shots, but the bear ignores the beans peppering it. It steadily approaches, white teeth flashing as it growls its determination, but never opening its mouth.

The closer it comes, the harder the beans hit, but it's like the bear knows what they're trying to do. Its muzzle remains shut as it leaps. Grips. Steadily comes closer.

Sam can smell the wet, animal hide. See the bloodlust in its eyes. Hear the growls that are far more terrifying than the thunder.

Hawk stops and Sam realizes he's run out of ammunition. He glances over his shoulder, obviously trying to hide his fear as he asks the question. "How many are left?"

"Three," Sam whispers.

Hawk's face hardens. "I won't let it get you, Sam."

A fresh wave of fear spears through Sam. There's no doubt in her mind Hawk intends on sacrificing himself for her. Possibly leaping down and trying to take the bear with him.

She wraps her arms around his waist. "Try again."

Turning back, Hawk once again takes aim.

"Two in the eyes. One in the mouth," Sam says quietly. Determinedly.

Hawk nods. A second later, he releases the first bean. It pelts the bear in the corner of its right eye. The bear grumbles as it blinks away the sting. Hawk waits for it to steady again, then rapidly releases the second bean.

It spears right into the bear's left eye, this time harder and with unerring accuracy.

The bear roars in indignation, the eye tightly shut.

"Now, Hawk," Sam breathes.

The last bean flies through the air and lodges straight in the polar grizzly's throat. It cuts the roar short as the massive animal chokes and splutters.

And then the bean is gone. Journeying to its stomach. About to be digested.

Except now the bear's furious. It roars again, droplets of water exploding with the force of its anger.

Hawk presses back, his arms reaching behind him to grip the trunk, trapping Sam. Protecting her.

The bear leaps then leaps again. This time, it swipes with a monstrous paw. It whooshes past Hawk's leg, hitting nothing but air and water. The bear grips the trunk again, the powerful claws impaling the tree in the same way they would human flesh.

Sam whimpers. The poison's taking too long.

Maybe it wasn't enough.

She's about to watch Hawk die.

Another leap. A violent swipe, this one only a hairbreadth from Hawk's thigh. Sam screams, and she's not sure if she's more terrified or angry that they came this far, only for it to end like this.

A flash of lightning, this one so much closer than the ones before, shoots another jolt of terror down Sam's spine. It dazzles her for a moment, but as she blinks furiously, she sees the bear has stopped.

It holds itself still, no longer climbing or swiping. Suddenly, its body contracts like it was just gripped by a spasm of pain. It moans, its arms loosening. The grizzly scrabbles to tighten its grip again, but it can't seem to get a hold. Shards of bark splinter and tear away, falling to the ground far below.

Hawk steps forward and lashes out with his foot. The grizzly rears back, its eyes shooting wide open as it realizes it just released the trunk. Blood gushes from its mouth, coating its lips as the poison destroys its insides.

The polar grizzly's massive body tumbles backward, slamming into a branch beside it. The bough shatters under its weight and the bear falls.

More branches break, with greater and greater frequency as the bear gains momentum. There's a thud. Then nothing but the thrum of rain.

Sam's arms loosen from around the trunk, disbelief coursing through her body. Her eyes trace the outline of Hawk's shoulders, noting the way they rise and fall with each panting breath.

He's breathing. He's unhurt. But, for some reason, she needs to touch him. To hold him. To make sure.

Hawk spins around, the same need bleeding from his eyes. In a blink he's holding her, and they kiss. Passionately. Desperately. Gratefully.

There's no more crashing, roaring, snapping of branches. The bear's dead.

Hawk draws back and rests his forehead against hers. Rain streaks down their faces in rivulets as they stare at each other, breathing hard.

They're alive. But it came at a price.

The Calabar beans are gone.

How will they save Askala now?

MERCY

*T*he wait for midnight is torture, mostly because Mercy has no idea what the time is. It's impossible to tell without a window to see the stars. It has to be soon. She *hopes* it's soon. Because sitting in a small hut in scorching temperatures with three other living bodies, one dead man, and a decaying bird is taking its toll.

Before the last of the daylight had disappeared through the cracks in the timber walls, Mercy had seen Tarquin asleep on Alyx's lap. Her gentle snoring indicates she's still sleeping. Nobody else is. Not when they're so acutely aware that these may be the last minutes or hours of their lives. It wouldn't seem right to waste them with their eyes closed.

Mercy is sitting up, leaning against one of the walls with Luca beside her. Their hands are clasped together despite the sheen of sweat coating their skin. The closeness of him is the only thing keeping her calm right now.

"You should've gone," Mercy tells him again.

"Not this again." Luca squeezes her hand in the dark. "I told you I'm not leaving you. Besides…"

"Besides what?" asks Alyx in a croaky voice.

"Grace may not be my mother," says Luca. "But I'm certain I'm important to her, somehow. She doesn't want to see me killed, which means the three of you are safer if we stick together. Then it's only Corbin we have to deal with."

Mercy nods even though Luca can't see her.

"I'm so sorry, Luca," says Alyx. "I want you to know I regret—"

"Alyx." Luca shifts uncomfortably beside Mercy. "I already know. It's okay. I get why you did it."

Alyx sniffs. "It's just that if anything happens to us, I want you to know I'm sorry. I really am."

"You're a good sister," says Mercy. "You did it for Tarquin. That shows courage."

"I didn't want my life to turn out like this." Alyx sighs deeply. "Hawk told me about Askala. He said he'll teach me to read. And Tarquin. He said we can have a better life. That maybe I can even find love..."

"We have to get there first," says Luca, putting a pin in Alyx's hopes.

"There's still hope." Mercy tries to inject some enthusiasm in her voice. "I haven't given up yet. None of us should."

"I'm not jealous, you know," says Alyx. "Of Tarquin's bond with you two. It's a relief to know there's someone else out there who'll look out for her if needed."

Mercy's heart aches. "We love Tarquin."

"And she's fast learning to look after herself," Luca adds.

Tarquin yawns loudly. "He's right."

"I thought you were asleep," says Luca.

"Peregrines don't sleep," says Tarquin. "That's why Mercy's awake."

"I'm pretty sure you've been asleep all this time," laughs Alyx. "Unless you snore when you're awake."

"I was just tricking you so that you'd say nice things about me." Tarquin giggles and Mercy wishes she could see the cheeky look she knows is on her face.

"We say nice things about you when you're awake, too," says Luca.

"You've never said you love me," Tarquin points out. "And just so you know, I love you, too. All three of you."

Mercy hears Alyx give Tarquin a noisy kiss.

"Is Hawk really going to teach us to read?" asks Tarquin. "Because no offence, but he doesn't look like someone who can read."

Mercy smiles. "What does someone who can read look like?"

"Hmm." Tarquin thinks about this. "Someone with less muscles. Someone like Sam."

"Then maybe Sam will teach you," says Luca. "Because she sure likes books."

There's a rattle at the door when the bar is lifted.

Mercy's gut clenches as the food she never ate feels like it's about to come up.

A warm breeze winds its way through as the door creaks open. Mercy drags in deep breaths of fresh air that smell nothing like death or body odor.

"Raiden." Luca is already on his feet. "You came."

Mercy squints up at his shadow and joins him, creating a buffer for Alyx and Tarquin just in case Raiden tries something.

"The boat is ready to go on the beach," says Raiden, not bothering to keep his voice down. "Come on. We have a long journey ahead."

Mercy still doesn't like the idea of trusting this slimeball, but Luca's already following him out the door so there isn't much choice.

"Come on," Mercy says gently to Alyx and Tarquin. "It's time."

She steps out into the night and blinks up at the stars

lighting the sky. Whatever happens next is going to be significant. Soon she'll either be on a boat to Askala, or she'll be… dead. She can't imagine an option where she remains in the Newlands still breathing.

Luca reaches for her hand and she takes it, grateful for the contact.

"This way," says Raiden, leaning heavily on his spear as he limps into the line of trees.

Luca turns to Alyx and Tarquin. "Stay close."

"Don't worry about that," Alyx mutters, practically stepping on Mercy's heels as they walk.

It's dark under the canopy of the trees and Mercy squeezes Luca's hand, wondering how he can be so calm. He's had more exposure to life and death experiences, she supposes. Too much. And sadly, it seems she's catching up.

The walk down the path behind Raiden is painfully slow. Mercy wills him to hobble faster, just wanting to get this over with. If this isn't a trick and Raiden really wants to go to Askala, they're going to have a whole new problem on their hands. They can't trust him. And Sam will never be safe with the likes of him wandering around. But there's not a whole lot of point thinking about this too much now. Actually arriving in Askala still seems like a pipedream.

They eventually arrive at the beach and Raiden holds back.

"The boat's been covered in branches to disguise it," he says. "You go on ahead first. I've slowed you down enough already."

Mercy lets go of Luca's hand and steps onto the soft sand, squinting at the water. Her heart leaps to see a dark shadow in the shallows that's roughly the right size and shape of a boat. It looks like Raiden's told the truth for once.

"There it is," says Tarquin, her voice spilling over with excitement. "We're really going to Askala."

Mercy smiles widely as she takes a few more steps down the sand but Alyx tugs her back by her shirt.

"Luca told us to stay close," Alyx hisses in her ear.

"Luca?" Mercy spins around, realizing he's no longer by her side.

There's a loud *thump* in the trees and Mercy's feet are moving before she has a chance to think. She has to get to Luca.

But when she gets back to the tree line, she grinds to a halt. There are two shadows. One standing and the other falling to the ground.

"Luca!" she gasps, blinking her eyes into focus.

"Stay back!" Luca shouts.

Mercy breathes a sigh. Luca's not the one on the ground and that's all that matters right now.

Luca squats down, checking on Raiden's silent form and Mercy gasps as she tries to make sense of what she's seeing. "Did you kill him?"

"Quickly!" Luca doesn't answer her question as he ushers her through the trees. "Follow me."

"But I want to go to Askala!" Tarquin wails. "There's a boat in the water."

"That's not a boat," says Luca, urging them forward. "That's a trap."

"Hurry!" says Mercy, not completely understanding what just happened, but knowing enough that they need to listen to Luca right now.

Luca jogs into the forest, heading away from the Outlanders' encampment.

Mercy waits for Alyx and Tarquin to follow so she can take up the rear. Keeping Tarquin safe is her only priority right now. Every child deserves the right to grow up. Mercy isn't going to let that be stolen away from her.

They move with urgency, only just managing to keep up with Luca in the dark.

Branches scratch at Mercy's arms but she pushes forward.

Luca wouldn't be leading them anywhere without some kind of plan. He knows what he's doing.

They weave through the trees until Mercy has no idea where they are anymore, eventually taking a track down to the sand about a mile from where Raiden originally led them.

Luca falls to his knees beside a large rock and starts scooping sand away.

"Help me," he says. "I buried a raft here."

Mercy's eyes fly open and she drops to the sand to dig. Tarquin and Alyx are beside her in a moment and the four of them haul away the sand frantically.

"When did you do this?" Mercy asks, not pausing her flurried movements as she waits for a response.

"Ages ago," he says between panting breaths. "When we first got here and I was avoiding you."

"Oh." That feels like a lifetime ago, but Mercy remembers it well. Luca had disappeared for a long stretch after he'd first given into the magnetic pull between them. She'd thought he was hiding from her in the forest, but it appears he'd been far busier than that. The clever guy had thought to set up an emergency escape plan in case they ever needed it.

And they've never needed it more than now.

"I can feel something," says Alyx at the same time Mercy's fingertips hit solid timber.

They continue digging and it's only moments later that Luca starts to heave on a large dark shape that's emerging from underneath the sand.

"You're so clever, Luca," says Tarquin, clearly impressed.

But clever isn't the first word that comes to Mercy's mind as she watches him haul out the raft he'd built and drag it down toward the water.

Hot.

That's the word she can't get out of her head.

This guy is just so...hot! Who else would think to prepare

something like this in case they needed it? If they survive this experience and ever get to spend another moment alone, she's going to jump him so fast he's not going to know what hit him.

"Let's go," says Alyx, tugging on Mercy's sleeve.

Shaking her head back to reality, Mercy runs down the beach just as Luca sets the raft down on the damp sand to untie the oars he'd strapped to it. It's a small raft given there are four of them, and it will be a dangerous journey to Askala, but they can do this. They have so much more chance now than they had when they were locked in that stinking hut. Besides, Mercy would much rather be devoured by a leatherskin than someone like that awful Raggid.

Luca gets the oars free and hands them to Mercy as he pushes the raft into the shallows.

"Quickly, get on," he says, moonlight bouncing off that kiss-able face of his.

Alyx carries Tarquin over the water and puts her on the raft while Luca holds it steady. She climbs on after her and Mercy hands Tarquin the oars, finding a free spot at the back behind her.

Luca pushes them further out and tells them to hold on while he scrambles on board.

The raft tips wildly and Mercy steadies herself as Tarquin hands Luca an oar.

He digs the timber into the water and rows. Mercy takes the other oar and helps him. Together, they make a small amount of progress against the waves that seem determined to drag them back to shore. She can't wait to leave this hellhole and return home, even if they know they're going to have to fight to save Askala when they get there.

Because no matter how Mercy looks at it, the Newlands suck. Never in her life could she imagine a more miserable place. It's even worse than the Outlands, despite the fact it still has trees.

Mercy rows harder as they try to clear the break of the waves.

"We're going home," she says, smiling at Alyx. "We're actually going home."

"I can't wait to see Askala." Alyx smiles back at her and as the moonlight glints off her fair hair.

Mercy's heart surges to know that Alyx will finally get a chance to live a life where she doesn't have to trade the most precious parts of herself. Nobody should have to fight for their survival like that.

The smile falls from Alyx's face and her eyes widen as if she's been shocked by an electric current. She lurches forward, plastering herself to Luca's back.

"What the—" Luca tries to turn around and Mercy screams.

There's a long stick poking out of Alyx's back. A stick Mercy's seen before.

It's Raiden's spear. And it's gone straight through Alyx.

"No!" Mercy cries as the horrible realization washes over her.

She looks to the shore and sees Raiden standing in the shallows. He's grinning at them. A group of his men are standing behind him, their own spears at the ready.

"Alyx!" Tarquin has turned herself around on the raft and is cradling her big sister's head in her lap. "Alyx, wake up! No, Alyx. No!"

"You bastard!" Mercy screams at Raiden as she plunges her oar back in the water, watching as Luca does the same. No matter how much their hearts are broken right now, they have to keep rowing.

They haul their oars through the water with renewed focus, widening the gap from shore.

"Watch out!" screams Tarquin as a spear slams into the raft.

Mercy rows harder, wincing as she tries to prepare herself to meet the same end as Alyx. But it seems that a moving target in the dark isn't so easy to hit. More spears rain down, slicing into the water, but somehow none of them find their mark.

"They're swimming out to us!" cries Tarquin.

"They're not going to get us," says Mercy through gritted teeth.

Her throat might be burning with thirst and her muscles screaming with pain but Mercy rows on, knowing they have one big advantage here. Those men are in the acidic water, and they're not. And it seems they've thrown every spear they have.

The ocean pushes them back but each time they surge themselves forward until they manage to get the raft over the crest of a wave.

"We're over the break!" calls Luca. "Keep going."

Mercy has no intention of stopping. She keeps rowing, not looking back, not even once. That would waste precious seconds they don't have. The acid will be burning the skin of those men by now and slowing them down. They've got this.

They row on. Agonizing minutes pass like hours. But Tarquin's howls and pleas for Alyx to wake up spur Mercy on. This isn't a game. This isn't some test in a Proving. This is real life. And real death...

"We can slow down now," says Luca, turning to look back at the shore. "They've given up."

Mercy sets down her oar for a moment, a pain in her heart replacing the pain in her aching muscles.

"She won't wake up, Mercy," sobs Tarquin. "She's really dead."

Mercy looks over at Luca and he nods. They both know what they have to do. The raft will move faster without extra weight. And there's no saving Alyx now.

It's time to let her go.

"Tarquin," says Mercy. "Did you know that Peregrines are not only the fastest animal on Earth, but they're also the bravest?"

Mercy actually knows very little about the Peregrine falcon but the way Tarquin's nodding spurs her on.

"Which means we need to be very brave right now," says Mercy. "We need to thank Alyx for being the best sister in the whole world. And then we need to let her spirit fly free."

"Is Alyx a Peregrine now?" asks Tarquin, biting down on her bottom lip.

"She is," says Mercy. "She looked after you when your own mother couldn't. She fought for you. She waited for you. She protected you. And she saved Luca's life. She's the bravest Peregrine I ever saw."

"She was very brave," says Tarquin.

"She was," Luca agrees. "We'll never forget her."

"Are we putting her in the water?" asks Tarquin.

Luca nods. "I'm going to take the spear out first. Can you close your eyes for a moment?"

Tarquin squeezes them tightly shut.

Luca moves quickly, pulling out the spear, dipping it clean in the ocean and setting it down beside him. A weapon like that could be valuable if a leatherskin takes an interest in their raft. They can't afford to let it go no matter what heinous crime it was just used for.

Mercy reaches for Tarquin, upsetting the balance of the raft.

"I'm okay," says Tarquin bravely. "I'm being brave."

"You're so brave," says Mercy, glancing back at the shore, noticing they've been pushed back a little. They need to do this quickly so they can move on. "It's time to say goodbye now, okay?"

Tarquin leans over Alyx and kisses her on the forehead. "Thanks for being my big sister."

Mercy holds back a sob as her emotion builds in the back of her throat. This is so unfair. If Raiden didn't want to go with them, why couldn't he have just let them go?

Not only did Alyx risk her life waiting for Tarquin to return to the Newlands, but ultimately she sacrificed herself for the very guy she only just begged for forgiveness. It's all too much to take in right now.

"Hold on," says Luca, as he positions himself beside Alyx and removes the blue diamond from around her neck. He hands it to Tarquin who clutches it tightly as Luca gently rolls Alyx to the edge of the raft.

"Bye, Alyx." Tarquin puts out her hand as Luca tips her into the sea.

She disappears under the surface and Mercy can hold back her tears no more.

"Bye, Alyx," she sobs.

Luca returns quickly to the task of rowing but not before Mercy sees the pain etched across his face. Alyx had once meant something to Luca. She knows they'd been far more than just friends and allies. Perhaps they still would've been if Mercy hadn't come along.

"I'm sorry." Mercy reaches a hand out to the ocean, wishing it hadn't turned out like this.

Tarquin curls herself into a ball in the middle of the raft and falls silent.

That poor girl has so much to process. Her short life has been filled with so much pain and loss. Hopefully when they get to Askala that can change. It has to.

In their last conversation in the hut Alyx had asked Mercy and Luca to look after her sister if anything were to happen to her. It was almost like she'd known. And Mercy might not be able to change anything in the past, but she can respect Alyx's memory by granting this final request.

She's going to look after Tarquin like precious gold. She's going to keep her safe. She's going to make sure she learns to read. She's going to give her the life that Alyx never got to experience. Everything that Alyx gave up is not going to be for nothing.

Raiden and his evil goons have taken so much from them.

But today that ends. The tide has turned.

And just like Alyx, they need to be brave.

Mercy looks at Tarquin's small frame all curled up, and draws her in closer.

It's time for this Peregrine to fight back.

LUCA

*D*awn creeps over the horizon, creating the glorious backdrop Askala deserves. Something unwinds in Luca's chest as he gazes at the sliver of land, a sweet shade of green even at this distance.

Askala.

His home.

The family he always wanted is there.

And yet he couldn't see that at the time.

Mercy puts her oar down and wraps her arms around him. "They're going to be so glad to see you."

"I've caused them so much worry and stress," Luca says, his voice full of remorse.

"And yet you've given them so much more," Mercy says with conviction. She hugs him tighter. "Have I caused you worry? Stress?"

He snorts. "Yes and definitely yes."

"And was it worth it?"

Luca doesn't hesitate. "Every second."

Mercy looks at him triumphantly. "Exactly."

It takes a second or two for Mercy's point to hit, but when it does, Luca bursts into a grin. Hopefully, Kian and Nova think the same—that the stress was worth it.

Tarquin sits up, rubbing her eyes. She looks around, stilling when she sees land on the horizon. "We're almost there?"

Mercy releases Luca so she can turn a dazzling smile toward Tarquin. "We are! You're going to love Askala."

Tarquin stares at the steadily growing smudge of green. "Do they have water? Food?"

"Yes and definitely yes," Mercy promises with a twinkle in her eyes.

Tarquin pulls up her own blazing smile. "Then I love it already." The smile drops as quickly as it appeared. "Alyx would've loved it, too."

"She'd be happy to know you'll be seeing it," Luca assures her.

He dips his oar back in the water, Mercy doing the same on the other side of the raft. A look passes between them. They're all thirsty. All hungry.

All conscious of what Alyx sacrificed so they could be here. So Luca could be here.

Luca pushes the oar deep into the water. His last reserves of energy were spent some time ago, but he didn't stop rowing. The three of them are on a small raft in a giant ocean, surrounded by predators—both human and animal. Getting to Askala as quickly as possible was their only chance of survival.

Of ensuring Alyx's death wasn't for nothing.

"It's so pretty!" Tarquin shuffles to the front of the raft, watching with rapt attention as Askala grows larger and larger. She's as still as a statue as the tree line becomes visible, then the bleached sand of the beach, then the roofs of the huts peeking from the greenery.

Luca thinks back to his own arrival at Askala as a child. He thought he was dreaming. He thought he'd found somewhere magical and impossible. He spent days thinking this wonderful place was going to disappear any moment.

And now Tarquin's going to discover somewhere so special is well and truly real.

"Look! There are even purple flowers in the treetops!" says Tarquin, her eyes wide. "And birds everywhere! Listen to them. They're so noisy!"

The raft has barely scraped over sand before Mercy leaps out to run up the final few feet. The moment she's away from the lapping waves, she throws her hands into the air as she spins around.

"We're home, Luca!"

Tarquin joins her, giggling as she runs circles around Mercy. The instant the raft jams into sand, Luca's off, too. He runs to Mercy and scoops her up, maintaining her momentum and spinning them both as she squeals with joy.

Chuckling, Luca places her down. "We're home, Mercy," he murmurs.

Her beautiful eyes shine up at him, overflowing with so much love that it takes his breath away. They're here thanks to the power of determination, love, luck. Sacrifice.

Tarquin pushes between them. "Can we eat now?"

Luca ruffles her matted hair. "Do you remember the pteropods?" he asks, reminding her of the harvest they undertook together. "There are lots of those here."

Tarquin wrinkles her nose. "Great."

"Luca?"

The choked voice has Luca spinning around. It's a voice he knows. A voice he wasn't sure he'd ever hear again.

Kian is standing at the edge of the trees, rooted to the spot. "Luca," he whispers. "My son."

Luca's heart splinters with joy and regret. He runs to the only man who's ever been a father to him, and they embrace for long, hard seconds.

Kian slaps him on the shoulder. "I can't believe you're back."

Luca pulls away. "I was always going to come home."

Kian's eyes pool with moisture as he nods. He looks over Luca's shoulder, his face splitting into a smile. "Mercy."

Mercy rushes forward to hug him, too. "It's so good to see you, Kian."

She steps back, holding out a hand to Tarquin. For the first time, Luca sees uncertainty in the little girl's face. Tarquin chews on her bottom lip before lifting her chin. She strides up to Kian and looks him in the eye.

"My name's Tarquin and I've come to live here. In peace, apparently."

Kian's face fills with delight as he chuckles. "Lovely to meet you, Tarquin. I'm Kian, Sam and Luca's father." He glances out of the corner of his eye toward Luca. "And goodness, do you remind me of someone I know."

Tarquin brightens at that. "The Falcon? Or the Peregrine?"

Kian glances quizzically between Luca and Mercy, wondering what Tarquin is referring to. Luca opens his mouth, unsure how he's going to explain all this, when he looks around. "You're alone?"

Kian's face instantly sobers. "There's much we need to talk about."

Mercy's hand flies to her chest. "My parents?"

"They're fine," Kian assures. "But many...aren't."

Luca scans the area. He's not surprised that Kian was the one who came across them. For as long as Luca can remember, Kian and Nova have taken an early morning walk each day, connecting with the beauty that is Askala. But Kian's alone.

Dread is like a rock in Luca's gut. "Where's Nova?"

Kian's face drops, deep lines that Luca's never seen before appearing. "At home. She's not well, Luca."

"Not well?" What does that even mean?

Kian grips Luca's shoulder. "I think you came back just in time."

The rock in his gut bottoms out painfully. "What are you talking about?"

Mercy brushes his arm. "I'll take Tarquin to meet my parents," she says quietly. "You go see Nova."

Luca nods mutely, scared of what he's going to find. This isn't what he was expecting to return to.

Kian turns and Luca follows him down the familiar path. How many times did he run down it, wanting to show Nova something he found? Needing her to tend to a scraped knee? Wondering whether she had some treat set out on the table, waiting for him?

"What's going on?" he asks Kian.

Kian glances over his shoulder. The lines in his face now look like they've been gouged into his skin. "I'll tell you everything once you've seen her."

Luca frowns. Kian's talking as if they don't have much time.

The hut is quiet as they approach it, and Luca glances around. There are fewer people around than he expected to see. Everything seems...subdued, somehow.

Inside, Kian pushes open the door and steps back. "She's going to be so happy to see you, Luca." He pauses. "She tires quickly, though."

Luca strides in, panic starting to flutter up his spine. The kitchen area is empty, the other place Luca would've expected to find Nova at this time of day, so he heads straight for Nova and Kian's bedroom.

He stops at the doorway, shocked into stillness. He barely breathes as he takes in the pale waif in the bed.

"Mom?" he whispers.

Nova's lids flutter, looking like translucent, veined butterflies. Her brows crinkle.

She knows his voice.

But Luca's never called her what she's always been to him. His mother.

Her eyes open and she searches the room, struggling to focus. A few blinks and her gaze settles on Luca. She draws in a shocked, shallow breath as her face lights up. "Luca?"

He's by her side in a few short strides. Falling to his knees, Luca takes her hand, noticing with alarm how cool and thin it feels. "It's me."

A tear trickles from the corner of Nova's eye, tracking its way down her temple. "You're home," she breathes.

"I'm home." He squeezes her hand gently. "I can't believe it took me so long to realize that's what Askala is."

Nova's pale lips tip up in a smile. "You'll always have more than one home, Luca. We were just lucky to be one of them."

Luca's chest aches so hard it makes his eyes sting. He swallows, knowing he needs to ask. "What's wrong? Why are you so sick?"

"Kian hasn't told you?" Nova asks, her voice already losing strength.

"I just arrived. When he said you were unwell, I rushed straight here."

Nova's eyes flutter shut, like just these few words have exhausted her. "He'll fill you in. A lot...has happened... since the Seekers left."

Luca feels her hand relax in his, and he can't help but hold his breath until he sees her chest rise again. The movement is there, but barely.

"I love you, Mom," he chokes out.

Her fingers, barely more than skeleton and skin, twitch in his hand. "Say it again," Nova breathes, the joy apparent in her thready voice.

Luca knows what she's talking about. He's told Nova he loves her plenty of times. But for some reason, he always insisted on calling Kian and Nova by their names. Not by the roles they took on.

He believed he should save those labels for his biological parents. Not the people who loved and cared for him, no matter what.

"I love you, Mom."

Nova lets out a rattly breath, her face softening with happiness. A moment later, she falls asleep again.

Luca tries to get up only to find his legs aren't working. A part of him doesn't want to leave her side.

But he needs answers. He needs to find out if they can fix this.

Pushing up, he steps back into the kitchen, finding Kian sitting at the table. His shoulders are weighed down with everything Luca just saw.

Nova's dying.

Luca moves to the other side of the table, his hands clenched as he braces himself. "What's going on?"

Kian looks up, his eyes full of something Luca never thought he'd see—helplessness. He opens his mouth to speak only to be stopped by the sounds of footsteps outside.

They both turn to find Sam standing in the doorway, looking shocked. "Luca?"

She flies into his arms and Luca holds his sister tightly. They remain in their embrace for long moments, neither speaking.

Sam pulls back. "You've seen her?"

Luca nods. "What have you tried?"

He has no doubt Sam would've spent every spare minute researching how to help their mother.

Sam's hands twist together. "Everything. At first we couldn't figure out what was making everyone sick. So many died." Sam's voice cracks. "Including Seb."

Luca rocks back on his heels. "No, not Seb."

Grief engulfs Luca, making it a struggle to comprehend that

his fragile, sweet little brother is gone. But the soul-deep sadness in Sam's eyes is undeniable. Over at the table, Kian has his head in his hands, his body wound tight as he works to keep it together.

The truth slams through Luca. Seb's gone. Taken from them.

Sam draws in a shuddering breath. "Then we realized it was Charity. She was poisoning our food with deadly nightshade."

Luca's breath whooshes out. "Sweet Terra."

"We stopped her—she's being held in a hut as we try to find out what the Outlanders are planning." Sam glances at the doorway to their parents' bedroom. "But she did a lot of damage. People have died, and many more are still sick."

Like their mother. Luca glances at Kian, wondering how much losing Nova will break his father's spirit, especially after losing his son.

Especially with the threat Askala is facing.

"I know what the Outlanders are planning," Luca says gravely. "An attack." He grits his teeth, hating he's bringing this news at a time like this. "They're building a fleet of boats. We have about two weeks to prepare."

"Two weeks," Sam repeats, trying to process what that means.

Luca turns to Kian. "And Mom? Surely there's a way to help her now that we know what's wrong."

His father is pale as he holds his gaze, his cheeks devoid of color. "Not anymore."

Sam frowns. "We can find more Calabar beans, I know we can."

Their father pushes to his feet. "There's no time. Outlanders are coming, far sooner than we hoped."

"Calabar beans?" Luca asks.

"They're a known antidote to deadly nightshade," Sam explains. "It's late in the season, but Hawk and I found some."

Her cheeks pink. "We lost them trying to protect ourselves from a polar grizzly."

Luca wraps an arm around her shoulder. "I'm glad you did." He looks to Kian. "This way we can find more."

But their father is already heading toward the door. "It took two days to find the last ones. And now we know an attack is imminent. We need to prepare."

Luca can see how much it hurts their father to say this. Nova is dying only feet away, but Askala needs him.

It needs every able-bodied person left.

Their father leaves the hut and Sam and Luca look at each other. Then at the door to their mother's bedroom. They glance outside, seeing Hawk and Mercy making their way up the path.

The Seekers are about to be united.

And yet, it seems they're too late.

HAWK

*H*awk frowns as he watches Wren pace in front of the group gathered on the sand, each of them with a slingshot in their hand. These lessons are important, but he can't help wondering if they're enough. How can a peaceful colony fight off an army of savage killers with little more than a small piece of timber and a pocket full of rocks? It all seems so hopeless.

"You need to become one with your weapon." Wren plants her hands on her hips. "No, Alina, not like that. Relax your grip. The slingshot should be an extension of your body."

Hawk glances at Sam beside him. Her face is serious as she adjusts her grip, trying to follow Wren's instructions as closely as possible.

Mercy is on his other side. She's also trying hard but seems to be having trouble holding up her arms, clearly exhausted from her journey back to Askala.

Luca is beside Mercy giving Tarquin some extra tips. The poor kid looks terrified every time Wren comes near her. Which says something given she used to live on an island with the likes of Raiden.

It feels so good to have the Seekers back together at last. If the Newlands taught them anything, it was that they make a great team. They have Sam and her incredible intelligence, Mercy with her uncanny ability to read situations, Luca with his impossible courage, and Hawk with his strength. And he doesn't mean the strength of his body. He knows now that strength comes in many forms, and he's proven to himself that he's just as strong in mind.

Hawk pulls back his slingshot and lines up the target Wren's set up. It's a large piece of bark with leaves fanning out from a central point. A few people have hit the outer edges, but nobody has a bullseye just yet.

"Do it, Hawk," Sam whispers beside him. "Pretend it's the bear."

Hawk lets the small stone fly, watching as it sails through the air and lands right in the center with a ping. It seems having to fire at a bear to save the life of the girl you love makes you a pretty good shot.

He nods at Sam, then turns to Wren for his praise.

"Not bad," Wren says, dryly. "For someone aiming at a stationary target three yards in front of them."

Hawk sighs as he wonders what he has to do to impress his aunt.

Wren points out at the ocean and he sees another target he hadn't yet noticed, bobbing way out in the waves.

"You can move to level two," says Wren, focusing her attention back on Alina. "Good luck with that one."

Hawk shakes his head. So much for his praise. But it's nothing new for Wren to be short with her compliments. The fact she moved him to the next level is praise enough. And he's not here to be told he's doing a good job. He's here to learn how to protect Askala.

And according to Luca, they only have two weeks to do it. Which makes these lessons feel even more pointless. They need something more than this. But until someone figures out what that is, it looks like slingshot lessons are the best thing they can do right now.

"You're good at this, Hawk," says Luca, letting a rock fly, hitting the inner edge of the target.

"Close." Hawk puts his hands on his hips to mimic Wren. "But you need to let the slingshot become part of your body..."

Luca grins as he lines up another shot, this time missing completely.

"I'm just a little rusty," he says. "This next one will work."

But before Luca can fire his next shot, another stone comes flying from the group and lands right in the bullseye.

Hawk turns to see Mercy doing a little jig.

"The Peregrine strikes again!" laughs Tarquin. "Good shot, Mercy!"

Mercy gives Tarquin a high five, but Hawk notices her shoulders remain slumped as if weighed down by the same sense of hopelessness he's feeling.

Sam has another attempt, again failing to land a shot anywhere near the target. She bites down on her bottom lip as her brow folds into creases.

"I don't understand," she says. "I'm doing everything right. Why isn't it working?"

"Here, like this." Hawk stands behind her and she tucks herself in, possibly a little closer than necessary. But he's in no way complaining. He reaches over her warm body and places his hands on hers. "I'll show you."

"Just for the record..." Luca scowls. "I don't need any help."

"Even if it's from me?" asks Mercy, sidling up to him.

"Even if it's from you." Luca turns around and lets a quick shot fly, hitting the target right in the middle. "But I'll accept all offers of congratulations."

Mercy doesn't miss a beat in slipping her hands around his waist and stepping up on her toes for a kiss.

A few people give them a strange look, not yet used to this shift in their relationship.

Luca and Mercy left Askala as cousins of sorts. And returned as so much more. And neither of them is ashamed of it. It's everyone else who needs to deal with it.

Now Sam's the only one without a bullseye, and Hawk's not going to let that happen. He helps her line up the shot with his left hand and pulls back the stone in the tight band with their right hands.

"Ready?" he asks.

She nods. "Ready."

They let go together and the stone makes an arc toward the target. Sam gasps as it hits its mark.

Tarquin jumps up and down. "Bullseye! You're all on level two."

Wren approaches. "Don't celebrate too soon. Let's see how you go on the real target now."

Tarquin hangs her head. "I'm stuck on the first level."

"Let me help you." Wren positions herself beside Tarquin.

"But you're a bit scary," says Tarquin, her eyes wide.

"I'm Mercy's mom," Wren reminds her, keeping her voice unusually soft. "I won't hurt you."

"It's true." Mercy ruffles Tarquin's hair. "And I promise she's not scary at all. She's just a fierce woman. Like us."

Tarquin pulls back her shoulders and smiles. "Okay, you can help me."

Hawk wraps an arm around Sam and leads her to the water's edge, where Mercy and Luca are already lining up shots. He can feel the tension in Sam's body.

"I didn't really get a bullseye," she says. "I should stay and practice with Tarquin."

"Seekers stick together." Mercy loops a hand in the crook of Sam's arm.

"I'd be better off looking for more beans." Sam pokes at a divot of sand with her toe. "At least that would be useful."

"We've already been through this," says Hawk. "That could take days and yield nothing. And it's dangerous, as we found out."

"And Kian forbade you from going," Mercy reminds her.

Sam crosses her arms. "Which is exactly why we're still here. I just wish there was a way to get more Calabar beans. I'm so worried about Mom."

Hawk's heart breaks at the distressed look on Sam's face. But he knows there's nothing he can do to fix the situation for her. All he can do is hope like sweet Terra that Nova is strong enough to fight the poison that's attacking her right now.

"I'm so completely hungry." Mercy lines up a shot and sends a stone flying out to the ocean, landing nowhere near the target. "I promised Tarquin we'd have a feast when she got here. Poor kid."

"We can't risk eating anything that can't be thoroughly washed," says Luca. "You know that."

Hawk's belly groans at the mention of food. They'll replenish their limited rations in time but it's going to take a lot of work. Which is energy they should be spending on training for the invasion they know is coming. But how can they fight an army without any strength in their bodies?

"Who knew Charity was such a bitch!" Mercy shoots her slingshot again, getting a little closer to the target this time. "I'm so glad she's not your sister, Luca."

"Mercy!" Sam's eyes are wide. "You can't say that."

"I can and I will." Mercy glares at Sam. "Stop being so nice. She killed your brother, and your—"

Hawk coughs to cover up Mercy's faux pas. Nova isn't dead. Not yet.

"I never said I liked her." Sam pulls her shoulders back as she raises her slingshot in front of her. She sends her small rock flying across the ocean, the stone fueled by anger as much as momentum.

Hawk's jaw drops as the stone hits the target directly in the very center.

"Sam!" he gasps. "You did it."

"Of course, I did," she says. "It was a simple matter of estimating the velocity of the stone and balancing that with the correct coordinates of the necessary trajectory."

Hawk smiles when he catches a glint in Sam's eye and realizes she's making fun of herself.

"In other words, it was a lucky shot." Sam winks at him—a simple gesture that has him turning to mush.

He pulls her close to his chest. "You're my lucky shot," he says into her hair.

"All right, you two," says Luca. "That's enough."

"Look who's talking!" Hawk drops a kiss on the top of Sam's head, pleased to see Luca give him a dirty look.

"This is just like the Proving and that stupid bet you two made." Mercy shakes her head. "I thought we'd all moved on from that."

"We have." Luca holds up his palms. "But that's still my little sister."

Hawk reluctantly removes his arm from Sam and lines up a shot. He falls short, so he tries again. Just as his stone is about to strike the target, a wave swells up, sending it spearing into the water. If Askala is going to be attacked by a flotilla of boats, he needs to get better at this. Wren had been clever to create a harder target. One that's far more realistic for what they're going to face.

"We need more than this, don't we?" says Mercy, voicing the words they're all thinking. "We saw how heartless the Outlanders are. We can't stop them like this."

"We have to try something," says Sam, as more people join

them, having achieved their first bullseye. "And progress is definitely being made."

"We have no chance," says Mercy, keeping her voice low so only the Seekers can hear. "You know it and I know it. And to make it worse, we have very little food for the healthy, and no antidote for the sick."

Hawk nods. *Weapons. And Calabar beans.* Mercy's right. Without those two things they've lost this war before it even has a chance to start.

"Sam," Hawk breathes, as an idea lights his mind. "We need to find more Calabar beans."

Sam frowns at him. "I'm sorry but are you the same guy who five minutes ago told me it's too dangerous?"

"What are you thinking, big guy?" asks Luca, stepping in closer.

"Weapons and beans," Hawk says, hardly able to get the words out fast enough. "We shoot Calabar beans at Outlanders. Just like Sam and I did with the bear."

Sam shakes her head. "We'd never find enough beans to do that. We can't even find enough to make the antidote."

"But what if we make a paste out of them?" asks Hawk. "Or a powder. Something that we can coat our stones with. What effect would that have?"

"It would cause extreme discomfort," says Sam. "Or death, depending on the location of the shot."

"We could test it on Charity," Mercy suggests, trying once more to hit the target and succeeding in landing it on the outer edges.

"We still don't know where to find any beans," says Sam, ignoring her cousin. "So, none of this matters, anyway."

Hawk's shoulders slump. Sam's right. Again. But he's not willing to let go of the idea so easily just yet. "Come on, we have to be able to find some more. We need to think harder. Where could they be?"

"Tell me again what they look like." Luca tucks his slingshot in the back of his trousers and tilts his head. "I'm not sure I've ever come across any. And I thought I'd come across everything out here."

"You probably have and just didn't know what they were," says Sam. "They're high up in the trees where there's sunlight. Which means they're not easy to spot from the ground. The pods are about six inches long."

"They don't have purple flowers, do they?" asks Luca.

Sam nods, her eyes wide. "They do. Although, they're near the end of their season so most of the flowers will have finished by now."

Luca turns to Mercy. "Do you remember what Tarquin said on the raft?"

Mercy raises a brow. "Tarquin said a lot of things on the raft."

"No, remember when we arrived, she was amazed to see purple flowers in the treetops?" Luca is hopping from foot to foot. "And now that I think of it, I'm sure they were coming from some kind of vine."

Hawk's heart thuds as he listens. Is this the hope they all needed to cling to?

"I didn't hear her say that." Mercy crosses her arms. "But we should totally check that out."

"Which part of the beach was it?" asks Sam, her focus intently on Luca now.

"We washed up about a mile west of the bridge," says Luca. "But Sam, I'm not certain about this. Like you said, it's late in the season for flowers. Maybe it was something else."

Sam is shaking her head in that adorable determined way of hers and Hawk already knows she won't rest until she checks this out.

"Sam and I will go," says Luca. "I know the location. Sam

knows the vines. You two cover for us. It's too obvious if we all disappear."

"Cover for you?" Mercy looks aghast. "I think Kian's going to notice if both his kids have gone missing."

"Make something up." Luca leans down and kisses Mercy gently on the lips. She goes visibly weak at the knees and Hawk already knows she'll agree to whatever Luca asks.

"Put your hand over your eye," Mercy says to Sam when Luca releases his grip on her.

"Why?" Sam looks at Hawk like he has any better idea what's going on.

He shrugs.

"Just do it," Mercy hisses before turning to Wren. "Mom! Mom!"

Wren looks over from the remainder of the group still working on the first target.

"Sam just hit herself in the eye with a rock," calls Mercy, just as Sam manages to slap her hand over her left eye. "Luca's going to take her to the infirmary."

Wren nods immediately, not seeming in the least surprised that Sam's managed to injure herself again. Hawk feels a little indignant. He'd thought Wren had seen just how much more capable Sam had become since being a Seeker.

"Be careful." Hawk puts a hand on Sam's back as she takes a step away.

"I'll be ok," she whispers with her hand still plastered over her eye. "And if Luca's right, then maybe Mom will be, too."

Hawk watches Luca lead Sam away.

Hope.

That's what they need.

Actually, no. They need more than that this time.

They need their hope to actually bear fruit. The kind that comes in six inch pods filled with beans that have the ability to both save lives and end them depending on how they're used.

And his clever girl is just the one who knows how to do that.

The future of Askala is in all their hands. But right now, it seems that Sam's hands are the ones that count most.

SAM

*S*am and Luca quickly weave their way through the huts toward the forest. The moment Mercy created their alibi, they were keen to get going. Both desperately hoping it was Calabar beans that were seen in the trees as Luca, Mercy and Tarquin approached Askala.

Everyone is conscious time is running out.

For once, Sam quells the hope that's smoldering like a banked fire seeking oxygen. All it will do is hurt more if they fail. It's just too far to fall.

Luca pauses as they pass another hut with no signs of life. "Aarov, too?" he mutters.

Sam nods. Luca's noticed every bare hut, each inhabitant lost to deadly nightshade poisoning.

Luca's hands tighten into fists as his brows slam down. They keep walking, Sam hoping that her brother is focusing on the fact they're on their way to find the final ingredient for the antidote. That they're doing what they can to make sure no one else joins the others who were sent to the bottom of the ocean. Any trace of them would have dissolved by now.

They pass another empty hut and Luca's frown only intensifies. "And Zali." It's no longer a question. Just a flat, grief-filled statement.

"Charity's in there now."

The moment Sam says the words, she knows they're a mistake. Luca takes a sharp right and strides down to the hut.

"Luca," Sam hisses. "We don't—"

Diesel is on guard duty, and he shoots to his feet as he sees Luca approach. He watches in mute shock as Luca walks straight past him and shoves open the door. Sam rushes after him, alarmed. She stops just inside as a crash reverberates through the hut.

Luca has Charity pinned against the wall to Sam's right, fury vibrating through his body as he shoves his face close to hers. "You're going to die for this."

There's no fear on Charity's face as she sneers back. "I did what I needed to do."

Luca pulls back and slams her into the wall again, making her grimace. "Mercy's right, you are a bitch."

Charity's eyes light up like Luca just gave her a compliment. "It's the people who do what it takes who'll be the winners in this war."

Sam steps forward, hesitating as she places a hand on Luca's shoulder, instantly feeling that his muscles are like corded steel. He flicks her hand away, not taking his gaze off Charity.

"I've seen the boats. We know your plans. And we'll be ready."

Charity's face twists into a smile. "Which beach?" When Luca doesn't answer, her smile grows wider. "You thought those were the only ones we're building?"

Sam grips his shoulder again, this time with more force. Luca's tenuous hold on his control is about to snap. "Luca! She's goading you on purpose."

For the first time since Luca stormed in, Charity's face loses a hint of its viciousness.

Sam narrows her eyes as she steps in a little closer. "That's what you want, isn't it? For him to end you."

Charity curls her lip, draws her head back an inch, and spits in Luca's face. "He's Askalan. He doesn't have the guts."

Luca's breathing hard as he stares at Charity, her saliva trickling down his cheek. His muscles coil and his hands tighten around her upper arms. Charity stills, anticipation filling her face.

"Damn straight, I'm Askalan," Luca growls. "And we don't choose to kill."

Releasing Charity, he watches as she collapses to the ground.

"No!" she screams, jumping up and running at Luca, her hands curled into claws. But Luca must've been expecting it, because he steps out of the way, taking Sam with him. Charity slams into the wall on the opposite side of the hut and crumples.

Luca grabs Sam's hand and heads to the door. He pauses, looking back at Charity as she folds into herself.

"Not easy to stay in the hut of one of the people you killed, is it? With nothing but the ghosts of everyone you murdered for company."

Charity doesn't answer, but even Sam knew she wouldn't. Charity murdered kind, peaceful people who took her in. It seems that's not easy to live with. They leave the hut, Sam locking the door behind her.

They find Diesel standing just on the other side, watching them. "You're a stronger man than me, Luca. I don't think I could've stopped."

Luca sighs. "Everyone needs a sister like Sam, somedays."

Sam bites her lip. She wonders if their mother had passed away during the night, whether Luca would've kept going. She bites down harder, welcoming the sting. She wonders if she would've let him.

Not wanting to know the answer now that she's realized

they live in a world where shades of gray exist, Sam presses a hand to Luca's arm. "We'd better get going."

Silently nodding, Luca turns away. They walk to the edge of the forest, the opposite end to where Sam and Hawk left two days ago. Sam glances over her shoulder as the trees engulf them in shadows and the scent of pine. She misses Hawk already, and she only saw him less than an hour ago.

At least they won't be gone as long this time. They can't afford to be.

Sam draws in a sharp breath as something strikes her. "Charity said there were more boats than just the ones you saw."

Luca draws back a branch and allows Sam to pass. "She was lying."

"Are you sure?"

"No. I doubt that girl knows how to tell the truth, so it's hard to tell the difference. But like you said, she was trying to goad me."

"So, it's possible this attack could be even bigger than we initially estimated."

"We've got this, Sam," Luca says determinedly. "No matter what comes at us."

Sam cocks her head. "Is this the Falcon talking?" Learning that her brother was a vigilante of sorts in the Outlands had been a shock, but not terribly surprising when Sam thought about it. Luca was a champion for the weak even as a child. Sam's pretty sure it's genetic just as much as it was molded by his early life experience of being abandoned and raised in Fairbanks.

Luca sends her a wry glance. "You're starting to sound like Mercy."

Sam grins. "I'll take that as a compliment."

She hasn't had much chance to reconnect with Mercy since they returned, but Sam saw the way people's faces lit up as they welcomed her. There's a sweet, determined strength to Mercy that others have always been drawn to. And her time in the Outlands only seems to have cemented that about her, judging by the fact they brought Tarquin back with them.

Sam cautiously steps over a log, and she sees Luca still for just a second before he continues again. She raises a brow as they keep moving. Her brother just suppressed his protective side. It seems Sam isn't the only one who's changed since becoming a Seeker.

They keep trekking, the ocean somewhere to their left. A mile from the bridge. It seems too good to be true that Calabar beans could be that close. And yet, what Tarquin saw could be nothing more than the pretty but innocuous *Lablab purpureus*...

"You and Hawk seem happy together," Luca says over his shoulder.

Sam almost trips even though there's not a log in sight. She quickly rights herself. "If you didn't see that Hawk and I are two halves of a whole, then you're more blind than me."

Luca chuckles. "There's a lot I didn't see while I was here."

Sam comes up beside him. "Like Mercy?"

Sam's watched the way those two seem to be each other's new center of gravity. It would be fascinating if it weren't her brother and best friend.

Luca scans the treetops as they walk, silent for several seconds and Sam assumes the conversation is over. Except his gaze flickers to her then back to the canopy. "Are you okay... with us?"

Sam winces, knowing she was the one who objected to their relationship not that long ago. And yet, after a few raised eyebrows, the people of Askala have already accepted Luca and Mercy's new status, probably realizing there are more important things to worry about right now.

"What did Dad say?" she asks, knowing she needs a bit of time to find the right words.

"That he wants me to be happy."

"And Mom?"

Luca's been spending any time their mother is awake by her side. It was inevitable that Mercy would be there, too. And Luca would've wanted the woman he now calls Mom to know, in case her eyes failed to open the next time they fluttered closed.

A smile trips up his lips. "That she's glad Mercy didn't give up."

Sam stops and Luca does the same. He looks at her quizzically. A little nervously.

She takes his hand and squeezes it. "Love doesn't know boundaries, Luca. That's what's so amazing about it. I'm happy you and Mercy found it with each other."

Joy dances to life in her brother's eyes, but it quickly takes a mischievous glint. "Like you did with your best friend?"

Sam wrinkles her nose at him. She realizes now how much Hawk must've hated hearing those words. "I think that might be a dirty word, now."

Smiling at each other, they continue trekking. Sam notes the trees are large here, which is encouraging. It's possible that the Calabar bean has expanded its distribution this close to the coast.

"You're different," Sam observes as she nudges Luca with her shoulder.

Luca nudges her back. "So are you."

"I like the changes."

Luca grins. "Me, too."

Luca slows down, paying more attention to the treetops, and Sam feels her muscles tense. They must be getting close.

Luca turns slowly. "I think it was around here somewhere."

Sam's eyes instantly look up, searching for the light green leaves and tendrils of the Calabar bean. They fall silent as they scan intensely, both trying to wish the vine into existence.

But the branches of each tree hold nothing more than pine needles. Sam almost falls over twice she's so focused on keeping her gaze up, that she slows even more. Luca is a few feet ahead when he plants his hands on his hips.

"You'd think there was more of it, considering how poisonous it is. It's not like it would be a snack of choice."

"From what I can tell, it hasn't evolved the bright color that's associated with deadly plants," Sam explains. "Animals don't know to stay away from it. It's too late once they're dead."

"No way!"

"Well, it's just a theory, but one that's quite plausible," Sam retorts, trying not to get defensive.

"No, not that." Luca's practically jumping up and down on the spot. He points to the top of a tree not far away. "I think we've found it!"

Sam's eyes widen as Luca rushes forward. With a quick grin over his shoulder, he starts climbing. "I'll be back in a sec."

He quickly disappears among the evergreen foliage. Sam cranes her neck, trying to get a sense of how high up he is, but it's like the mangrove pine has swallowed him.

A moment later a whoop so loud it scares away several birds echoes through the forest.

"I've got them!" Luca's voice is so full of excitement that Sam finds herself doing a little dance.

They've found Calabar beans! They can make the antidote!

"How many do you need? Ten? Twenty?" Luca calls down.

Sam gasps. So many! "As many as your pockets will hold," she shouts back.

"They're already full. I'll drop some down," Luca says.

Sam watches in amazement as one by one, Calabar bean pods rain down. She pictures grinding them to a powder, then carefully measuring the necessary amount before adding it to the mix. She'll wake her mother up and spoon feed it to her, no matter how bad it tastes.

The lines on her father's face will relax, he may even smile again. Sam realizes she hasn't seen that for quite some time now.

When the rain of pods stops a few moments later, Sam waits, assuming Luca's climbing to another branch to get some more. But no more pods come tumbling through the branches.

"Luca?"

When there's no answer, concern coils through her chest.

"Luca? Is everything okay?"

The sound of scrabbling and branches snapping has Sam leaping back. A moment later, Luca lands in front of her.

Sam's hand darts to her chest. Did Luca just fly down the tree?

He grabs her arm, his face full of panic. "We need to go."

"What? Why?" Sam looks around frantically, expecting to see another polar grizzly. Except then they'd be up the tree. Something else has happened. "Did you eat one, Luca?"

But Luca's already tugging her along. "We've run out of time."

Sam yanks her arm out of his grip and stops. It seems some things haven't changed, like her brother's tendency to act now, talk and think later. "What is going on?" she demands.

Luca stops, his familiar features tight with dread. "I saw boats. Out on the water." His jaw tightens. "They're coming."

Sweet Terra. They can finally make the antidote, but it doesn't matter.

It's too late.

The Outlanders are here.

MERCY

*M*ercy holds Hawk's hand as they walk back down the beach after slingshot training is declared over for the day. It feels different to holding Luca's hand. This touch reminds her of the comfort of her childhood. Holding Luca's hand evokes a set of feelings that are a lot more...adult.

"What's up?" Hawk asks. "You seem distracted."

"It's just good to be back home," she says, glad mindreading isn't one of Hawk's newly acquired skills as a Seeker.

He nods. "And it will be even better if Luca's right about seeing those beans."

"Did somebody say beans?" asks Tarquin, skipping along beside them. "I love beans!"

"Not these beans," says Mercy. "They're not for eating."

"We'll find you something to eat when we get back," says Hawk. "And how about I introduce you to my sisters? I think you're going to get along especially well with Dove."

"I prefer to be friends with boys," says Tarquin, fiddling with the enormous blue diamond hanging from her neck. "Do you have any brothers?"

"Sadly, no." Hawk smiles at her.

"Pity," says Tarquin, perking up. "I liked kicking Relic in the nuts."

Mercy puts on her best stern face. "No more kicking people, okay, Tarquin?"

Tarquin rolls her eyes before running off ahead, sending up a cloud of sand in her wake.

"She's a funny kid," says Hawk.

"Does she remind you of me?" Mercy tilts her head.

"Actually, she's more like Luca as a kid," he says.

Mercy is aghast. "But you never liked Luca back then!"

"I didn't understand him." Hawk lets go of her hand so he can hold up his palms. "I get him now. Which means I think I get Tarquin. Well, as much as it's possible to understand a female."

Mercy grins. "How's it going with Sam? Are you having trouble figuring her out?"

He shakes his head. "Actually, no. Things are great. It seems we're finally on the same page."

"Which says something given the number of pages Sam's read in her life." Mercy laughs at her own joke. "I'm glad you two are together at last. It feels so right."

She waits for him to say the same about her relationship, but he just nods his thanks instead.

Mercy almost walks straight into the back of Tarquin, not having noticed she'd stopped still.

"Luca's coming back," says Tarquin, pointing. "Except that's not the direction of the infamy."

"Infirmary," Mercy corrects, following her line of sight. There's a figure running down the beach. It could be Luca, but they're too far away to tell.

"That can't be him," says Hawk. "He wouldn't leave Sam by herself."

"That's Luca." Tarquin plants her hands on her hips. "Only the Falcon runs like that. And Sam's in the infrimpery."

"She's not," says Mercy, realizing if that really is Luca then their cover story has already been blown. "Sam went with Luca to look for something important."

Mercy's mom comes up behind them along with the rest of the group.

"Is that Luca?" she asks, her eyes as sharp as ever.

Mercy looks again, and this time Luca's dark mop of hair comes into focus, his long legs taking wide strides down the beach. Her heart rate picks up as her brain scrambles for what this could mean. Surely, Sam isn't hurt? They were only going a mile down the beach! Polar grizzlies don't normally come this close.

Unable to contain his concern for Sam, Hawk takes off, running toward Luca. Mercy launches herself after him, aware that Tarquin is behind her. Possibly the whole colony is following… Clearly, Luca doesn't have seconds to waste. The sooner they can close the gap between them and find out how they can help, the better.

Hawk gets to him first, but Luca runs past Hawk until he reaches Mercy. Grabbing her hand, he hauls her back down the beach toward the others.

"Need to talk to you all at once!" he shouts back to Hawk.

"But!" Hawk protests. "Sam—"

"Sam's fine!" Luca continues jogging. "She's taken the beans to the infirmary."

"Then what's happening?" Mercy asks, trying to get Luca to slow his pace.

Luca doesn't reply, so Mercy draws in a breath and heads back down the beach, collecting a confused Tarquin along the way.

They reach the people, who by now have figured out something big is happening. Mercy's parents are at the front, concern etched over their faces.

"The invasion," pants Luca, bending over to catch his breath as he draws to a stop. "It's happening. I saw boats. They're coming."

"Are you sure?" Mercy's mom asks.

Luca nods. "Four boats. I don't know how many people. They're far off the coast now but with the tides it won't take them long to reach the shore."

Mercy bites down on her lip as she shakes her head. This can't be happening! They were supposed to have two weeks to get ready and they needed every day of that! There's no way they can win any kind of battle right now. She's not even sure they could win in two weeks.

"We need to get Kian," Mercy's mom says. "Actually, we need everyone."

Mercy's dad nods, but instead of running to the colony, he races to what remains of the bridge. It takes Mercy a few moments to realize what he's doing.

The ancient bull's horn.

Used only in emergencies, in the right wind its high-pitched blast can be heard over most of the island.

Mercy's dad blows into the horn, sending the sound reverberating across the beach. She's never heard it used before and if she weren't so afraid, she'd almost be excited.

Within moments people come running from all directions, bursting from the tree line and streaming onto the beach. Dozens then hundreds of Askalans, all gathering with panicked looks on their faces.

"What's happening?" Kian shouts as he storms down the beach.

"Luca saw boats," Mercy's mom calls back. "The invasion's beginning."

There's a murmur across the crowd.

"Where did you see them?" asks Phoenix, flexing his muscles. "I'll kill the lot of them."

Mercy's brows shoot up to hear her uncle talking this way,

even though she's been told many stories about his behavior in the past.

Luca points. "About a mile west."

"Grab whatever weapon you can find," Wren tells the people. "Slingshots, spears, knives. Anything! It's time to do what we've been talking about. It's time to protect what's ours."

Mercy looks across the crowd, hoping to see anger and courage.

But, instead, she sees fear.

Which means they're all completely doomed.

Kian must see the same thing as he holds up a hand to get the attention of the people.

"We're a society of peace-loving people," he says. "I know this is hard for you. But Wren's right. It's time to protect what's ours or lose it to a race of people who treat the land with even less respect than they treat their own. All our work, and the work of our ancestors, will be for nothing if we don't hold these savages back. The last time the Outlanders tried to take Askala, we fought hard, and we won. We can do it again."

"My father's right," says Luca. "We can do this. We *must* do this. As Seekers we did our best to make peace with the Outlanders, only to discover this isn't possible. They don't understand the concept of peace. It's time to talk to them in their language."

"What about the boat you're building?" a woman with a baby in a sling asks. "For the vulnerable."

Jagger steps forward. "The boat isn't finished yet. If you're not able to fight, your best chance is to hide. Go to the old encampment on the cliffs. That's the safest place for you now."

This answer doesn't seem to placate the woman who pulls her baby a little closer to her chest. Mercy's heart breaks for her, but Jagger's right. Hiding in the huts would be suicide if the Outlanders win this fight. At least in the old encampment, the people stand a chance.

"We need to move," says Luca. "Now!"

The people fan out, some running west toward where Luca had pointed, others back to the colony to either fetch their weapons or make their way to the cliffs

"Hawk," calls Kian. "Go back to the colony. Tell the people to leave their huts. It's not safe for them there. Those who aren't well enough to hide in the forest should be taken to the infirmary. That leaves you one building to protect. Can you do that?"

Hawk nods as he retreats. Mercy knows he'll be relieved to be able to check on Sam for himself. It's no coincidence that Hawk's the one Kian chose to keep his daughter safe. There's nobody else who'd do a better job.

Mercy's attention is diverted as her dad grips her by the hand, looking deep into her eyes.

"Be careful," he says.

She nods up at him, her heart swelling with love as this situation becomes even more acutely real. "You too, Dad."

Then she's running down the beach with Luca, her heart pounding from both adrenaline and exertion. Tarquin has climbed on Luca's back and for a moment it feels like they're back in the Outlands.

The three of them against the world.

Except this time there's far more than just the three of them. They have an army of fifty at least. And they may not have had time to finish building their boat or coat their stones with poison, but they have the advantage of being the ones standing on land. And like Kian said, they must hold these savages back.

Mercy pats her back pocket as she runs, checking her slingshot is still there. Part of her hopes that Raiden is on one of the boats. After what he did to Alyx, there's nobody's else's eyes she'd like to aim for more.

The people form a line on the beach as they pant to catch their breath. Luca and Mercy ease their way to the front, Luca setting Tarquin on the ground and tucking her behind him. There's no point asking her to go and hide. They both know she's sticking with them. Telling her to leave would be about as successful as drinking water out of a sieve.

The boats are still a way out, but close enough now for Mercy to count four of them, and they look to be crammed full of men waving their fists in the air.

Mercy glances up at Luca. "We can totally do this."

But he doesn't hear her. He's too busy frowning.

"What's wrong?" she asks.

"They're not the boats we saw being built." He scratches at his head. "The ones we saw were larger than that. These look almost more like rafts."

"Isn't that a good thing?" Mercy squints, trying to figure out what the problem is.

"Charity said they were building lots of boats," he says. "More than what we saw. I thought she was lying."

"Hang on a second." Mercy jams a hand on her hip. "When did you talk to Charity?"

"On our way to get the pods," he says, not taking his eyes from the ocean. "I popped in for a chat."

Mercy lets out a long sigh, able to imagine exactly what kind of chat he'd had with the girl who killed his little brother. But she can't see any bruises on him, so that's a positive sign, at least.

The group gathered on the sand grows as people return with their weapons. Each person who joins them gives Mercy hope. They can do this. They've totally outnumbered the people about to land on their shore. Especially if they're in smaller boats than Luca first thought.

"We might need to split up," Luca says to Kian, who's come to stand beside him with a spear in his hand. "There could be more boats arriving from another direction."

Mercy's heart sinks as she listens to Luca explain what he'd just told her. He's totally right. If these aren't the boats they saw being built then it's completely possible they're about to be attacked from multiple angles. And if they split up, they'll no longer outnumber the Outlanders...

A sinking feeling settles in Mercy's gut. This wasn't supposed to be how things played out.

"Phoenix," calls Kian. "I need you to return to the settlement. Make sure Hawk has everyone out of their huts. Help him protect the infirmary. Can you do that?"

Phoenix hesitates but then nods, realizing he's the best person for the job. If Mercy were going to be desperately unwell in an infirmary during a battle, she'd want Hawk and Phoenix as her guards.

"Jagger," says Kian. "I want you to head up to the cliffs. Take the bull's horn with you. Scan the horizon and sound the alarm if you see any other boats out there. I need someone up there who can keep the people safe."

Jagger is gone before Kian can even draw another breath. Mercy knows many people in Askala have questioned Jagger's loyalty, which makes him an interesting choice. But Kian clearly trusts him. Which means they need to as well.

"Good thinking," says Luca, nodding his approval.

"The rest of us stick together." Kian bangs his spear on the sand. "Our numbers are our strength right now."

A few more people emerge from the tree line and Mercy's surprised to see some of the older generation clutching knives from the kitchen, including Mercy's grandmother, Avis, and her constant companion, Thea. Even Amity has made her way down from her home, her dark hair wild as she holds a sharp stick in front of her. These people have seen war before. They're not prepared to hide in the forest while what's theirs is taken from them. They know just how important it is to fight.

"Mercy," says Luca, drawing her attention back to the ocean. "Look."

She squints, beginning to wonder if there's something wrong with her eyesight, when she sees what he's pointing at.

As the boats are drawing closer, she sees they're more like complicated rafts woven together from a collection of wide roots and branches. And the people upon them aren't groups of angry men. There are women and children amongst them. And they're not waving their fists in the air. They're just...waving.

"Fairbanks." Luca is grinning now. "It's the people of Fairbanks. Look, I can see Dharma and Finn."

"Is Relic there?" Tarquin squeezes herself out from behind Luca. "I see him! I see Relic! Do you see him, Mercy?"

Mercy smiles as all the stress wooshes out of her body. They're not being attacked! These are reinforcements. Their army just grew a whole lot in size.

"I see him." Mercy puts a hand on Tarquin's back. "And I see Annabel."

"Do you think she brought her treasures?" Tarquin asks, jumping up and down.

"Definitely," says Mercy, looking across at Kian who's smiling broadly. They're not the only ones with a connection to Fairbanks. Kian spent some time there with Nova once. He knows these people, too.

But there's one person who has a greater connection to them than anyone standing on the shore.

Avis.

Mercy turns to see her grandmother walking down the sand, enraptured. These are her people. She established this colony and would never have left them if it weren't for her desperate longing to be with the children who were stolen from her. Tears prick at the back of Mercy's eyes and she thinks of all the suffering her grandmother experienced at the hands of the man the Outlanders once called the Commander.

A role now taken by the woman they know as Grace.

"Put down your weapons," Luca calls across the crowd.

"These are friends, not enemies. These are the people of Fairbanks. They've come to help us."

There's some cheering and a few sighs of relief.

"You did well," says Kian. "I'm proud of you all. We should think of this like a drill. When the attack comes for real next time, we'll all be better prepared."

People nod their agreement. It goes without saying that they'll take their weapons training more seriously. It's obvious now where their weaknesses lie. This is their chance to fix that.

"Who's the man with the blond hair?" asks Luca, frowning as he points to the boat on the far right. "We don't know him."

Mercy's heart skips a beat as she studies the man. His face isn't familiar but she's certain she knows who he is. She's seen a flash of that blond hair. And there's something about the way he's holding himself separate from the rest of the people on the boat.

"It's the ghost," she says. "The one who gave me the knife."

"The one who carved my shell?" Luca's eyes are wide.

Mercy knows just how important this is to him. He hit nothing but dead ends when talking to Grace about his parents. But this ghost of a man must know something if he carved the shell that was tucked inside Luca's blanket when he was abandoned. Perhaps he's going to get his answers after all.

The rafts crest on the waves and are pushed toward shore, moving quickly now.

Luca and Kian wade out to help pull them onto the sand. Mercy's never seen such strange-looking rafts before. They're more like a hybrid of raft and boat.

Avis walks out into the shallows and Dharma leaps into the water and flies into her outstretched arms. The two women hold each other for long moments before Annabel jumps off the side of her raft and calls out their names. She has a bag strapped to her back, no doubt filled with treasures, that's making it hard for her to walk.

Avis goes to Annabel and embraces her.

"The water stings!" cries Annabel. "Ouch!"

Luca is behind Annabel in a moment and scoops her up, treasures and all, and carries her to the sand.

"Thank you, Falcon," says Annabel, clapping her hands. "I always wanted to be rescued by you."

"Relic!" cries Tarquin, skipping from foot to foot on the shoreline in front of the raft Relic is climbing off with his dad.

Relic takes one look at his friend, waves with one hand and covers his groin with the other, anticipating the greeting Tarquin's likely to want to give him.

Annabel sees Mercy and flies at her. Mercy squeezes her tightly, drawing in her warmth.

"Welcome to Askala," she says. "I'm so glad you've come to help us."

"We didn't really come to help," says Annabel. "Fairbanks fell down. We had nowhere else to go."

"We also came to help," says Finn, overhearing and touching Mercy gently on the arm.

"What happened?" Mercy looks at the rafts being hauled onto the sand. "Are those made from—"

"Our tree!" says Annabel, proudly. "We took the fallen roots and branches and made these boats instead."

Mercy feels a sad pull in her heart to imagine that gentle giant of a mangrove pine no longer exists. It gave these people shelter and comfort in times where nothing else could. And then it took them to safety here. All the memories and secrets of Fairbanks are embedded into those lengths of gnarled timber sitting innocently on the shore.

She wants to tell them they should have come years ago but holds her tongue. She knows better than anyone how hard it is to leave the place you call home.

"How did you know how to build the rafts?" she asks.

"Ghost helped us," says Annabel, pointing at the blond man. "He can make anything out of wood. I told you he was real."

"And I believed you," Mercy reminds her.

Finn is pulled away by people who remember him from his time in Askala, while Annabel catches sight of Tarquin's necklace and goes to her as if drawn there by a magnet. Finally, a real treasure for her to look at. Except it's one Tarquin will never part with. It may have once been worth a fortune, but its value now lies in Tarquin's love for her sister.

Avis catches Mercy's eye and goes to her.

"I'm so happy for you." Mercy takes her grandmother's hands. "Your people are here."

"My people were already here," says Avis. "But you're right, now I have *all* my people. For the moment, anyway."

Mercy nods, knowing why she added that last part. Her grandmother's scarred face is stark evidence of her knowledge that nothing in this world is ever guaranteed. It could all be taken in an instant.

"Kian! Kian!"

Mercy spins around at the sound of Hawk's voice calling from the top of the beach, having seen that they're not under attack.

"Kian! Come quickly!" Hawk shouts more urgently. "Sam made the antidote. Nova's awake!"

LUCA

*L*uca stops the moment he enters his family's hut, not quite believing what he's seeing.

"Good morning." His mother smiles at him from where she's sitting at the table, Luca's father beside her.

She's still too pale and far too thin, but she's up. Alive. And smiling.

Luca's grin feels like it could stretch across half the globe. "And a good morning to you, too." His grin does the impossible and grows a little more. "Mom."

Her eyes mist over, and Luca's father presses a kiss to her temple. "Don't overdo it, remember?" he murmurs quietly.

Flashing him an admonishing look, his mother presses her lips together. "I smiled, nothing more."

His father raises a brow. "You were thinking of getting up and hugging him."

Luca chuckles as his mother's cheeks flush pink. Seeing color on her skin makes his heart do a little happy jig.

He walks over and engulfs them both in a tight embrace. "You both need food and rest."

Luca's father looks just as exhausted as his mother does after spending countless sleepless nights by her bedside, trying to keep her alive by sheer force of will.

His father straightens. "We have training this morning. And the food reserves to review. And then there's the leaders' meeting."

Luca rolls his eyes. "Dad, I'll be at the training and I'll report back. We have carrots and pods, which is enough for the time being. You can rest until the leaders' meeting."

His father blinks. "Well, I suppose..."

"That's exactly what I could do," Luca finishes for him. He turns back to the door. "I'll let you know how it goes."

His mother's voice reaches him as he's stepping outside. "That's our boy, Kian..."

Luca rolls his eyes again, although his grin never diminishes. It feels good to make his parents proud.

And speaking of parents.

His smile diminishes as he makes his way down to the beach. An image of the blond man who came with the people of Fairbanks floats through his mind. The man who possibly carved his shell.

Luca runs his fingers over the finely etched lines on the fragment he always keeps in his pocket. Just because he's acknowledged Nova and Kian are the parents he always dreamed of, doesn't mean the desire to know his roots has waned.

And that man could have the answers.

The beach is already filling up with people—both those from Askala and Fairbanks. They shift around uneasily, all conscious that things just got serious.

The 'drill' as Luca's father called it yesterday showed everyone exactly how much work there is to do.

And how vulnerable Askala really is.

Luca scans the crowd and quickly finds what he's looking for. Mercy is sashaying toward him, a smile curving her full lips.

She slips her arms around his waist, sending shivers rippling over his skin.

"Good morning," she purrs, memories of last night heating her hooded gaze.

Although they maintain the pretense of separate sleeping quarters, Luca built them a small hut not far from the beach. Tucked up in the tree line, it's not visible from the village, but close enough that they're still just a shout away.

It's where they spend the darkest hours of the night, each sneaking back to their respective huts just before daybreak.

Luca's looking forward to the day they have their own hut, not far from their families...talking of growing one of their own.

"It certainly is a good morning," he murmurs, allowing himself the barest of brushes against her lips. The promise of their hut has meant their chemistry is constantly simmering beneath the surface.

They straighten to the loud sound of someone clearing their throat. Wren is striding toward the crowd, glaring at Luca and Mercy.

Luca rubs the back of his head, guilt and the refusal to be ashamed of loving Mercy warring inside him. But Mercy seems to have no such difficulty. She grins and waves at her mother, clutching Luca to her like a prize.

Wren's lips twitch before her frown slams back into place.

Focusing back on her task, she hikes her hands on her hips, pacing in front of the people lined up on the sand. "Thank you everyone, and welcome to the people of Fairbanks. After yesterday, we'll be training longer and more often."

The people all nod solemnly. Luca notes the blond man is standing a little aside from everyone else, his arms crossed as he watches intently.

"Let's break up into our usual groups," Wren orders. "Fairbanks people, come with me and we'll get you up to speed on the basics."

The people split up, taking their places on the beach. Luca joins Hawk and Mercy at the edge of the water, the target waiting patiently as it bobs on the surface. Sam would be in the infirmary, continuing to make the antidote, as well as the poison to coat their stones.

Everyone's quiet and focused as they line up and lift their slingshots, conscious their aim needs to be accurate. Each and every time.

Stones fly out, most peppering the target with variable accuracy, too many still going wide and splashing into the water.

Gritting his teeth, Luca focuses harder. Everything and everyone he loves depends on them being able to defend Askala.

Mercy sighs beside him. "Why does this feel...not enough?"

"If it's not, we have a plan B," Luca says quietly.

Luca checked out the boat they're building last night. The frame is complete, the sheets of timber have been prepared, the scarf joints sanded down. With people working as hard at building it as they are training, it should be ready in time.

Mercy glances at Tarquin as the little girl lines up another shot, her tongue peeking out from the side of her mouth. Her jaw set in determined lines, she aims for the target once more.

Luca knows he should be doing the same, but like Mercy just said. It doesn't feel...enough. And yet, it's all they've got. That, or retreating.

Luca frowns as he realizes something. Getting Mercy on that boat is going to be his biggest challenge. Running away isn't in her blood.

But that's possibly exactly what they're going to have to do.

Looking around, he tries to find something to pin some hope on. Everyone is working hard, brows furrowed, slingshots pulled back as far as possible. Even the people of Fairbanks are wielding slingshots, some already walking down toward the waterline to join the others.

Everyone except the blond man. He's still standing where he was, except now he's shaking his head.

"I'll be back in a sec," Luca says to Mercy before walking away.

The man watches him approach, his face impassive.

Luca comes to stand beside him. "You're not joining us?"

"No."

Luca waits to see if the man will say anything else, but the quiet simply stretches out.

"So…what's your name? Ghost?"

The man inclines his head. "Ghost will do just fine."

He continues to watch the people as they train, and Luca tries to get a read on this guy. And comes up with nothing. The guy's lean and strong, like many of the Outlanders are, but his face is practically devoid of emotion. It's hard to tell if he's happy to be in Askala.

Luca decides he may as well just come out and ask. After all, he has some other questions for this man…

"Why aren't you interested in taking part…Ghost?" Maybe he's injured?

Ghost's gaze flickers toward Luca, then, almost as if he's dismissing him, returns to the people training. "Slingshots?"

"They're better than spears." The only other weapon the people of Askala have any familiarity with. "Considering most people here don't have the strength to throw them as far. This way we can defend ourselves before the Outlanders reach our shores."

"With stones?"

Luca's spine stiffens. "They'll be coated in poison."

"So, they need to swallow them? You'll be aiming for their mouths?"

"If the stones break the skin, they'll be affected." Luca

wonders for the first time how much that will incapacitate the Outlanders. And how quickly…

"Slingshots don't have an extended reach," Ghost says. "Your enemy will be quite close by the time you can hit them with your poisoned pebbles."

Luca feels as if his back is about to snap, it's so taut with indignation. "We're doing everything we can to defend Askala and our people."

"This is your strategy? A defensive one?"

"Very few of our people know how to fight. It's all we have right now. And we're building a boat, so we can leave if we need to," Luca adds, his jaw tight.

Ghost's brows hike up. "You're going to run?"

This is why Ghost isn't taking part? Because he's pretty unimpressed with what he's seeing? Luca's gaze settles on Mercy as she releases another shot. She's so intent, so sure she's doing the best thing to defend Askala.

And yet Ghost doesn't believe it's enough, and Luca's wondering if he's right.

"What do you suggest?" he asks tersely.

Ghost slides a glance Luca's way, almost as if he didn't expect the question. "You need to be more offensive. Bows and arrows are your best chance of doing that. You'll be able to attack the Outlanders before they get too close."

"We have no one—" Luca stops his statement that there isn't anyone with that sort of knowledge in Askala. He turns to Ghost. "Can you use one?"

"I grew up in the Outlands," he states flatly. "You fight for everything there, including the right to be alive. War is in our blood."

The words are an ominous threat. The people of Fairbanks are as familiar with battle and violence as the people of Askala. That gives the Outlanders an advantage they may never be able to overcome.

"All you had to do was say yes," Luca states dryly.

Ghost lets out a huff, and Luca guesses that's the closest the man's ever come to a laugh.

"What will we need?"

"Long, supple branches for the bows. Straight lengths for the arrows. The fibers of the mangrove pine bark can be used to make a cord. I'll show you how to construct them."

Luca's gut clenches at the difference these bows and arrows could make. "Thank you," he says simply.

Ghost looks away. "Well, you took me in and offered me food, water, a home, what else would I do?"

Luca doesn't mention that's exactly what they did with Charity, and that ended up with dozens of them dead. Ghost has nothing to do with Grace and the Outlanders.

The people down at the beach begin to make their way back as Wren calls a short break. It's time for water and some pods— getting everyone healthy and strong is a priority.

Ghost goes to move away, just as Luca thought he would. The man doesn't seem to like being around people. Knowing he still has one more question to ask, Luca pulls the fragment of shell out of his pocket and holds it up.

"Did you carve this?"

Ghost stills. "Where did you get that?"

"It was tucked in my blanket when I was abandoned as a baby. It was a gift from my mother."

Ghost's eyes widen so imperceptibly, if Luca wasn't watching so closely, he would've missed it. But this conversation could be pivotal, which means every detail counts.

Luca takes a step forward. "You carved it."

"I'm not the only one who can carve in the Outlands, boy."

"But—"

Ghost shoves his face close to Luca's. "I. Didn't. Carve. It."

The words are said with such certainty that Luca knows he's telling the truth.

Ghost holds himself there for a few more moments, as if making sure that Luca gets it. Then, with a snort, he turns and walks away.

Luca tucks the shard of wooden shell back in his pocket, frustration creeping up his spine.

But he's not ready to give up.

The Ghost may have been telling the truth that he didn't carve the shell, but his reaction suggested something else.

The Ghost knows who did.

HAWK

The boat is bigger than any boat Hawk's ever seen. And he's not sure if that's genius, or a mistake. On one hand, they're going to be able to fit many people aboard to keep them safe. On the other, it's going to take them days to finish. Days that he's not sure they have.

The false alarm when the Fairbanks people had arrived was a big wake-up call. Had that attack been real, Hawk's sure they would have lost the fight. While their so-called army had gathered on the beach, Hawk had run back to the colony so fast his heart had almost exploded. But when he'd found Sam in the infirmary with the antidote in her hand and a smile wider than he'd ever seen before, his heart had broken in half instead.

Hawk and his father had worked together to carry people to the infirmary, including Nova who'd been so frail Hawk had barely felt her weight in his arms. And now here they are, working together, once more. This time, protecting the colony in a different kind of way by providing them a means of escape.

"We're making a habit of this," his father says, banging two pieces of timber into place using one of his signature scarf joints.

"I'm just sorry it's a new habit," says Hawk, feeling responsible for the distance that sat between them for so many years.

"I was playing the long game with you." His father grins. "I knew you'd come around eventually."

Hawk continues his work. They make a great team. Their progress in the early hours of the morning when neither of them could sleep had exceeded both their expectations.

"Hey, Phoenix!" calls Luca from the other side of the boat frame, his hair still mussed from sleep, or whatever else he's been doing during the night. "Want me to start from this end?"

Hawk's dad nods. "Yep! Deniel, can you give Luca a hand?"

Zali's son nods his agreement, picks up a sheet of timber and goes to Luca who issues him with a set of detailed instructions.

Hawk pushes down yet more guilt. He should be his father's right-hand man, yet Luca knows so much more about building than he does. But instead of feeling resentful toward Luca, he finds that for the first time, he feels grateful. They need Luca's skills right now. And besides that, Luca earned his place. He was the one who followed Hawk's dad around like a shadow when he was younger, while Hawk was busy trailing Sam around.

Before long, Jagger joins them along with that strange man they call Ghost. Apparently, he knows how to work with wood. Hawk's not entirely sure he trusts him just yet, but now's not the time to turn down any offers of help. Jagger and Ghost begin filling out the frame on another section of the boat's skeleton.

Kozue and Cleo join them next and are given the task of sourcing more sap from the mangrove pines—an important job given the boat won't last long in the water without its protective coating.

More people arrive, and Hawk's surprised when his dad turns them away, instructing them to work on their fighting skills.

"We have all the people we require," his father says, noticing the confused look on Hawk's face. "We need to keep control of the quality of this build.

Hawk nods. "Learning to fight is just as important as providing a means to flee."

"I've been thinking…" His father lowers his voice so only Hawk can hear. "What if this boat wasn't a means to flee?"

"I don't understand." Hawk lowers his hammer. "We need to keep the vulnerable safe."

"Exactly." His father moves a little closer. "And the best way we can do that is by preventing the Outlanders from coming ashore. Not sending our people out in a boat where they'll likely perish. I've already told your mom and sisters not to go aboard. They'll be safer in the old encampment. It served our people well in the last battle."

Hawk's jaw falls open. "You told Mom not to leave? But Dad, why are we racing to finish this thing if you don't think it's a good idea?"

"Hawk, think about it." His father grips his forearm. "These Outlanders have been raised to fight on solid ground. What if we use the boat to fight? What if we meet them out on the water before they ever reach us?"

Luca clears his throat. "It's a good idea."

Hawk's dad spins around, his eyes wide with surprise at having been overheard.

"Phoenix, you couldn't whisper if you tried." Luca holds up a hand and smiles. "And I can see that you were trying."

"I think it's a good idea, too," says Jagger. "We take the fight to them, instead of waiting for them to bring it to us."

"You would say that," mutters Deniel.

"What's that supposed to mean?" Jagger sneers.

"My mother didn't trust you," says Deniel. "And I don't either. Once an Outlander, always an Outlander."

"Hey." Hawk's father leaves his side to go to Deniel, shoving a finger into his chest. "Can I remind you that I'm also an Outlander? As is my sister. The same sister who's teaching our colony how to use slingshots. Do you not trust us, either?"

"You're different." Deniel drops his gaze. "Jagger has—"

"Been nothing but loyal since he set foot on our land," Hawk's dad finishes. "And if you can't learn that same loyalty, then you're done here for the day. We'll find someone else to help."

"Fine." Deniel nods at Jagger. "I apologize."

Jagger nods in return, although he hasn't managed to wipe the sneer from his face.

Ghost remains quiet as he watches this exchange and Hawk wonders what he's making of it. From what Hawk's heard, arguments like this would be rare in Fairbanks. Not that Ghost is technically from there. He could be from anywhere, really.

"What makes you think we'll be any better at fighting on the water?" Hawk asks his father, still unsure about this suggestion.

"Hand to hand combat is never going to be a strength of a peace-loving society," his father says. "Killing a man with your bare hands is far harder than you could possibly imagine. We're better to fight them from a distance."

Hawk remembers his fight with Raiden in the Tournament and how, when it came down to it, he hadn't been able to deliver that final deadly blow. Perhaps his father has a point.

"It's more about removing their advantage," says Luca. "Than giving us an advantage."

Hawk nods, starting to see the sense in this as an idea.

"I already told this one," says Ghost, pointing at Luca. "You need bows and arrows, not slingshots and stones. It will give you further reach."

"Wren's already collecting the materials we need for those," says Luca, a little defensively. "I did hear you."

Ghost nods, returning to his work on the boat, seeming to have used up his quota of words for the day.

And to think Hawk thought he himself was quiet! It seems he's met his match in this Ghost of a man.

"How about we finish building the boat before we decide how to use it?" suggests Hawk, looking back to his father. "Either way, we're going to need it."

Mercy chooses that moment to appear from behind the large pile of wood beside the boat.

"And you say girls talk a lot," she says, walking up to Luca, her gaze firmly on his bare chest as she bites down on her bottom lip. Hawk knows they think they're being subtle in that love shack Luca built them, but he knows what's going on...

Luca drops a quick kiss on Mercy's lips. "What's up?"

"I come bearing gifts," she says, producing a wrapped parcel from behind her back. "Of the cornbread variety."

Hawk's mouth instantly waters as Mercy passes out slices of bread. "The corn was thoroughly washed before baking. It's safe to eat."

The bread is gone in a matter of moments and Hawk pats his belly contentedly.

"And now that you have full stomachs, I have news." Mercy smiles sweetly. "There's a leaders' meeting. And it's sort of been brought forward...to now."

Hawk's father groans. "That's half my workers."

"Yeah, sorry about that," says Mercy. "Kian said he'd send you a few people to take their place."

Right on cue, three people approach the building site, already rolling up their sleeves.

"Fine," Hawk's dad huffs. "Go. But don't mention anything about what we just talked about. Kian's more likely to agree to it if I explain it properly."

They nod their agreement while Mercy narrows her eyes, trying to figure out what she's missed.

"I'll be there in a minute," says Jagger as Luca and Hawk set down their tools. "I just want to finish this little bit. I'm right behind you."

Hawk, Luca and Mercy head up to the path that leads to the Oasis gardens.

"So, what did you just talk about?" asks Mercy, as soon as they're out of earshot. "The thing you're not supposed to mention?"

"It's a secret, apparently," says Hawk.

Mercy rolls her eyes. "Which is exactly why I want to know. I like secrets. I hardly want you to tell me how to build a boat."

"You'll be disappointed then," says Hawk. "Because it was about the boat."

"Boring," says Mercy, faking a yawn. "Are you trying to figure out if you use a scarf joint or a glove joint? Because I'm totally a fan of the hat joint."

Hawk gives his cousin a playful shove, hoping she'll drop the subject.

"Phoenix wants to use the boat to attack the Outlanders," says Luca.

"Hey!" Hawk's eyes widen. "We weren't supposed to say."

"But it's Mercy." Luca's brows pull together, like it hadn't occurred to him that when Hawk's dad said not to say anything that it might also include the girl he loves. Which is kind of a good thing now that Hawk thinks about it. He knows for sure he'll end up telling Sam.

"A water battle." Mercy whistles "That's cool!"

"You like the idea?" asks Hawk, wondering if he's the only one who had initial reservations.

Mercy shrugs. "It might give us the advantage we need. It's got to be easier to kill someone at a distance than up close."

Hawk rolls his eyes. "That's what my dad said."

"You don't think it's a good idea?" Mercy seems genuinely concerned.

"It's growing on me," he says.

Luca puts an arm around Mercy. "A bit like the way I grew on him."

"That's still a work in progress," Hawk mutters.

"Like the boat," says Mercy, hearing him perfectly well. "Although, even with just a few boards in place now it's looking more finished."

"Yeah, shouldn't take much more than a couple of days," says Luca. "And then it's just about getting enough sap to coat it with."

"So, why doesn't Phoenix want us to mention it?" Mercy asks Luca.

"You heard him," he says. "He thinks he has a better chance of convincing Kian himself. Although, I'm not sure that's wise. If we're changing our strategy, we really should do it now, so we have time to prepare."

"Does it bother Phoenix he's not a leader?" Mercy directs her question at Hawk this time.

"Nah." Hawk shakes his head. "He never even went to a Proving. He's not interested in that kind of thing."

"He contributes in other ways." Luca sweeps out his hand at all the huts they're passing. They all know they wouldn't live as comfortably as they do if Hawk's dad hadn't built their shelters.

They find the leaders gathered around the large table in the outdoor ballroom. It seems the meeting has already started.

"Thanks for coming," says Kian, noting their arrival.

Hawk slides into the seat Sam saved for him and takes her hand. She looks both exhausted and exhilarated from the work she's been doing. She may not be as skilled as her mother at caring for people, but it seems she's found her place in the infirmary after all as Askala's very own alchemist.

"There's a lot to do," says Kian.

"Yeah, like building the boat," says Jagger taking a vacant

chair and panting to catch his breath. "How long's this going to take?"

"Not long," says Kian. "We just need to make sure we're capitalizing on every spare minute right now. Would you like to give us an update on the boat?"

"Should be finished soon," says Jagger. "Few days at most."

Kian writes something down. "Do you have all the labor you need?"

Jagger nods. "Phoenix has it all in hand."

"And training?" Kian asks, turning to Wren. "How's that going?"

"Making progress," she says. "Most of the colony can fire a slingshot with accuracy now. We're moving on to bows and arrows to increase the range of fire. I could use some help to gather what we need to get them built."

Hawk finds himself distracted as he listens to Kian organizing a team of people to assist Wren. It's so hard to concentrate on anything when Sam has her hand in his. He just wants everyone else to fade away so they can be alone for a few moments. Maybe he should ask to borrow Luca and Mercy's shack...

"What's funny?" Sam whispers. "You're smiling."

"Nothing." Hawk pulls his face into a more serious expression, knowing Luca's love shack isn't their style. Once this battle is over, he and Sam can start building their life together properly. "Just thinking about you."

"I'm right here," she says.

"Yes, you are." He rubs his thumb across the back of her hand and notices the goose bumps that appear on her arm.

"Sarah, how are the food supplies going?" asks Kian.

Hawk's ears prick up at this. He hadn't realized a replacement for Zali in the kitchen had been found. He just hopes Sarah sticks at it longer than she did at the Proving.

"We're getting back on track." Sarah pulls back her shoulders. "All food that could be washed, has been dealt with. Everything else has been disposed of. No new illnesses in the colony reported so far."

"And you have enough workers?" Kian asks.

Sarah nods. "We can always use more, but we're coping."

Not satisfied with that answer, Kian organizes more people to help out.

"Can we have an update on the infirmary please, Sam?" Kian turns his gaze to his daughter. The warmth that floods his eyes unmistakable. It seems Hawk isn't the only one who's proud of her.

"The antidote has done its job," says Sam. "No more deaths since it was administered. The patients continue to improve."

"Have you begun the paste to coat the stones with?" Wren asks.

Sam shakes her head. "Not yet. The antidote was the priority. I'll start work on the paste next."

"Does anyone else have any other business to discuss?" Kian asks. "Because I'd like to talk about strategy."

Luca catches Hawk's eye and nods at him.

Hawk's brows jump up. He's not telling him to speak on behalf of his father, surely? His dad had been very clear with what he wanted them to do. Or rather, what he didn't want them to do.

Luca clears his throat. "Hawk has something to say on behalf of Phoenix."

All eyes turn to Hawk and he freezes. For a start, speaking now will go against his father's wishes. And then there's the fact that talking in public has never been his strong suit...

"You tell them, Luca," he says.

"You're Phoenix's son." Luca nods encouragingly. "You're better to speak on his behalf."

"My dad wanted to talk to you himself," says Hawk. "I'm not sure this is a good idea."

"If we're changing our strategy, we need time to get it right," says Luca, repeating what he said earlier.

"He's right," says Jagger. "You should speak for your father. We don't have time to waste."

Hawk draws in a deep breath, and lets go of Sam's hand, needing to keep a clear head.

"My father believes we should use the boat to attack," says Hawk. "That we should take the fight to the water and prevent the Outlanders from reaching the land where their fighting skills are best. He thinks we're more likely to be able to kill them from a distance than with our bare hands."

There are a few gasps around the table as people absorb this news.

"And what do you think?" Kian asks.

"I agree with him." Hawk looks Kian directly in the eye as his voice gains volume. "We should meet these savages in the ocean they're attempting to cross. If we let them onto our soil, we're all as good as dead."

Kian turns to Wren and they stare at each other for long moments. Once enemies themselves, these two have formed a friendship built from respect and trust over the years. Kian would never make a decision like this if Wren didn't think it was a good idea.

Wren nods slowly at Kian, indicating her agreement.

But even though Kian takes control when needed, he doesn't see himself as the leader. They all get a say in this. Hawk knows what will come next.

Kian stands. "All those in favor of using the boat to attack, please raise your hand."

Hawk casts down his gaze, frightened of what he might see. His relationship with his father has come so far since he returned from the Newlands. And now he'd not only gone against his wishes, but he'd spoken on his behalf.

Hawk lifts his eyes to find a sea of hands in the air around him.

It seems he did his father proud.

The vote is unanimous.

The escape boat just became an attack boat.

And the fight for Askala has never felt more real.

SAM

"*H*awk, could you give me a hand?" Sam calls out from the doorway of the infirmary office.

Hawk looks up from where he was helping someone sip the antidote out of a cup. "Sure."

Sam watches him approach, wondering which Hawk she loves more. The man she surreptitiously watches as he helps his father build the boat—sweat glistening on skin, curls catching the sun. Or the tender guy who helps her in the infirmary any break he gets—so gentle, always smiling and encouraging.

He smiles his Sam smile, and her heart expands exponentially.

"What's up?" he asks. "Did you need something lifted off a shelf?"

Sam steps back so he can enter and closes the door behind them. She presses herself against it, her breath already picking up in anticipation.

"No, I just wanted to tell you I've been doing some research."

Hawk grins, pride shining from his warm eyes. "Yeah, I know. About how to seal the sails."

"Well, yes, I have been researching that," Sam concedes.

"Everything's ready for this afternoon. But I've also been researching something else."

Hawk glances around the office. "Great.

"It's been fascinating," Sam says huskily as she slides closer. "I've learned all about the science of attraction."

Hawk stills. "Oh."

She steps in so they're only inches apart. "It explained so much. Did you know high levels of dopamine and norepinephrine are released during attraction?"

Hawk's eyes heat, his lips softening and molding into a sexy smile. "I didn't."

"Those chemicals make us giddy, energetic, and euphoric," Sam breathes. "In fact, I can feel them right now."

"Me, too," Hawk says, his voice low and husky.

"They even lead to decreased appetite and insomnia."

It's true. Sam lays awake at night, thinking of Hawk. Remembering their moments in the marriage tree. Missing his comforting warmth, his enticing heat.

"That explains a lot, actually."

Sam presses herself against him, glorying in the sensations that multiply in every place they touch. "Attraction is like a total eclipse of the brain."

"Sam," Hawk groans.

She pushes up on tiptoe, holding her lips millimeters away from his. "And I love it."

When she's with Hawk, like this, she's never wanted to think less. All she wants to do is feel.

Hawk's mouth crashes onto hers, claiming her lips. But Sam asked him in here so she could claim him.

Her hands wrap around his back, climbing beneath his shirt and spearing over the corded muscles of his back. Hawk groans again, and Sam uses the opportunity to deepen their kiss.

Thought is obliterated. There's nothing but passion exploding. Heat scorching trails through her mind.

Love soaring and rejoicing.

Sam clings to him, no longer the temptress she was trying to be. She's falling, drowning, clinging to the one person who can do this to her.

The sound of something clanging onto the floor out in the infirmary has them jolting. They reluctantly pull apart, still holding each other.

Hawk studies Sam, hot eyes full of admiration. "What brought that on?"

Sam smiles, loving the way they're both a little out of breath. "It was an experiment."

"How long it takes for you to turn me into mush?"

Giggling, Sam shakes her head. "My hypothesis was that you've awakened a part of me I never knew existed." Hawk blinks at her, seemingly speechless. "I was right. There's a Sam that can never get enough of you, Hawk."

"Best experiment ever," Hawk breathes before kissing her again.

They keep this one short, reining in the passion that's been sparked. Sam presses her hand to his heart. "I just wanted you to know..."

Hawk wraps his arms around her, holding her tight. They both sober, conscious the attack from the Outlanders is imminent.

"We're going to be ready," Hawk says with conviction.

Sam nods. Everyone is working toward that goal.

It's whether it'll make a difference or not that's less guaranteed.

"Sam? Are you in there?"

Sam draws back, surprised to hear her grandmother's voice.

"Just coming now," she calls back.

Hawk grips her hand as she goes to move away. "I love you, Sam."

Sam smiles. "That's why my hypothesis was going to be proven true."

Attraction can only be intense as it is between them because it's a product of two hearts fanning the flames. Sam's hand tightens around the doorknob. That love is one of the few things giving her hope right now.

Askala won before because of love. Because everyone here cares—it's firmly etched in their DNA.

It's the only advantage they have over the Outlanders.

Opening the door, Sam finds Amity on the other side, about to open it herself. "Ah, there you are."

Her eyes widen a little as she sees Hawk behind Sam. Sam steps out, shoulders back as she refuses to feel like they've been caught out. Except her cheeks flush as her grandmother looks at her knowingly.

Hawk smiles. "Hi, Amity. Great to see you."

Since the Fairbanks people arrived and everyone assumed they were under attack, Amity has spent less and less time in her hut up on the hill. The threat to Askala has ended her years of reclusivity.

She steps back to let them pass, holding up a jar. "I've brought pods for everyone."

"Wonderful," Sam says warmly. "They're just what everyone here needs to get their strength back."

With Sam's mother sick, her father no doubt needed help looking after the pods, and everything he knows about pods he learned from Amity.

And right now, everyone needs to be strong.

Speaking of getting strong. "How's Mom?"

"I checked on her on the way here. Her progress is impressive." Amity's eyes glow. "Your antidote saved her life."

Sam flushes again. "Getting that antidote together was a team effort."

Hawk squeezes Sam's hand, telling her he knows she's being modest. "I'd better get back to my dad."

Sam nods. "Take a pod before you go."

Amity holds out the jar and Hawk scoops out a luminescent, wriggling body and pops it in his mouth. He grimaces—the bitter flavor of pods is something he's never been able to get used to, just like the crunch of cockroaches—pulls up a smile and leaves.

Amity's eyes sharpen as she glances around the infirmary, no doubt noting that several of the beds are now empty. "How are the other preparations going?"

Sam takes the jar of pods and places it on a nearby table, nodding at Rose to start handing them out. "We're stabilizing our food sources now that everything that could've been poisoned has been destroyed. Between you and Dad, we have an ample supply of pods."

Sam walks over to an adjacent table. "I've prepared the glue for the bows and arrows, along with the solution we'll need to coat the cords."

Sam thinks back to yesterday, when Ghost had come in with a list of instructions. The glue for the feathered fletches had been straightforward, the recipe similar to the sap they'll be coating the boat with, just not as concentrated.

Then Ghost had told her, with as few words as possible, what they'd need to treat the pine fibers so they could be woven into strong, tensile cord for the bows.

Sam had nodded, her mind calculating where each ingredient was in the storeroom. But as Ghost had turned to walk away, obviously done, she'd called out.

"Wouldn't the ratio of sap to water need to be higher?"

Ghost had turned back, his face stony. "No."

"It's just that—"

"Are you familiar with war, girl?"

"Well, no, of course not," Sam had said, feeling a little

chagrined. "The people of Askala are ethically opposed to the use of violence to satisfy personal gain."

Ghost had grunted. "Exactly."

With that, he'd turned and left the infirmary.

She'd shaken her head at the retreating back of the silent, gruff man, thinking that whatever he's endured in the Outlands has indelibly defined him.

"Excellent," Amity praises. "And everything is ready for today?"

Sam smiles, moving onto the next table, where the largest urn yet is sitting. "This one took a while, and a bit of research, but I think I've got it right."

Amity runs her hands over the urn. "Kian said the weavers have been working hard to have the sail complete."

"Yes, they have. Weaving such large swathes of fabric while maintaining a tight weave is time consuming. Then the key was to make it water repellent—or the material becomes saturated and heavy—but also not weighing it down."

"And what did you come up with?" Amity asks, obviously harboring no doubt Sam has managed this.

Glad she has, Sam smiles. "I got the idea from Fairbanks, actually. They use a unique mixture of resin and sap to make candles and coat their bowls to make them waterproof. I figured that a diluted mixture of the same should work nicely." Sam pats the urn. "We'll paint it on today when it's hoisted for the first time."

Everyone's been looking forward to this moment. It feels pivotal, because once the sail is up, the boat they'll use to defend Askala is almost complete.

Amity raises her brows. "You've been busy, granddaughter."

Sam shrugs. "Everyone has."

They have no choice. Askala, and the lives of everyone who lives here, depends on them.

There's the sound of footsteps, ones that Sam instantly recognizes, and Hawk appears in the doorway. "They're ready."

Excitement tingles down Sam's spine. "Wonderful."

Hawk enters and lifts the large urn, the muscles of his arms bulging in a way that has dopamine increasing in Sam all over again.

"Shall we? There's been quite the turn out," says Hawk.

Sam smiles. "It'll be good for people to see this."

The massive sail rising and unfurling will be a symbol of hope. One they desperately need.

They make their way down to the beach, joining the crowd that's already there. Sam's surprised to see how far the boat has come along since she saw it yesterday. The sides seem complete, and now a large mast spears high into the air.

Her father greets them, taking the urn from Hawk. "Thank you." He smiles a little wistfully. "Your mother would've liked to have seen this."

Amity rests a hand on her son's arm. "You told her to stay home?"

"She still gets tired so easily."

Amity raises her brows. "She always did have a mind of her own."

She's gazing over his shoulder, meaning Sam's father spins around. Her mother is making her way slowly to the beach, clinging to Luca's arm. Their father rushes over, seeming to offer to carry her, but she vehemently shakes her head.

Something in Sam's chest softens and warms as she watches her parents make their way to the beach, slowly but surely. Seeing them together, here, is another wonderful symbol of hope.

Jagger clears his throat. "Now that we're all here," he says with a grin. "We can get started."

The sail is already on the boat, one end tied to some rope. Jagger turns to Phoenix who's standing inside the vessel.

"When you're ready."

Phoenix nods and this time, it's Sam's turn to squeeze Hawk's hand. She can practically feel the pride pulsing from him as he watches his father step up to the mast.

The boat that will defend Askala, the one that will ensure the Outlanders never step foot on the beautiful land they've worked so hard to protect, is here thanks to Phoenix's craftsmanship.

Hope flares bright and hot inside Sam, making her bounce on her toes. The boat will be coated with sap today. The sails painted with water repellent. And everything will be ready.

Phoenix grips the rope which reaches a pulley right up to the top of the mast and starts to haul. The edges of the pale brown material flutter in the breeze, as if the sails are just as impatient to be up as everyone else.

He must decide to do it quickly, maybe wanting the dramatic sight of the sail expanding as it catches the breeze just as much as everyone else. The rope yanks up fast, the material rising into the air. The sail unfurls.

Hawk freezes. A few people cry out. Sam blinks, disbelief making it hard to process what she's seeing.

Long, jagged gashes run down the length of the sail. It flaps about uselessly in the breeze, the air moving straight through the gaping lacerations.

"No," Amity moans. Sam's father catches her mother as her legs give out.

Someone has shredded the sail. Destroyed it.

Sabotaged their chance of attacking the Outlanders.

MERCY

Finally, since returning from the Newlands, Mercy sees her chance to do something useful. Because while Sam's been busy curing the sick, and Hawk and Luca have been building the boat, Mercy's been…floating. Nothing had made that more obvious than when Kian asked her to go and gather the leaders for the meeting. She's little more than a messenger.

No good at building. No good at making antidotes. No good at fighting. Not even any good at getting Charity to talk. And everyone knows that talking's her thing.

But all that's about to change.

Because Askala has an enemy in its midst. Someone is sabotaging their efforts to protect themselves from the imminent attack. And Mercy is going to find out who it is.

She looks around the crowd gathered on the beach to see the unfurling of the sail. Surely, whoever tore it to shreds has to be here to see the devastated reaction to their handiwork.

The people of Fairbanks stand off to one side. Tarquin is with them, glued to Relic. Those two have become inseparable since the people of Fairbanks arrived. Mercy suspects it's because Relic understands what it's like to be an outsider here. Their bond reminds her a little of Hawk and Sam when they were young.

She studies the faces of these new arrivals. The people who gave her shelter in the Outlands and treated her like one of their own.

There's Annabel but there's no way she can be a suspect. She wouldn't hurt a mosquito.

There's Finn and Dharma—two people who are impossible to put in separate categories given their closeness. But they wouldn't have done it either. They want a better life for their younger son than the one that was stolen from their first.

She looks at the other Fairbanks faces, lesser known to her but all seeming equally as shocked by what just took place.

No, these are peaceful people. They would never sabotage Askala like that.

Although...the man they call Ghost isn't technically one of them.

Ghost is standing off to the side of the group. He's looking at the ground, deep in thought. Mercy can't tell if his odd behavior is because he's not used to being around so many people, or if he's just...suspicious.

Then she remembers how Ghost saved her life by dropping that knife in her lap when Gunner and Vitron held her captive. It can't be him!

Determined not to let her personal feelings get in the way of this serious investigation, Mercy adds Ghost to her list of suspects. Although, it's not shaping up to be much of a list so far.

Scanning the crowd, her eyes land on Deniel next. She's never trusted that guy. His mother was always so busy accusing everyone of everything—especially Jagger—that it makes Mercy wonder if some of Zali's attitudes rubbed off on her son. Luca had mentioned only last night that Deniel had said some pretty uncomfortable things about Jagger as they'd been working on the boat.

She adds Deniel to her list, deciding he's definitely worth further investigation.

Which brings her to Jagger. Had Zali been suspicious of him with good cause? Again, this seems unlikely. But she might make some enquiries just to be sure.

As the people disperse, absorbing the shock of what they just witnessed and needing to get back to the urgent tasks that await them, Mercy's eye is caught by one more person. Another lonely soul who holds themself apart from the rest of the colony. Someone who pledged her love to a man who once tried to sacrifice them all for the sake of the planet they live on.

Amity.

Is she trying to finish what Magnus started? Who knows what's been going on in her mind while spending all those hours alone in her hut.

Amity turns to leave the beach and Mercy jogs over to her, deciding to start right there. She doesn't know Sam and Luca's grandmother very well. Now that she thinks of it, they don't seem to know her all that well either. But she needs to find out if there's more to her suspicion, if only to rule her off her list.

"Hi," says Mercy, approaching her.

Amity looks up with a startled expression. "Hello, Mercy."

"Terrible what happened to the sail, isn't it?" Mercy smiles as sweetly as she can manage.

Amity nods, her brows still knitted together as she must surely be trying to figure out what Mercy wants with her.

"I was wondering if I can help you with the pods?" Mercy asks, wincing slightly. She's not in the least bit interested in the breeding center, something Amity would know.

"Sure." Amity nods toward the path that leads to the breeding center. "I was just about to check the tanks. I could use a hand."

"Great!" Mercy attempts to inject enthusiasm into her voice as she falls into step beside her.

They walk in silence as Mercy tries to think of something she can ask that will provide the answers she needs. But being a Seeker has taught her to hold her tongue. After all, that was how Hawk got Charity to talk. He just sat there, looking at her until she spoke.

But Amity doesn't seem much in the mood to talk. It's like she has a weight sitting directly on her shoulders that just won't shift. Could that weight be made from guilt? Did she slash the sail and is now regretful? It's too hard to say right now. But that's exactly why Mercy is here.

They reach the breeding center and Amity quickens her pace as she rushes to the tanks, her relief obvious as she moves between them, declaring the pods to be safe.

"You were worried?" Mercy asks as something important clicks into place. She's just not sure what it is just yet.

Amity nods and Mercy can't help but notice how beautiful she is. It's not at all hard to believe that once two brothers had fought over her so passionately that their own relationship had been destroyed.

"You asked about the sail," says Amity. "It's not the first time Askala's been sabotaged. I thought that maybe…"

"The pods had been targeted as well," Mercy finishes when Amity's voice trails off.

She nods, her eyes filling with tears. "I couldn't bear to see that happen again. Especially not now when I've only just redis-covered my love for them."

Guilt winds its way through Mercy's gut. Amity didn't destroy the sail. She's a gentle soul. She cares about Askala like it's a child of her own.

"It was my grandfather who did that," says Mercy, even though Amity is well aware of her blood connection to Ronan.

"He destroyed the pods. Then he came back and tried to destroy us."

Amity nods. "And that's no more your fault than what Magnus did is mine. We can't wear the guilt of the sins of those who are close to us, do you understand me? Believe me, I've tried. It doesn't work."

Mercy nods.

"You're your own person, Mercy." Amity hands her a thermometer and nods for her to dip it into one of the tanks. "You can make your own future."

Mercy checks the temperature of the tank and calls it out to Amity, who writes it down in a logbook. She moves onto the next tank, noticing that Amity hadn't double checked the accuracy of her reading. It seems she trusts her. Which only makes her feel more guilty.

Despite needing to get through her list of suspects, Mercy finds herself enjoying the work with the pods. Amity is a good teacher. Kind. Patient. And her enthusiasm for these strange gelatinous creatures is infectious. The way their transparent butterfly wings flap in the water as they circle their tanks, safe under the protection of the layers of phytoplankton, is calming. Watching them makes Mercy feel like nothing else in the world matters.

"You're a natural," says Amity. "Maybe when all this is over, you can help Kian here."

"What about you?" Mercy rests the net she's holding on the edge of one of the tanks.

Amity smiles at her. "I'm old."

"Hardly," Mercy laughs.

"I like helping here but the pods are Kian's now. He'd hoped Sam might take over from him one day, but it's clear we need her elsewhere. As for Luca, I can't imagine him enjoying this, can you?"

Mercy laughs. "It's far too peaceful for him."

Amity nods her agreement. "Seb may have enjoyed it, but…"

Mercy's smile evaporates. "I'm so sorry about what happened to Seb."

"Thank you." Amity pulls back her shoulders in a practiced way of a woman who's used to dealing with grief. "He was a good kid. What happened to him was unfair. Which is why we can't let them win. We have to—"

"Win." Mercy goes to Amity and puts her hands on her shoulders. "We have to win. And we will. And when we do, I'm going to help you here with the pods."

Amity nods. "I think I've got this under control now. You have a job to finish."

Mercy tilts her head. "What job?"

"More suspects to interview," laughs Amity. "I must say that initially I was a bit surprised you made a beeline for me, but I suppose it's best to leave no stone unturned."

"I…but…it…" Mercy's jaw hangs open as her hands fall to her side. "Was I that obvious?"

"Only to someone who knows how to read people." Amity reaches for her hand and squeezes it. "So, have I cleared my name? Or am I still a suspect?"

"It wasn't you," says Mercy. "I apologize for even entertaining that thought."

Amity waves her apology away.

"Who do you think it was?" Mercy asks, deciding that perhaps starting with Amity might have been a smart idea after all. Her insight here could be invaluable.

"I think it was the Ghost," she answers without hesitation.

"I thought it might be Deniel," says Mercy, not wanting it to be the man who saved her life.

Amity shakes her head. "He's too loyal to his mother's memory to do anything as foolish as that."

"What about Jagger?" Mercy raises a brow.

Amity laughs at this one. "What else does that poor man

have to do to convince you how deeply Askala runs in his veins? It wasn't him."

"So, why the Ghost then?" Mercy asks on a sigh, fast running out of options on her list.

"He's up to something," says Amity. "I'm not sure what yet, but I'm watching him."

Mercy opens her mouth to protest then slams it shut, deciding that perhaps now is the time to listen. It's a known fact that you can't possibly learn a single thing when you're the one who's talking.

"I could be wrong." Amity frowns. "So, tread carefully. But there's more to that man than meets the eye."

Mercy nods. "I might go and talk to him."

"Good luck." Amity closes the logbook and walks toward the cricket enclosures. "Thanks again for your help today. I meant it when I said you're a natural."

Mercy leaves the breeding center deciding perhaps it was Amity who'd helped her and not the other way around. Mercy's gut instinct about Ghost may just be right if Amity has been sensing the same thing. But why would he help build the boat and give them the idea of the bows and arrows if at the same time he's working against them? It makes no sense.

There's a strange mood in the air as Mercy makes her way through the colony. As people rush about getting their tasks done, there are suspicious glances and hushed voices. Clearly, she's not the only one trying to figure out who was responsible for this.

"There you are!" Luca rushes up to her and loops an arm around her shoulders. "I've been looking for you everywhere. Where were you?"

"Helping Amity with the pods," she says as if that were a normal occurrence. Perhaps one day it will be.

"Okay..." He leans over to look at her. "What brought that on?"

"They're interesting," she says, not wanting to tell him that she'd suspected his grandmother. "It's about time I made myself useful around here."

"Hey." Luca pulls her into a hug. "You do loads around here."

"Who do you think did it?" she asks, changing the subject to one that's sure to get his attention.

"I don't know." He kisses the top of her head then loosens his embrace. "But it's all anyone can talk about."

"We need to unite at a time like this!" Mercy pushes away from Luca and scuffs at the ground with her foot. "Not be torn apart by suspicion."

Luca shakes his head. "Maybe that was the whole point."

"What do you mean?" Mercy asks.

"The sail can be mended," he says. "It's a setback but we can overcome it. Our weavers know how to work fast. We can fix that. But if our people are divided...that's a whole lot harder to fix."

"We can't win the war if we're not all on the same team." Mercy nods, her eyes filling with tears. "We have to find out who did this!"

"What are your thoughts?" Luca asks. "Now that you've ruled out Amity..."

Anger bubbles in Mercy's gut. Not him, too! Is she really that transparent?

"How did you know?" she asks, resisting when he tries to hug her again. "No, don't tell me. Be quiet."

"You've never shown an interest in the pods before," he says, pulling his face into an innocent expression. "And I know how your brain ticks."

She looks him in the eye, trying to come up with something smart to say in return but is instantly lost in the dark pools of his eyes. He does know how she ticks, in more ways than one. All her negativity evaporates as she steps forward and lands a kiss right on his lips.

That's one way to shut him up.

Possibly her favorite way.

He kisses her back with restrained passion, saving that for when they're in their hut in the cover of darkness. And just like when she got lost in the world of caring for the pods, she's lost in him.

There's a giggle as two small children run past them and they break away, breathless. But Mercy feels a little better. A teeny bit more like the world isn't about to end.

"Who's next on your list of suspects?" Luca teases.

"Why does everyone think I have a list!" Mercy crosses her arms. "I totally do not have a list."

"Admit it." He puts his arm around her again. "You one hundred percent have a list."

She huffs. "Okay! I have a list but it's in my head and it's short, so it completely doesn't count."

"I knew it." Luca fist pumps, his affection for her clear in his eyes.

"Mercy! Luca!" Tarquin comes running at them at top speed, her wild hair flying behind her.

"What's wrong?" Luca bends down to catch her as she flies into his arms. "What's happened? Where's Relic?"

Tarquin is panting hard and pointing, as her words struggle to find a way out.

They immediately start walking in the direction she's pointing.

"Where's Relic?" Mercy asks again.

"He's stuck," says Tarquin with wide eyes. "On Charity's roof."

Now they're no longer walking. They're running. Zali's old hut comes into view, and sure enough, perched on top of the thatched roof is Relic, looking terrified.

"What's wrong?" asks Reggie from his position at the door.

"What's wrong is that you're supposed to be guarding this

hut." Luca sets Tarquin down. "And there's a kid on the roof and you haven't even noticed."

"What the—" Reggie steps back and gasps as he sees Relic.

"Get me down," Relic pleads. "It's too high!"

"What are you doing up there?" Mercy asks.

"I can't get down," he says, not answering her question.

Luca reaches up and Relic jumps into his open arms.

"What were you doing?" Mercy asks again.

"It was a dare." Relic looks to the ground.

"Tarquin!" Mercy glares at the small girl beside her.

"He never said I dared him," Tarquin complains.

Luca sets Relic down on the ground. "He didn't need to."

"I think you'd better go and find your parents," Mercy says to Relic. "And tell them about this before I get a chance to."

"But…" Relic looks up at Mercy. "But I need to tell you something first."

"What is it?" Luca asks.

"The hut," Relic says. "Tarquin told me it was a prison, except I looked through the thatch and…"

"And what?" Mercy squats down to get at eye level with the small boy.

"And there was nobody inside," he says. "Why are you guarding an empty prison?"

Luca races to the door and flings it open.

His gasp is enough to confirm that what Relic is saying is true, but still, Mercy goes up behind him to check, needing to see this with her own eyes.

The hut is empty.

Which means that somehow, Charity has escaped.

And Mercy's list of suspects is suddenly useless.

Because she now only has just one.

LUCA

"Sweet Terra," Luca's father gasps as he hears the news. Luca's still breathing hard from their run to find him. "Reggie last checked on Charity at dawn when he started his shift. We don't know how long she's been missing."

Mercy pants beside him, her hands hiked on her hips. "She's probably the one who sabotaged the sail."

Dex comes running up, no doubt after seeing his daughter run frantically toward Kian's hut. "What's wrong?"

"Charity escaped," Luca's father states flatly.

Dex's brows hike up. "Ah, that's not good."

"No, it really isn't."

Luca turns to his father. "We need everyone in their huts. Who knows what Charity is planning—she's on the run and desperate. From what I can tell, she went into the forest. I might be able to track her."

His father nods. "Good thinking." He looks to his cousin. "Dex, get the word out. Everyone has to remain in their huts until we've given the all-clear. Every person in Askala needs to be on high alert."

Luca grabs Mercy's hand. "We'll go pick up the trail. When

that's done, send every able-bodied person to help with the search."

His father's frown is ferocious as he nods. "Be careful, son."

Luca grins even though every muscle in his gut feels like iron. "Isn't careful my middle name?"

He's gone before his father can respond, taking Mercy with him. The sooner they pick up Charity's trail, the sooner the people of Askala will be safe.

"What do you think she's planning?" asks Mercy as they run back to Zali's old hut.

"Nothing good," Luca mutters. "Charity no longer cares if she lives or dies."

Or how many she'll take with her.

They reach the hut where Reggie is pacing, pulling at his hair as he berates himself under his breath.

"Reggie," says Luca. "You need to get your family safe in your hut."

"But this is my fault, Luca," he wails. "She escaped on my watch."

Luca shakes his head. "We should've had two people each shift—we're a peace-loving society. We assume people are better than this." Luca indicates the path he and Mercy just came down. "Now, you need to go look after your family. Once you've done that, find my father, we're going to put together a search party."

Reggie nods, his jaw tight as if he's determined to get at least this right. He leaves quickly as he jogs down the path.

"Now what?" Mercy asks, looking around. "You said she went into the forest."

Luca walks around the hut, finding again the small hole that Charity had dug beneath one of the walls—and had probably been hiding for days as she progressively made it bigger—and points to the footprints leading away from it.

They lead straight to the tree line not far away.

161

Luca squats beside the nearest footprint. "See how each one is spread apart? That means she was running." He frowns. "And she was running on the sides of her feet."

Mercy frowns. "Why would she do that?"

Straightening, Luca heads to the edge of the forest. "She's trying to avoid being tracked."

Mercy joins him, her face set in determined lines. "Well, she didn't take into account that the Falcon would be tracking her."

"I'm not the Falcon here, Mercy."

She raises a brow. "You *are* the Falcon, Luca." She turns back to the forest they're about to enter. "No matter where you are."

Luca squats down, running his fingers over a bent blade of grass. "Except there are no trees in the Outlands. I haven't done a lot of tracking in a forest."

Mercy joins him, watching as his hand drifts over to a small pebble. One that's been overturned, the underside a little darker than the other stones around it. "Tell me what you see."

"She came this way. See how the grass is bent?" Mercy nods, her brows scrunched in concentration. "It tells us which direction she went. And this stone's been overturned, like it was flicked backward."

Mercy's gaze follows the trajectory of the clues as if they're an arrow pointing into the trees. "She used this animal track," she breathes.

Luca straightens, pride sparking in his chest. "She sure did. We don't know how much of a head start she has on us, but it can't be more than a couple of hours or the underside of that stone would've been dry."

Mercy eyes heat with admiration. "Between your face, your body, and that sharp mind of yours, I never stood a chance."

Luca brushes past her, running a finger down her nose. "Ditto."

Returning his focus to tracking, Luca alternates between scanning the area just in front of them and the path ahead. Just as he expected, the clues continue—still showing Charity was running, still on the sides of her feet.

Several times they have to stop as Luca loses Charity's trail. Each time, he backtracks, checking for any signs he missed. Each time, Mercy's by his side, wanting to know what he's looking for.

They've walked for several feet with no sign of a print and Luca stops again, ready to repeat the process, when Mercy angles her head.

"She's staying on the track. Wouldn't it be quicker to keep going until we come to another sign?"

But Luca's already squatting, bringing his face close to the ground. "She's still hiding her tracks. Preferring to step on rocks, randomly changing her gait, that sort of stuff. She could've turned off and headed into the trees at any moment."

Mercy's eyes widen. "Because she wants us to assume that she'd just kept following this track."

"Yep," says Luca, straightening and dusting his hands off. "She's planning something. I can feel it." Looking around, he scans the shrubbery they're surrounded by. "She might also be disguising her tracks because she's planning an ambush."

Mercy spins around, doing her own sudden scan. "You're telling me this now?"

Luca wrinkles his nose apologetically. "Sorry, only just thought of that."

Finding what he was looking for—a slight scuff on some tree bark—he takes Mercy's hand and they begin walking again.

"I know it's tempting to rush on ahead—no one wants Charity on the loose—but the more thoroughly we do it, the more likely we are to catch her."

Mercy's lips edge up at the corners. "Did you—Luca, the boy who probably named the dare tree, the man who saved damsels and asked questions later—just advise me to slow down and think things through?"

Despite the tension that's permanently knotted through his muscles since they discovered Charity had escaped, a little burst of delight shoots through Luca.

He presses a quick kiss on Mercy's lips before making a point of rolling his eyes. "You don't know me at all."

They've only been walking for a couple of minutes when Luca hears it. The gentle sound of water tumbling over rocks has his heart plummeting. He jogs ahead, Mercy right behind him, turning a bend in the track to see the gurgling trickle.

"Dammit," Luca mutters. "If Charity chose to continue walking through the stream, it's going to be almost impossible to track her."

They both race forward, seeing that Charity's last footstep is just before the water's edge.

Mercy shakes her head in determined denial. "No, we haven't lost her." She splashes into the water, looking around frantically. "We can't afford to lose her."

Luca stands at the edge of the stream, eyes narrowed. "No, we can't."

Mercy reaches the other side of the small waterway. "Luca, look! Another footprint!"

Splashing over, Luca joins her, even though he already sees what Mercy's seen. There is, indeed, another track on the other side.

"She must've kept going." Mercy tugs on his hand.

"Just wait a sec," Luca says thoughtfully, remaining where he is. "That footstep is the clearest one so far."

Scanning their surroundings, Luca can't ignore the tingling in his gut. Why has Charity tried to cover her tracks, but then stopped?

A second later, he realizes what had caught his attention. He points to the silvery threads reaching across the path. "See that?"

Mercy squints, takes a step closer to him so she can try to figure out what Luca's trying to show her, then stills.

"There's a spider's web."

Luca holds his breath, suspecting Mercy's already figured out why the gossamer trap is significant. "And?"

"It's unbroken. Charity couldn't have gone that way."

"I have a feeling the Peregrine is going to outfly the Falcon, one day."

Mercy's smile is blinding. "I have a feeling they both soar higher when they're together."

Wishing there was time to kiss those amazing lips of hers and show her how much her words touched him, Luca brushes a hand down her cheek. "They most certainly do."

He turns back to the stream. "She's trying to trick us. We need to spread out, going a little further out with each loop. See what we can find."

Mercy nods, her gaze already on the ground and vegetation around them. They spend long minutes, circling from the last footprint, trying to find some sign of which way Charity's gone.

Only to find nothing.

Frustration has Luca grinding his teeth. Every moment spent searching is another moment Charity is roaming through the forest, scheming and planning.

No doubt intent on hurting as many Askalans as she can.

They don't have time for this.

"Luca?" Mercy's voice reaches him from the other side of the stream.

She's standing several feet away from the path they arrived on, staring at the ground.

He's by her side in an instant, not liking the edge of worry he heard in her voice. "What's up?"

She points down.

The clear outline of a foot has been pressed into the moist soil. A small, slender female foot. One facing Askala.

Luca's stomach clenches painfully. Charity walked several feet down the stream and came out on the same side. She led them on a useless, wild chase.

And the whole time, she was heading back to Askala.

Simultaneously, they break into a run. Tracking Charity back to Askala is easy. She's no longer hiding her tracks like she was before—the clues that were nothing more than a decoy. Instead, her prints are deep and easily spotted, even wider apart than the last ones.

Charity was in a hurry to get back.

Luca and Mercy burst out of the forest further east of where they entered, breathing hard. Luca points to the trail, and they continue, slowing, but not losing momentum.

They reach the first huts and have to stop because there are now several tracks crisscrossing the ones they were following. Several people have walked around here, no doubt going about their tasks for the day.

Except now, the colony is eerily quiet with everyone tucked away in their huts, waiting for a murderer to be caught.

"There!" Mercy exclaims.

Luca sees what she's pointing at. The footprints continue to their left, now following a path. The size and shape match the ones they've been tracking.

He's about to take a step when Luca stops. He follows the indents in the soil, his gaze creeping up the path and to the hut at the end of it.

"Jagger's hut," Mercy states, horrified.

Once again, they're running. Except the mishmash of tracks outside the door has Luca pausing. The same narrow footprints facing both ways.

Mercy frowns. "She left again."

Squatting, Luca runs his fingers over the most recent track. "But it looks like she came back."

"Are you sure?"

Luca shakes his head, knowing it doesn't make sense. Why would Charity do that?

He shoots to his feet. Unless she came back looking for him! It makes sense that Charity would target Jagger first. He can probably track better than Luca, and he's big and strong.

More of a threat.

Luca bursts through the door. "Jagger! Are you okay?"

Mercy appears behind him, just as Luca realizes the hut's empty.

He shakes his head, realizing he needs to think more clearly. "Jagger's probably part of the search team."

"Yes," agrees Mercy. "Of course, he wouldn't be in his hut."

Frightened and trembling, like many of the other Askalans would be.

"But I am," comes a quiet voice from the corner of the room.

Luca freezes, his heart feeling like it just came to a standstill. He spins, slowly with senses on high alert, to peer in the gloomy corner behind the table.

Charity steps out, her straggly lengths of blonde hair plastered to her head with sweat. "Whoever's hut this is, it was a good choice to come to," she says with a smile.

Something glints in the shadows she's standing in, only heightening Luca's focus. Whatever it is, he has no doubt it's a weapon.

"Charity," Luca says, keeping his voice level and low. "If you come quietly, no one will get hurt."

Her lip curls. "Which would defy the point of escaping, wouldn't it?"

Luca tries to indicate behind his back for Mercy to leave, but she moves up beside him instead. "Charity. You're scared, just like you were that time up the tree. Remember how I helped you?"

Another step, and Charity toes the edge of the light streaming through the door. "And yet, if you'd let me jump, we wouldn't be here. Think of how many people you could've saved."

Mercy shakes her head, refusing to take responsibility for Charity's actions. "I wanted you to know we cared."

Charity's face turns away so sharply, Luca would've thought Mercy just slapped her. When she turns back, her features harden until she looks like they're carved from marble. "All you did was make everything worse."

Luca blinks as he realizes that's exactly why Charity looks so…unhinged. In the Outlands, it's easy to kill. Everyone is your enemy. They want to see you dead as much as you do them.

But here in Askala, she killed good people. People who cared. People like Seb. Now, she's cracking under the weight of what she's done.

Which only makes her even more dangerous.

Another step and Charity reaches the table, allowing herself to be completely seen. Mercy gasps, but it's not Charity's sweaty, panting state that has the cold sound of fear detonating through the hut.

Charity's holding a knife. One of the biggest Luca's ever seen.

She waves it menacingly, but also with pride. "Told you this was a good hut to find. Not only was it empty, but this knife was right here on the table, waiting for me."

Luca's eyes flicker to the table between them. A slice of material is lying, rumpled, in the center. His gaze quickly returns to Charity—the one with death in her eyes—but not before he registers the shredded, tattered edges of the cloth.

Or the color. The same as the sail.

Charity smiles, pulling in a deep breath. "Finally," she hisses, the word full of anticipation.

And relief. Because Charity wants her own death as much as everyone else's.

Which means there's no way they'll be talking her down.

And that's why Luca decides he's going to move first. He runs and leaps, shooting straight for Charity like an arrow.

A split-second later, Charity does the same, as if she was waiting for this. Welcoming it.

She climbs onto the table and surges at him, teeth bared and eyes crazed, the knife glinting in the beams of sunlight pouring through the door.

"No!" Mercy screams, bolting forward, too.

Charity must've been expecting that, because she twists mid-air, changing her trajectory. She screeches, slashing the twelve-inch blade across Mercy's chest.

Mercy instantly sucks in her torso and the knife slices through her shirt and across her shoulder. Her scream of pain is cut short as Charity brings her hand back, slamming the hilt of the blade across Mercy's temple.

Mercy's head twists sharply with the impact, her body following. Her eyes are closed, her face pale, as she tumbles and falls. And doesn't get back up.

"Mercy!" Luca shouts, his heart splintering.

But she remains still and lifeless, crumpled on the floor.

Charity's already coming at Luca, meaning there's no time to check on Mercy. There's no swinging of the blade this time, just an unerring accuracy for his chest and a violent hunger in her eyes.

Luca catches her and her momentum has him stumbling backward. He trips over a chair and falls, the timber splintering beneath him. Charity lands on top of him. Seeing the opportunity for what it is, she puts all her weight behind the deadly blade she's holding.

And spears it straight into Luca's shoulder.

He roars in pain, trying to buck her off. The knife slips back out, now painted in blood—his blood—and Charity quickly brings it back down, trying to impale him again.

Luca's hands shoot up, grabbing the hilt where both of Charity's hands are holding it. He locks his arms, trying to keep the blood-soaked tip away.

But the pain in his shoulder is burning away his strength, his torn muscles unable to take the strain. His hands drop an inch and Charity's eyes flare with excitement as the blade moves closer to Luca's face.

Grimacing, Luca channels everything he has into keeping his arms locked, knowing his life depends on it. Against his will, the blade comes another inch closer.

Charity may be smaller, but she's been driven mad with guilt. Luca's injured. And she wants to kill with every fiber of her being.

Mercy!

"Once you're dead, she is, too." Charity sneers, as if she read his mind. "Along with anyone else I can take down with me."

And Luca won't be able to stop it. The knife is now a silver point only a breath from his face.

Mercy.

His family.

Askala.

Luca's failed them all. Lost them.

Suddenly, Charity's eyes widen. Her mouth pops open. She arches her back, pain slicing across her face.

Then she's falling sideways, body stuck in its agonizing curve and the blade still clutched in her hands, as she hits the ground with a *thud*.

Luca swallows, trying to get moisture back into his dry mouth. What the Terra just happened?

A man appears above him, his face almost expressionless.

"Ghost?" Luca croaks.

Ghost straightens, looking around the room. "I heard a commotion," he says, his voice flat. As if he didn't just kill someone.

Luca scrabbles to his feet, desperate to check on Mercy. He

stumbles around Charity's body, her eyes still open and lifeless, the leg of the broken chair piercing her back like a stake.

Ignoring the lancing pain in his shoulder, he collapses beside her. "Mercy. Mercy!"

Her pale lashes flutter as her eyes open. "Luca?"

"Thank Terra." Luca goes to lift her head into his lap, only to yelp in pain. He grabs his shoulder, feeling nothing but sticky blood. The same wine-colored red that's now coating his arm.

"Luca!" Mercy pushes herself upright, wincing. "You're hurt!"

"I'm okay," he mumbles, his vision darkening. "As long as you are..."

Blackness clouds his vision and Luca doesn't fight it. Mercy's okay. Charity's dead.

Askala is safe for now.

But as consciousness seeps from his mind, a sound splinters through it, sharp and loud. Four words of denial echo through his foggy brain before he blacks out.

No! The bull's horn!

HAWK

*T*he sound of the bull's horn echoes around Askala, sending dread winding through the trees and circling the huts in a cloud of panic. It travels over the colony and to the beach, twisting and clawing its way across the sand as it reaches Hawk.

"Not yet," he breathes.

The weavers had only just carried the repaired sail down to the beach, ready to coat with sap so it can withstand the effects of the ocean. But there will be no time for that now. They'll need to take their chances and use it as it is. It's just pure luck the timber boards had their sap applied this morning. The boat hasn't dried properly but it's going to be better than nothing. The alternative is to stand on the beach and wait to be killed.

Hawk looks across at his father who pauses his frenzied movements. They lock eyes and his father's brows raise slightly in concern.

Hawk nods to let him know he's okay even though he's not. It wasn't supposed to be like this. He hasn't even had time to say a proper goodbye to Sam. It feels like everything that's ever happened in his life is going to come down to the next moments. The outcome is going to determine whether he gets to live the life he dreams of with Sam, or...well, perhaps not live the rest of his life at all. These Outlanders aren't coming to their shores to make friends.

His father grabs the sail and Hawk helps him lift it from the sand and carry it onto the boat. Their footsteps are fast and with each step they're joined by more of Askala's strongest and bravest—those who are willing to fight to protect what belongs to them. The sense of urgency hangs in the air like a dense fog. There's not one person unaware of the gravity of the situation they find themselves in. And the fact they're having to do this well before they're ready is only adding to this.

"We need the weapons!" shouts Jagger as he helps shift the sail into position. "And the poison for the arrows."

"It's too late for the poison," says Deniel, climbing aboard. "We don't have time. We have to leave now."

"Hawk will get it." His father glares at Deniel. "Be quick, Hawk. We launch in ten minutes. Five, if we're fast."

Hawk doesn't hesitate, leaping from the boat and hitting the sand with such force his feet disappear underneath the grains. He knows why his father asked him. It's not because he's the fastest. Or the strongest. He was giving him the chance to see Sam before they head out to what could likely be their death. And whether or not that's a valid excuse, Hawk doesn't care. He's taking this gift. And quite literally running with it.

He pounds across the sand, hits the tree line, and takes the path to the infirmary.

People pass him going the other way, carrying all kinds of weapons.

"Keep going!" Hawk shouts, as they look confused to see him going in the wrong direction. "The boat is getting ready to leave! Run!"

The people rush past, their panic clear in their frenzied movements.

Hawk bursts out into the clearing and races toward the infirmary.

"Hawk!" Wren calls, her arms laden with arrows. Ghost is beside her with at least half a dozen bows threaded over each arm. "Dex has taken the slingshots to the boat. But we need the poison paste!"

"That's what I'm getting," he shouts back. "You go ahead. Dad's almost ready to launch."

Everywhere Hawk looks, there are people running. Some are heading up to the cliffs to wait this out. Others to the beach. And yet more are securing their huts and readying themselves to defend the village. At least this time, the sick have been healed. There's no need for anyone to lie helpless while Askala is attacked.

Hawk pushes open the door to the infirmary and gasps. He'd expected to see Sam, so that's no surprise. But instead of her preparing the poison paste for the arrows, she's tending to Luca and Mercy.

"What in Terra?" Hawk asks.

"We're okay!" Luca jumps to his feet, wobbling slightly. His hair is wild and his eyes dart across the room. He's not wearing a shirt and has a large bandage on his shoulder with blood seeping out. "We just needed a quick patch up."

Mercy slides off the bed and stands beside Luca. The top buttons of her shirt are undone and the upper half is stained a dark red. She pulls it closed. "We're as good as new."

Hawk's torn between wanting to know more and aware that they don't have time. There's no way either Mercy or Luca are as good as new, but it seems they're as good as they're going to get for now.

"The boat's about to leave," Hawk says, trying to keep his focus. "I need the poison for the arrows. And I sort of need it five minutes ago."

"I'll get it." Luca heads for the office.

"Like hell you will." Hawk steps in front of him. "You and Mercy go to the beach and tell my dad I'm coming. That is assuming you're well enou—"

"We're well enough." Luca takes Mercy's hand, and they disappear out the door.

"I haven't had time to put it in smaller jars yet," says Sam, pushing past Hawk and going to a large bucket on one of her workbenches. "I thought we had more time."

"I can carry it." Hawk wraps his arms around the bucket.

"It's too heavy," says Sam. "Let me get another container and we can divide it up."

"We don't have time." Hawk leaves the bucket where it is and puts his hands on Sam's shoulders. "They won't wait."

"Hawk." Sam's bottom lip quivers.

Hawk quickly drops a kiss on her rosebud mouth, silencing whatever she was about to say, and tears himself away. He hauls the bucket off the bench, clutching it against his chest. This poison could make the difference between winning this battle and losing. But only if he can get it to the boat in time.

"What did you mix in with this stuff?" he asks as he takes some steps toward the door. "Rocks?"

"Actually, there are rocks in there," she says, looking a little guilty. "Hot rocks. I needed their slow, steady heat to help with the chemical reactions."

"Can we take them out?" he asks as she holds the door open for him.

She shakes her head. "The heat will also keep the paste thin, making it easier to paint on the rocks. Sorry."

Hawk grunts as Sam follows him down the steps of the infirmary. "What else did you put in there?"

"I used beeswax left over in the kitchen from when Zali last collected it for honey," she says. "It's the perfect carrier."

"I thought that was me," says Hawk.

"I don't get it…" Sam looks confused. "Oh, yes. The perfect carrier. Very funny…"

"Sam, I think you should go to the cliffs," Hawk says, knowing the days of trying to protect her from danger have long passed but still wanting to give it one last shot. "That boat isn't safe. Stay here. Please?"

"Like hell I will!" She storms off ahead, taking the path to the beach, and he smiles at her determination. It's just one of the reasons he fell in love with her. And he doesn't think he's ever heard her curse before, so he knows for certain that she means it.

He follows, slowed down by the weight of his load, yet finding the strength to keep up. He can do this. He has to do this!

Sam turns to him on the path ahead with fire in her eyes, clearly not finished cursing at him yet. "I'm a Seeker, Hawk. And a good one at that. I've earned my place on that boat."

He's about to apologize when the bull's horn sounds again.

Two blasts this time.

Whoever's acting as lookout at the cliffs is letting them know the Outlanders are getting closer.

"Hurry!" Sam goes to Hawk to help him carry the bucket, but he shakes his head.

"It's easier to carry alone." He stumbles on a tree root but pushes forward. "Sam, run ahead. Make sure they wait. That last warning will have them edgy. We're so close now."

The last thing he wants is to get to the beach only to have missed them by a few minutes. Not when this bucket of poison is the thing that could make all the difference.

"*You* might want to leave me behind, Hawk, but we're sticking together." Sam grips his arm and urges him forward.

"Go and tell them to wait!" he begs. "Or we'll both be left behind!"

Sam huffs, gives his arm one last squeeze, and dashes ahead.

"And I know you're an amazing Seeker!" he calls after her, uncertain if she can hear. "I'm sorry!"

There's a crashing noise ahead and for one moment Hawk thinks a polar grizzly has chosen the worst possible moment to make a move on him. He reminds himself that grizzlies can't get beyond the colony walls, and continues to move forward. He has no time to wait.

But it's only Kian, bursting through the trees. Sam must have sent him.

"Hawk!" Kian rushes at him. "Give it to me for a bit."

Hawk is about to say he can handle it, but now isn't the time for his pride to get in the way. They have to get to the boat as fast as they can. And a fresh set of muscles is exactly what they need.

Kian takes the bucket with a grunt and Hawk stretches his aching arms as he walks.

Dirt turns to sand underneath their feet as they break through the tree line. The boat has been dragged into the water and is loaded with a dozen of Askala's best sharpshooters. While this vessel was initially built to handle many more passengers, they'd be foolish to overload it now. They need to keep their weight light for agility and speed, as well as allowing enough space to line up their shots.

Hawk's dad and Wren are in the water, guiding the boat as they prepare to leap aboard.

"There they are!" shouts Sam, pacing the sand.

"She wouldn't get on the boat without you." Kian is puffing now, his biceps straining from the heavy load.

Hawk nods. "Which I assume is why you wouldn't get on it, either."

"I'm not going with you," says Kian as they hit the damp sand. "I'm staying behind to protect Askala. Just in case we get some unexpected visitors. Which is why I need you on that boat."

"To protect Sam," Hawk says, understanding more than Kian is letting on. Nova isn't well enough to go on the boat. Kian can't bring himself to leave her when she's still so weak.

"And Luca, too," says Kian. "He's more injured than he's letting on. I need you to look out for him."

Hawk's father comes rushing from the water just as they reach Sam. He takes the bucket from Kian.

"Hurry!" he shouts to Hawk. "We leave *now.*"

Sam kisses Kian on the cheek and takes Hawk's hand, practically dragging him into the water.

But before her feet get a chance to get wet, Hawk scoops her up, cradling her in his arms. He glances back at Kian and nods, letting him know he'll do as he asked. He'll look out for Sam. And Luca. He would have done it, anyway. The Seekers have each other's backs. Always.

"I can walk," Sam protests, wriggling.

"Your skin is sensitive." Hawk wades into deeper water. "Part of knowing your strength is recognizing your weakness."

Sam stills at these words and lets him carry her. He pushes through the water, his legs stinging from the acid as he closes the gap to the boat. This whole thing has taken far too much time. But it had to be done. With their poison paste, they now have everything they need to put this plan into action.

Jagger is leaning over the side of the boat beside Wren who's climbed on board. He takes the bucket from Hawk's dad and passes it to Dex while Wren helps Sam scramble up the side of the boat.

Hawk and his father nod at each other then begin pushing the vessel into deeper water. It's burning at Hawk's waist now, but he ignores it. They have a job to do here.

The boat tips wildly as the people aboard work to get organized. The sail is being hoisted and weapons are being assembled. Everyone seems to have a job to do and they're doing it as fast as they can.

"That's deep enough!" Hawk's father calls.

Jagger leans over the side of the boat once more and Hawk grabs at his hand, pulling himself upward and swinging a leg over the gunwale. Once safely aboard, he reaches for his father and helps him up.

"You did good, son." Hawk's father grips him in a brief hug before making his way to the sail to get it properly into place.

The boat surges with new momentum and Hawk squints at the horizon, seeing several dark smudges in the distance. Whoever sounded the alarm on the cliffs was right. They're most definitely boats.

"How many are there?" someone behind him calls.

"I can count at least a dozen," someone else replies.

A sick feeling winds its way through Hawk's gut as he looks around their one and only boat, hoping it's enough. A dozen of Askala's finest are aboard this vessel that's slicing over the waves. Including the girl he loves.

Sam is bent over the bucket of poison paste, carefully applying it to the tips of the arrows and shouting at people to be careful not to touch them.

Mercy is sitting quietly with a hand across her blood-stained shirt, her face a little paler than Hawk would like to see.

Luca is beside her, his eyes focused on the horizon, holding his body in the same way Hawk did when his ribs were broken and he didn't want anyone to know the pain he was in.

Dex is sorting out the weapons, preparing to distribute them.

Finn is clutching a spear, a fierce look of determination on his face. It wouldn't have been easy for him to leave Dharma behind. But someone had to look after Relic and Tarquin.

Hawk's dad and Jagger are at the sail, while Deniel pulls on a rope, adjusting their course.

Ghost is at the bow, keeping as far away from everyone as he can in such a cramped space. Hawk wonders if he's cut out for the battle that lies ahead.

"What in Terra?" Wren is studying one of the arrows and frowning at the end of it. Not the sharp end, but the one with the feathers. She puts it down and picks up another.

"What's the problem?" Hawk asks, an uneasy feeling crawling across his skin.

"The feathers aren't attached properly." Wren holds an arrow out to him. "These aren't the arrows we used in training."

"Do they need feathers?" Hawk asks, taking the arrow from her, careful not to touch the tip.

"If you want to take an accurate shot, they do," she says, lowering her voice.

Hawk looks back to the arrow he's holding and sure enough the feather falls away and flutters to the floor of the boat.

"Someone did this on purpose, Hawk." Wren's whispering now. "Because I know the arrows I set aside weren't like this. Somebody switched them. And I don't think it was Charity. She would never have had the time."

Hawk sets down the arrow. "Then who?"

"Let's just hope it's not anyone on this boat." Wren looks around.

Hawk shivers as the fight ahead suddenly feels so much harder. How can they possibly win this battle if the enemy is already amongst them?

SAM

*S*am looks over her shoulder when another arrow doesn't appear in her hand. Her stomach clenches, as if several more Newtons of force just clamped around it, when she sees Hawk and Wren's shocked faces.

Or is that fear stamped across their features?

"What's wrong?" she asks Hawk's pale, wide-eyed face.

Hawk raises the arrow he's holding and tugs on the feathers at the end. They slip out as if they were never glued in.

"But the arrows need fletches for aerodynamics and stabilization!" Sam gasps. "They enable the arrow to shoot straight!"

Wren's jaw works. "We know that."

"Who?" she whispers, seeing the same question blazing in Hawk's eyes.

Wren's lip curls. "Once we find out, they're dead. But right now, we have more urgent concerns."

Sam looks back the other way, and the dozen boats approaching have already grown. The horizon is now behind their fleet, and the miles of ocean between them and the Outlanders are shrinking far too rapidly.

"What's going on?" Phoenix asks, no doubt sensing his twin's alarm.

Wren shoots to her feet. "Someone sabotaged the arrows, that's what's wrong."

The collective gasp from the people on the boat could almost power the sail. Mercy clutches Luca's hand as they both try to comprehend this. Finn visibly swallows. Jagger's frown is twisted with fury. Ghost doesn't move, but Sam didn't expect he would. The man is carved from stone.

Sam doesn't understand how the knowledge hasn't even sparked a flicker of response from him. The arrows were their one way to fight off the Outlanders before they got too close.

"Can we still use them?" Mercy asks.

"They'll be very inaccurate," her mother responds.

Jagger snorts. "We'll look like fools as the arrows hit the ocean more than them."

All that work. Wasted.

Deniel shoots to his feet, making the boat tip sharply. "He did it!" he screeches as he points at Jagger. "This is exactly what you wanted. You want us to look like idiots before they slaughter us!"

Jagger launches at Deniel, and Sam grips her bench seat as the boat rocks far more wildly. He grabs the man by the shirt, his face red as he shakes him. "I'm tired of your accusations! I've had enough of *you*!"

Luca and Phoenix quickly jump between and separate the two men. Luca plants himself in the middle, pressing a hand to Jagger's chest. "The tension is getting to all of us, but this isn't what we need right now."

"Exactly," sneers Deniel. "Violence isn't the answer, Outlander."

Jagger leaps again but Luca acts as a barrier. He hides the flinch of pain it causes him to stop the mountain of a man that Jagger is, and Sam's pretty sure she's the only one who sees it.

Probably because she's one of the few who knows exactly how badly injured Luca is.

Phoenix shoves his face close to Deniel's. "That's enough. It's time you began acting like someone born and raised in Askala before you start throwing those sorts of words around."

Deniel flushes then steps back. He sits down again, crossing his arms. "We never stood a chance, anyway."

Ghost grunts, and Sam looks at him more closely, taking in his emotionless features. All this started when he arrived—the sail, now the arrows—and yet he's done nothing but help them, including killing Charity and saving Luca and Mercy's lives.

Looking away, Sam's gaze returns to the bucket. Like Wren said, accusations aren't helpful right now. They have Askala to save.

Despite the insurmountable obstacles.

The thick, dark sap glistens. The hot rocks would've cooled by now, meaning the mixture will start to thicken and coagulate. Sam's spine straightens as she realizes something.

"The poison! We can use it as glue!"

Hawk's face lights up, only to darken again. "But it's....poison."

Sam dips the narrow brush she was using into the thickening tar and dabs it onto the end of the arrow where the feathers once were. "Yes, we'll have to be careful." She holds up the painted grooves. "But this will hold the fletches."

Wren takes the arrow, then carefully, her fingers pinching the feather so she doesn't brush the deadly poison, slips the feather back into the groove. Twirling the arrow gently, everyone on the boat watches as the feather stays where it is.

Wren looks to Sam, eyes heavy. "It works."

Sam nods. It does. The arrows will now be able to fly straight. Except they could be quite dangerous to the user if they get the poison on their hands.

"I'll keep the glue"—Sam can't bring herself to call it by what it really is...poison—"contained to where the fletches are notched into the arrow." She looks at the others. "When drawing back to shoot, hold them at the end as much as possible."

There's a round of slow nods as everyone processes this.

Sam smiles weakly. "And don't touch your faces, especially your mouth, afterward."

The sound of a faint shout carries on the wind, fracturing the heavy tension. There's no time. The Outlanders are drawing irrevocably closer.

"Everyone, take your places!" Jagger orders. He looks to Sam, Wren and Hawk. "Can you finish the arrows?"

In answer, the three jolt into action. Sam holds out her hand. "Pass me the feathers. I'll paint the tips of the arrows and then glue the fletches."

Hawk frowns but Sam holds his gaze. He knows, just like Sam does, that it's best that only one person handles the poison. But he doesn't like that it's Sam who just volunteered to do it.

Wren passes her the feathers. "We need to hurry."

Sam takes them, and they begin a frantic pace.

With each arrow repaired and poisoned, the Outlanders come progressively closer. The fewer miles between them, the thicker the air feels. The more cloying the danger. Sam has to focus harder and harder on keeping her hands steady. No one can afford for her to accidentally drip the poison anywhere else along the length of the arrow.

"Sam."

It's Hawk, his voice low and heavy. She looks up to find him close, his handsome face drawn with lines of worry. Sam stills, knowing what he's here to say. A part of her is aching to hear it.

A part of her wishes they weren't in the situation where he wants to make sure she's heard these words. They both know they're about to face people who want them dead.

She nods, wishing she could touch those drawn cheeks. But right now, her fingers are as deadly as the Outlanders.

"I love you," he breathes. "No matter what. Forever."

Sam's chest expands and constricts all at the same time. She swallows, hard. "And I love you." She tries for a smile. "Probably for longer than forever."

His gaze flickers to her mouth and she knows he wants to seal their words with a kiss. She bites her lip and looks away, wanting that, too.

But they can't. War is looming.

"Look!"

It's Luca, standing at the bow of the boat, pointing toward the Outlanders. Sam squints, trying to see what has him practically vibrating with energy.

The Outlanders have spread out, their boats stretching from left to right across the red ocean. But Luca's staring at the one in the center. Sam gasps when she sees it. A raft is a few feet in front of it, with three people on it.

And they're rowing toward them.

Mercy frowns. "What are they doing?"

Luca watches the raft intently for several seconds. "I think they're coming to talk."

"Like an emissary?" Mercy asks in disbelief.

Except, that's exactly what the raft seems to be. It steadily grows as it covers the distance between them. It seems the Outlanders have a message.

"They're pretending they have honor," snorts Jagger.

Deniel curls into himself even more from his place at the back of the boat. "And we all know Outlanders don't have that," he mutters.

Jagger tenses, but ignores the barb. He turns to Sam. "How many arrows do we have?"

She surveys the two piles. "About half are complete."

"Everyone take a few. Be careful. Only grip them in the middle or the very end. If this is a trap, we need to be ready."

Hawk shuffles past Sam to take his place at the front of the boat. His hand brushes her cheek, the touch gentle and fleeting. But it reverberates through Sam with all the ramifications of what they're about to face.

What will their world look like when this is all done? Sam almost whimpers as another question slices through her.

Will they both be here to see it?

Phoenix lowers the sail, then joins Luca, Mercy, Hawk, Wren and Jagger at the front of the boat. Finn slips back to sit beside Sam, whilst Deniel remains where he is. Ghost hasn't twitched a muscle, remaining at the furthest point at the back of the boat. Sam wonders why he even came.

The vessel bobs gently in the ocean, each rise and drop counting down the moments until the Outlanders reach them.

"Of course, it's her," Luca mutters.

Sam looks up from where she was furiously dabbing more poison on the arrows. She registers who is on the raft just as Mercy gasps one name.

"Grace."

And Corbin.

And Raiden.

Sam almost drops the arrow she's holding. The Commander is coming, along with her husband, and the one who killed Nikita right before Sam's eyes, reveling in taking a life.

Telling Sam he intends on marrying her.

"Hide the weapons," Wren orders quietly. "We don't want them knowing what we have."

Quickly and carefully, Sam tucks the arrows beneath her seat. The others lay their bows on the floor behind them. Out of sight, but within easy reach.

Sam watches as the raft draws nearer. Corbin and Raiden are rowing as Grace stands in the center, feet planted wide enough that she absorbs the movement of the waves. She holds her chin high, her gaze never wavering from her target—the single boat of Askala.

They're a few feet away when they stop. Silence echoes over the water and Sam can see Luca's back winding tighter and tighter.

"We come with an offer," Grace calls.

There's a sound behind Sam, maybe a gasp, but far more strangled, although she doesn't turn around to see who or why. There's no way she's taking her eyes off the raft.

Raiden's gaze is roaming over the boat. It pauses when he sees Sam, and even across the distance she sees the way it flares. A second later, he's obscured from vision as Hawk subtly moves left.

"I doubt you have anything we want," Luca says, steel laced through his voice.

Grace's nostrils flare. "Your life?"

"You're the one threatening it," Mercy states flatly. Almost angrily.

Grace's eyes flicker toward Mercy, then scan the others. "You've kept Askala and all its riches from us for long enough."

Corbin growls beside her. "Get this over and done with."

Ignoring him, Grace looks at Luca once again. "Surrender, and no blood will be shed."

Sam blinks. *Surrender?*

"If Askala yields to us, then there will be no fighting," Grace continues. "You could save countless lives."

So, there would be no battle, after all? Sam straightens. No one needs to die? Except...

Jagger crosses his arms. "What are your terms?"

Sam almost gasps. Jagger's considering the offer?

Grace's lips soften just a touch, allowing the edges to bow up. "Cede Askala to us. Your people may remain if they wish, but the Outlanders now reign."

They'll take the huts. The food. Whatever they can or want.

If the Outlanders were in control of Askala, they'd destroy everything. Generations of work. Hectares of land. Years of healing.

And they wouldn't stop. Not until Askala is as desolate as their hearts.

"Take it," whispers Jagger.

Wren's hands clench. "No. We can't let them have Askala."

Luca and Mercy look at each other for long moments, words they no doubt want to say hanging between them. Mercy imperceptibly nods.

Luca turns back to Grace. "We reject your offer."

Jagger reels back. "Luca—"

"No. We're fighting for far more than our lives. We're fighting for what Askala stands for." His hand wraps around Mercy's. "We're fighting for the future that every life on this planet deserves."

Raiden's hands clench around his oar. "Fools." His angry glare lands on Sam again, looking almost…hungry.

"Go back and tell your people Askala will not surrender," Luca states loudly.

For some reason, Sam can't look away from Raiden. His fingers are twitching around the handle of the oar. She's seen those restless hand movements before. A quick glance down shows Sam what she suspected. Raiden's spear is resting between the planks of wood of the raft. Waiting.

Hawk takes a step back, then another, never breaking his focus on the three Outlanders. Another two shuffles and he's in front of Sam, completely obscuring her.

Sam can just imagine Raiden's face turning a furious purple, but she's not peeking around her protector to find out. Right now, it's best if she's out of sight.

But a gasp, one so laced with pain that Sam instantly wonders if Raiden used his spear, has her shooting to her feet.

The voice was female. No, not Mercy!

But Mercy is still standing strong beside Luca. It's Grace whose mouth is slightly parted, like something was just wrenched out of it and she lost the ability to move immediately after. She looks like she's turned to stone.

Sam frowns. Hawk's movement cleared a line of sight, and Grace is staring at the back of the boat. She's staring at Ghost... as if she's seen a ghost. A quick glance over Sam's shoulder shows Ghost is just as frozen as Grace is, his face contorted with the same aching pain.

"Commander," Corbin growls, the word laced with contempt.

All emotion washes from Grace's face. She flicks her fingers, indicating to her husband and stepson that it's time to leave. Turning around, she holds her shoulders back as Corbin and Raiden do the same.

Except, Corbin is far from emotionless as he scans the boat and those within it. In fact, Sam doesn't think that she's ever seen his face so alive. It ripples with excitement.

He's relishing what's about to come.

War.

MERCY

*M*ercy is holding her bow so tightly it's in danger of snapping as she watches Grace, Corbin and Raiden row their raft back to their boat.

"They insult us," Mercy's mom sneers. "First, they ask us to surrender, then they turn their backs on us like they don't think we have the balls to take aim."

"We kinda don't." Mercy nods her head at their motley army, all frozen in fear.

"Screw that." Jagger launches into action, leaning over the side of the boat and readying his bow. "You want to kill a snake, first you need to cut off its head..."

Grace.

He's aiming at the Commander.

Mercy's eyes widen. Maybe it's time Grace was taken out, no matter what relationship she may or may have to Luca. Killing her would be a clear message that they're serious about defending Askala. Although, to be honest, Mercy would prefer Jagger take aim at Corbin or Raiden...

But just as the deadly arrow is about to be ejected, Ghost

flies at Jagger, sending him toppling into the water and the arrow shooting for the clouds.

Mercy blocks out the sound of the Outlanders hooting and laughing.

Luca curses as he readies his own arrow, waiting for Grace to turn around. Mercy knows he has too much honor to shoot her in the back. But before he can fire, Ghost is on him, too, and the arrow spears into the water, only narrowly missing Jagger who's flailing in the waves.

"No!" Mercy screams, her heart leaping out of her chest. Luca's injured. Hand-to-hand combat isn't going to be his specialty right now.

Luca attempts to flip Ghost to his back, but as they saw earlier in Jagger's hut, it seems that although Ghost may be quiet, he knows how to fight. Luca is pinned to the floor of the boat, with Ghost sneering above him.

"Get off him!" Mercy grabs the back of Ghost's shirt, but it's like he knew she was going to be there before she'd even decided to move. He flicks her off with ease, sending her sliding across the boat and landing at her father's feet. Whoever taught him to fight, taught him well.

Realizing he's gone too far, Ghost throws his hands in the air and steps off Luca. "I'm trying to save you from yourself, that's all."

Hawk positions himself between Luca and Ghost with a murderous look in his eye that Mercy's never seen before.

"You're a liar," sneers Hawk.

"Throw him from the boat." Mercy crawls back toward Luca, not understanding why Ghost would save Luca one minute and try to kill him the next. "Let him swim to the Commander he was trying to defend."

"You swapped the arrows, didn't you?" Mercy's mom steps up and shoves her finger in Ghost's chest like she hadn't just witnessed his superior fighting skills. "You're the enemy in our ranks."

Ghost sizes up Mercy's mom. "I can help you. But not if you kill the Commander. That's not how things are done. Trust me, if you kill her, you've already lost."

"Trust you?" Mercy's mom's eyes flare. "Why exactly would we trust you?"

Mercy narrows her gaze at Ghost, remembering the look of pain on Grace's face when she saw him.

"You know her, don't you?" she accuses. "You and the Commander mean something to each other."

But before Ghost can even open his mouth to answer, there's an almighty bellow from the water.

"Get me out of here!" Jagger shouts, his voice filled with unusual panic.

Mercy's mom picks up her bow and feeds in an arrow coated with Sam's poison, aiming directly at Ghost's chest.

"Don't move," she tells him.

Ghost swallows. He's seen enough of Mercy's mom in the short time he's been in Askala to know she never misses her target. His fighting skills are no use here.

Mercy and Luca haul themselves to their feet and rush to the edge of the boat to help Jagger.

But Hawk's already there, leaning over the gunwale with his arms outstretched.

"Take my hand!" he shouts to Jagger.

"I can't!" Jagger cries back. "There's something in the wa—"

The rust color of the ocean around Jagger turns crimson as he thrashes about, hitting at something Mercy can't see. Surely, if that were a leatherskin, they'd have seen the giant fin by now?

"Someone help me here!" calls Hawk. "We need to pull him out."

Luca goes immediately to Hawk's side, but the moment he leans out, Mercy hears him stifle a groan.

"He'll tear his stitches," says Mercy, aware of how much her own injury hurts, and she wasn't cut anywhere nearly as deeply as Luca. "Someone else! Quick!"

"I can do it," Luca protests.

"And then be useless when we need you most?" Hawk looks to his other side. "Deniel, get here and help!"

Mercy urges Luca back. "He's right. We need you."

Luca grits his teeth, clearly not happy with the situation and what Charity's earlier attack has cost him.

But Deniel is backing away, shaking his head. "I'm not helping him. He's a traitor."

"For Terra's sake!" Hawk shouts. "He's not the traitor here."

"It's okay," Phoenix pushes Deniel out of the way to get to Hawk.

Father and son lean out, just like a mirror image, reaching for Jagger.

"Get close enough so we can grab your shirt!" Phoenix calls over Jagger's screams.

Mercy looks across at their enemy, wondering why they haven't taken this moment to attack. They're watching with open mouths at the chaos unfolding. Grace's raft has made it back to the boats now and she's safely back on board.

"They're waiting for us to implode," mutters Luca, seeing Mercy's confusion.

A sick feeling winds its way through Mercy's gut. He's right. The way things are going, it's very possible the Outlanders will win this war without having to make a single move, other than just showing up. That way, they get to make it to land with their army fully intact.

Mercy goes back to the edge of the boat, needing to see what's going on with Jagger as his screams worsen.

His arms are thrashing about as the waves drag him under for long seconds before he manages to fight his way back up to the surface. Jagger's a big guy. Strong and determined. Whatever's attacking him in those crimson depths won't get him, Mercy's sure of it.

"Jagger!" she shouts. "You can do this!"

Almost as if by divine intervention, the waves push him toward the boat, and he slams into the hull.

Phoenix and Hawk waste no time in grabbing his shirt.

The boat tips wildly as the others reposition themselves to counterbalance the weight.

But Mercy's unable to move. Her jaw has fallen open as a tremor spreads its way through her limbs.

Because it's not only Jagger who's being dragged from the ocean. Attached to his legs by their teeth are a dozen infant leatherskins. Mercy understands that even the biggest leatherskin must have been a baby at some stage, but she's never seen one before. Let alone a whole school of them!

Phoenix lets go of Jagger with one hand to try to brush off a leatherskin that has a mouthful of Jagger's forearm. Only slightly larger than the size of Mercy's outstretched hand, the leatherskin holds on, refusing to let go of the soft flesh it's feasting on. Dozens more of these hideous creatures swarm in the bloodied water, all seeking their share of the prey that Jagger's become.

"Don't let him on the boat!" Deniel shouts. "Those things will kill us all."

"Shut up, Deniel!" Hawk mutters as he strains to lift the weight of Jagger and the sharks feeding off him. "They can't survive out of the water."

"Good work, Jagger!" Mercy shouts, hoping Jagger can't hear what's going on. "You're doing so well."

Others in the boat cheer as their spirits buoy and Jagger becomes a symbol of everything they're fighting for here. Never will they leave a man behind, no matter how many frightening baby monsters he's bringing with him.

Phoenix and Hawk manage to get Jagger high enough to

swing him over the edge of the boat when a movement catches Mercy's eye.

"Watch out!" she calls as she turns her head far too late. A spear twists its way through the air and slams into Jagger's back.

As the air is sucked from Jagger's lungs, so is all their hope. Instead of being a symbol of what they're fighting for, the sight of Jagger's lifeless body is now a symbol of everything they're about to lose.

"Raiden!" Sam screams, her voice bouncing across the ocean as her eyes fix on the guy they all knew they couldn't trust. It makes sense that he'd be the one to take the first shot.

Mercy sees Raiden smiling at Sam with the same satisfied look on his face he had when he killed Alyx. It makes Mercy's blood boil! She's not sure how or when Raiden will be killed in this battle, but she vows right then and there to make sure that happens. Even if the Outlanders win, Raiden will not.

Phoenix leans forward and yanks the spear from Jagger's back before he and Hawk lower his body back into the water. Within moments, dozens of small fins surround him, dragging him down until it's like he never existed.

But there's no time to reflect on Jagger's life and all the things he did to protect Askala, no matter what Deniel might think of him.

Phoenix straightens his back and hurls Raiden's spear right back at his smug face. The move is as unexpected as it is impulsive. The spear is propelled across the expanse of water, fueled by Phoenix's anger at having just watched his friend die.

Raiden's mouth falls open and Mercy can only hope he doesn't have enough time to react.

Except, he does.

He grabs the man standing beside him and pulls him in front like a shield, catching the spear right in his throat.

The gurgle echoes across the ocean and Mercy gags as she sees the spray of blood spurt over the Outlanders' boat. Raiden removes his beloved spear and pushes the man forward, sending him diving headfirst into the water. Another meal for the baby leatherskins. Or perhaps their mother will show up and take Raiden's man in one bite.

Arrows fly from the Askalan boat, and Mercy turns to see her mother and Alina firing at the Outlanders. Mercy's dad joins them using the specially made sling he constructed so he can shoot with one hand. Pride swells in Mercy's chest. Her dad never lets his missing hand hold him back, determined to prove he can fight just as hard as anyone else. Often, even harder.

And that's what they need to do now. Be like Mercy's dad. They must turn their disadvantage into an advantage. Because the more determined you are to prove your worth, the harder you're going to fight.

Mercy ducks as a spear flies toward her and it slams into the mast. She's only glad there was nobody standing behind her.

"Get back." Luca tugs on her arm.

She raises her eyebrows at him, wondering if he knows her at all, and reaches for a bow. It's time to put everything her mother taught her into use.

Luca takes a bow, too, and Sam hands them each four poison arrows.

"Be careful how you hold them," Sam hisses as she immediately works on readying the next one.

"Keep low!" Hawk calls as he retreats to get his own weapon.

Mercy can see the pain written across her cousin's features. Lowering Jagger into the sea like that wouldn't have been easy for him. But underneath the pain, she sees the same anger that had his father throwing Raiden's spear. The Askalans have found their hope once more, except this time, it's hope that's fueled with rage.

"Shift your weight back!" Phoenix calls, and Hawk drags Sam's heavy bucket of poison to balance the weight of everyone crouched at the edge of the boat as they fire off their arrows.

Mercy remembers what her mother taught her as she lines up her first shot, positioning herself side-on so she's less of a target. Raiden is keeping himself out of direct line, no doubt rattled by Phoenix's attempt on his life. Grace and Corbin are being similarly protected as other boats move ahead of them, creating a shield. They've missed their chance for now.

Mercy sets her sights on a man she recognizes as one of Corbin's men. She pulls back her arrow and watches as it pings toward him.

"Got him!" she shouts as it pierces his shoulder.

The man howls and Mercy wonders if it's from the arrow or the poison seeping into his system. It would have to be both.

"Good shot." Luca pushes Mercy's head down as a spear flies over them.

"Remember to keep low!" Luca calls out as more spears rain down.

Phoenix is collecting the spears and throwing them back, using the Outlanders' own weapons against them. This makes the bows and arrows even more genius. They can't exactly be launched back at the Askalans once they've been fired, not to mention they're coated in poison. And to think the arrows were Ghost's idea...

Mercy glances back at the man her mother called their enemy. He's neither working for them or against them now that Grace is at a safe distance, instead sitting at the back of the boat, helping to keep them from capsizing. That's something at least.

"Keep firing!" Mercy's mom shouts. "It's working!"

Mercy sees the man she shot in the shoulder wobbling as he throws a spear that lands well short and disappears into the ocean. He collapses into his boat and Mercy feels a horrible pang to know she's responsible for what she imagines will be his very unpleasant death.

Or is she? After all, it was Raiden who threw the first shot.

All they're doing is protecting themselves. The responsibility is all on him.

She lines up another shot, although this one misses, landing in the timber of the Outlanders' boat. With any luck it won't be wasted. The Outlanders don't know they're stained with poison. If they pull it out and touch their face, it will be as deadly as taking an arrow to the heart.

"They're going around us!" Deniel calls.

"Crap." Luca spins around to take aim at one of the boats that's making a dash for it. This must be the Outlanders' strategy. Use a few boats to keep the Askalans occupied, enabling more to reach the shore. It's just as well that Kian and a few others stayed behind to fight.

Mercy thinks of Tarquin hiding up on the cliffs and hopes she's smart enough to stay put. Now isn't the time for her to be fierce. She needs to do what she's told. Not that Tarquin seems to know where to begin with that.

"We're running out of arrows," Sam calls. "Be careful with your shots."

Mercy screams as a spear sails toward Sam, but Hawk has reacted even faster than that, launching himself in front of Sam and knocking the spear out of the way. It clatters to the floor of the boat and Phoenix dives on it, dipping it into the poison and sending it straight back where it came from.

A harrowing noise has Mercy spinning to her left and she sees Alina clutching at her stomach, a spear sticking right through her middle.

"Get it out of me!" she screeches and Mercy's not even sure how she's still alive to use her voice. "Get it out of me!"

Phoenix pulls Alina to his broad chest, cradling her head with one of his large hands while he swiftly removes the length of the spear. Alina's scream is cut short as she blacks out and Phoenix lowers her to the floor, blood pooling around her.

"Keep fighting!" Phoenix shouts at anyone who's watching.

He's right. They don't have time to watch this, or they'll all end up dead.

Mercy lets a third arrow fly, taking her time to line up her shot. It's difficult on a boat and she's glad her mom made her practice in the ocean on a moving target.

She sees her arrow find its mark, this time landing in the chest of a man she doesn't recognize.

"Alina!" gasps Sam. "No!"

Mercy knows she shouldn't turn, but instinct kicks in and her head snaps around to see Alina with a handful of poison. She lifts her hand and pushes the goop in her mouth.

"Oh, Alina." Mercy fights the tears that threaten. Alina knew she was dying and clearly wanted to speed it up. But that can't be a nice way to go.

Within moments, Alina has her wish and is lying still on the bottom of the boat with foam pouring out of her mouth.

Without fuss, Phoenix lifts her up and drops her into the ocean. He knows they can't afford a distraction like this. It's crucial they stay focused.

"Hold fire!" Mercy's mother shouts.

Mercy lowers her bow, keeping one eye on the Outlanders for incoming spears.

"We don't have many arrows left," her mother says. "We need a better plan."

A bubble of fear sits at the back of Mercy's throat.

"We need to get closer," her father says.

"Are you crazy, Dex!" Phoenix rakes at his hair. "That's exactly what they want."

"He's right," says Luca, shaking his head. "If we're close enough, we can use the slingshots."

"Watch out!" cries Sam, as a spear pierces the side of the boat.

Phoenix sighs loudly, goes to the mast, and without a word, he hoists the sail.

Mercy looks at Luca who wraps his arm around her shoulder, placing a kiss on top of her head. He doesn't say anything and nor does she. Words aren't needed right now to know that what they're about to do comes with a great deal of risk.

They either get close enough to kill every last Outlander, or they join Jagger and Alina and become fish food.

"Let's do this." Mercy's mom starts handing out the slingshots.

Mercy takes her weapon.

"I'm proud of you," her mom says, moving onto Luca before Mercy can reply.

She just hopes her mom is saying that because it's true, and not because deep down she fears it might be the last thing she ever says.

LUCA

"*D*eniel!" Luca calls out. "Make straight for the Commander."

The boat angles as Deniel adjusts the rudder. It's the only reason they brought the sullen man—he's far more skilled at sailing than anyone else on the boat. If Deniel had any fighting ability whatsoever, Luca would tell him to keep an eye on Ghost, who's sequestered himself at the back of the boat again.

But Deniel doesn't. Which means there's no one to keep an eye on the guy who saved Luca's life one moment, then betrays them the next. Everyone's too focused on what they're about to do.

The vessel jolts forward as if it's impatient to reach the Outlanders. Luca's heart jerks painfully. Mother Nature wants this over and done with, and he can't blame her.

But...is she pushing them to victory?

Or their death.

Luca glances down at Mercy as she stands beside him, her slingshot ready. Somehow, he regrets nothing and yet regrets everything. Falling for Mercy is the most wondrous, amazing, life-changing thing that ever happened to him.

And yet, their actions brought them to this moment. To a fight where they're outnumbered and outskilled.

Their chances of surviving this are low...

Mercy glances up at him before focusing back on the rapidly approaching Outlanders. "How's your wound?"

Luca's been doing everything he can to ignore the slicing pain in his shoulder. Luckily, there hasn't been much time to dwell on it. Or the knowledge that a couple of the stitches tore when they tried to save Jagger.

He's about to shrug but he quickly changes his mind. The less he moves the better. "Is your wound okay?"

Mercy rolls her eyes. "Is yours?"

Grunting, Luca looks away. "Just focus on what you have to do."

On keeping herself alive.

Mercy shoots him another quick glance, this time with one eyebrow raised. "And you weren't thinking about me?"

Luca blinks. "I'm always thinking about you."

Mercy's the reason his heart beats.

She lifts her slingshot and draws it back. "It's the same for me, Luca," she says quietly, her voice full of husky determination.

Luca's heart simultaneously swells and clenches. Mercy's telling him she'll be doing everything she can to save him, just as much as Askala.

In the same way he's promised he will for her.

Mirroring her actions, Luca lifts his own slingshot, not even wincing as pain jolts through his chest and down his arm. He's going to do everything he can to make sure Mercy comes out of this alive.

There's a cry across the water, a hoarse, angry sound of battle. The Outlanders had fallen silent as their enemy approached, no doubt saving their ammunition just as the Askalans are. But the cry breaks the silence. Shatters the brief period of peace.

It signals the birth of a new kind of battle.

A spear slices into the water before their boat. Another scrapes the side. A third has Sam gasping as it impales the floor beside her feet.

"Not yet," Wren says levelly. "We're not close enough."

Luca's entire body stills, coiling in preparation. On either side of him, his friends and family do the same, making an unflinching wall, waiting to attack.

The next spear sails through the air in an arc, far more deadly with its aim. Dex shoves Wren hard enough that she slams into Phoenix, then leaps back himself. His left arm swings back just in time for the spear to miss.

He blinks, holding up his stump. "Wouldn't want to have lost a hand," he says wryly.

Wren grins at him as she straightens. "Thanks."

"I only have to save your life about ten more times and we'll be even," he says lightly, although Luca hears the gruff edge of relief. Dex turns back to face the Outlanders. "We're almost there."

Tensely, they wait. It's only a matter of time before a spear hits its mark. Luca keeps his gaze on Grace's boat, seeing the way they're readying themselves. Corbin and Raiden have their spears raised, also waiting. Even at a distance, Luca can see that Grace is pale.

The other Outlander boats are moving. Five bob steadily closer to their Commander's vessel, which Luca expected. The other six, though, are rowing out wider. Away from the defensive line around their leader.

Luca frowns, not liking that because it doesn't make sense. The plan they were concerned about is playing out.

But there's no time to dwell on it. Wren raises her slingshot, drawing her arm back another inch. "Now!" she shouts, releasing her poisoned rock.

Everyone armed on the boat does the same, and a hail of stones fling into the air. They pepper down on the Outlanders, many of them splashing into the water like raindrops, but a good proportion hitting the men and women on the boats.

The Outlanders wince and duck, but once the assault is finished, they straighten and look at each other, surprise etched across their faces.

"Again," commands Wren.

Luca and the others are just lining up their shots when a new sound fills the air. Laughter. Raucous, mocking laughter.

The Outlanders jostle each other, glancing back at the Askalans, their faces twisted with amusement and scorn.

"They're laughing at us," moans Deniel. "I should've run to the shelters with the others."

Luca grits his teeth. At least they're fighting, no matter how futile it is.

Deniel gasps. "The other boats! They're going around us!"

Luca's gaze flickers left then right before returning to his target. Deniel's right. Half of the Outlanders' fleet aren't even bothering to attack the Askalans' boat. They're so little a threat, that the Outlanders are heading straight for Askala.

"Now," snaps Wren.

They unleash another volley of pebbles, even more hitting the Outlanders this time. The men and women laugh even louder.

One of the men on the boat beside Grace's lifts his fist and shakes it. "You think your measly rocks will win this war?"

He wipes away at a dot of sticky sap on his forehead, leaving a smear across the bridge of his nose. A second later he clutches his eyes, letting out a hideous scream. He stumbles and the others around him leap out of his way, not wanting him near.

The man hits the gunwale and tips over, splashing into the water.

The sea thrashes as the countless juvenile leatherskins discover their next meal and the screams reach fever pitch, only to suddenly stop.

The smiles wipe from the Outlanders' faces.

"Go for Grace," Wren says coldly.

They all change their focus, everyone's slingshots now aiming at one target. The Commander.

A pang echoes through Luca's chest, and it has nothing to do with the stab wound in his shoulder. Whatever Grace knew about his mother, it's about to die with her. Although, maybe it's not only that. There was a softness to Grace, hidden by years of fighting to survive and all the choices that go with it, but it was there. A shred of humanity.

But she's the Commander. The leader of the greed and hatred that's threatening Askala.

Luca draws back the slingshot another inch, stretching it to capacity.

If the Commander is gone, then the Outlanders will crumble. It wasn't until they had a leader that they were finally able to coordinate an attack.

"Fire."

Wren's command is soft. But heavy with the knowledge that she's ordering someone's death.

"No!" shouts Ghost, realizing who their target is. Except it's too late. Luca, Mercy, Hawk, Wren, Dex, Phoenix and Finn release their ammunition, the poisoned rocks finding their mark with unerring accuracy.

They all know this shot has to count.

That if this fails, so will they.

Half a dozen boats are already on their way to Askala.

Grace's arms fly up to protect her face as she turns her head. The rocks pelt her forearms and torso, leaving smudges of poison. She holds there for several seconds, and even from here, Luca can see her arms are trembling. The same arms that are covered with leather guards.

She lowers them, seeing that Corbin and Raiden had leaped to the side. Luca's lips twist. Of course the cowards did.

Grace throws her shoulders back and lifts her chin, her unbroken skin clear of sap. Their plan failed.

"Finish them!" roars Corbin. "They tried to kill the Commander!"

"Take cover!" shouts Phoenix.

Luca yanks Mercy down as they hide behind the side of the boat. There are *thumps* and *twangs* as spears slam into the wood. There's a scream from the back of the vessel and Luca recognizes the voice as it twists with agony—Deniel.

Luca glances over the edge of the boat, his heart a painful drum in his chest. The Outlanders are preparing for another wave of spears to hit them.

Mercy tugs on his shirt. "Get down, Luca!"

But there's no way he's going down like this, hiding. Cowering in the same way Corbin and Raiden did. Luca yanks out a spear embedded in the side of the boat. The fewer Outlanders there are, the fewer bastards will be a threat to Mercy.

Maybe she'll be taken back to Askala. The moment there's an opening, she'll be able to run. Find sanctuary in the forest.

Have a chance at living.

Luca's shoulder screams with pain as he lifts the spear, trying to find Grace. He sees her, bending over the side of the boat as she frantically washes away the poison she's now peppered with.

Her back's to him, but if the choice is between honor or Mercy, Luca will choose Mercy. Every. Time.

Corbin's large body steps in across his line of sight and Luca almost growls with frustration. Now's the moment the bastard decides to protect her?

But Corbin isn't looking at him. His gaze flickers over the Outlanders as they grab more spears. He takes a step back. Then another.

And without a flicker of hesitation, pushes Grace into the ocean.

Her scream is cut short as she disappears beneath the surface.

She paddles desperately, her hands trying to grip the side of the boat, only to slip off. "Corbin! Raiden! Help!"

Corbin and Raiden glance at each other. Then turn away. The Outlanders still, unsure how to process what they're seeing.

Neither Corbin nor Raiden are lifting a finger to save Grace.

"What are you waiting for?" Corbin screams. "Attack!"

The Outlanders jolt into action. Turning back towards the Askalans, preparing to fight even though Grace is still in the water.

Not one of them is willing to sacrifice their life to save her.

"Bastards!"

A moment after the word is screamed with more fury than Luca's ever heard in his life, Ghost leaps into the water. He powers over the distance between their vessels, obviously intent on reaching Grace.

Despite the fact it brings him closer to the Outlanders.

Despite the fact the water is alive with young leatherskins.

He kicks and thrashes, trying to keep them at bay as he swims. Grace must see him, because she paddles toward him.

Ghost reaches her and scoops her up, never breaking momentum. He makes it to the side of the boat, which is now holding a shocked Corbin and Raiden, and pushes Grace toward them.

Her torso lifts out of the water and she grips the side, determinedly dragging herself into the boat. Corbin hesitates, then quickly kneels over her, the image of a solicitous husband.

Ghost treads water as he makes sure Grace is okay. Then he looks around, as if he suddenly realizes where he is. And what he's surrounded by. Leaping into action, he starts swimming again.

Toward the Askalans.

"He's coming back," Phoenix says in amazement.

He's returning to the people he sabotaged.

There are so many leatherskins surrounding him, the water looks as if it's boiling. Small, triangular fins peek out of the water as they dive and thrash, competing for food.

Ghost continues to swim, and each time his arm comes out of the water, one of the young predators is attached to it. The sea around him turns a darker shade of red as Ghost steadily becomes their next meal.

The man doesn't shout once. There are no screams of pain, only stony determination. Or is that acceptance of his fate? Is he feeling like Luca was? Prepared to die now that he's done what he can to save the woman he loves...

Ghost reaches the side of their vessel, his hand reaching up to clamp onto the side. His skin is riddled with bites, the flesh raw and bleeding. He looks up at Luca, and they both know he can't get up on his own.

And yet, there's no regret on Ghost's face. No apology.

Without giving himself time to think, Luca reaches down and grabs the man's arm.

"What are you doing?" Phoenix demands.

Luca doesn't answer, knowing it's obvious. He's not going to let Ghost die. He owes him one.

He pulls, discovering exactly how heavy the injured man is. Luca feels the wound at his shoulder strain, the flesh screaming for him to let go. Luca tightens his hold around Ghost's hand, and bracing his legs, pulls up. Hard.

A scream is wrenched from his throat as the wound tears open again. Blood trickles down his arm, blending with Ghost's. But he doesn't let go. He won't watch this man be eaten alive.

Suddenly, Mercy's beside him, grabbing Ghost's other arm. Then Hawk. Then Phoenix.

With one great heave, they pull Ghost into the boat.

Luca falls backward, his arm a useless mass of agony as he cradles it to his chest.

"Luca, what were you thinking?" Mercy's hands flutter over him, like she's not sure where to touch. He looks down to see blood steadily pooling on his torso. He glances over at Ghost, seeing that he's covered in crescent-shaped bite marks as he lays motionless. He raises his head, his gaze finding Luca's once again. With a curt nod, he drags himself to the back of the boat.

"Sam!" Mercy calls out, her voice tinged with panic. "What do we have to stop the bleeding?"

His sister says something, and there's movement around him, but it feels too far away. Luca's head hits the wooden floor, and he stares up at the clear blue sky.

There's no doubt in Luca's mind that Ghost loves Grace. Why or how, he has no idea. What's more, that love is why Ghost sabotaged the arrows. He sympathizes with the Outlanders, and not just because he was one of them. Their leader holds his heart.

And although that means Ghost is one of the enemy, one who infiltrated Askala, Luca couldn't let him die. Isn't everyone in Askala doing this for love? Protecting the ones they care about. The ones they would die for.

One more word reaches Luca before blackness takes hold. It's a command from Wren, but this time, said far more quietly. Almost solemnly.

"Retreat."

HAWK

*H*awk stares at his aunt. Did she just say *retreat?*

"Wren!" Hawk's father gasps. "What are you thinking?"

"It's no use," Wren says through gritted teeth. "Our strategy isn't working. We're better off to retreat and figure out something else."

"She's right," Ghost mutters from the stern of the boat. He's badly injured but it seems he's used to pain. "You'll never win like this."

"Nobody asked you," Wren snaps, even though he just agreed with her.

Hawk moves over to Sam. She sets down the stone she's holding and looks up at him, her eyes filling with tears.

"It can't all be over," she says as yet another spear is thrown into the side of the boat. "It can't."

A lump appears at the back of Hawk's throat. They have to make the only decision they can right now. And that is to live. The Outlanders have outplayed them, just like they did in the Newlands. How did Askala ever think they stood a chance?

"Luca," sobs Mercy, crouched beside him as she gently strokes his face. "Wake up, Luca. You have to wake up."

As much as he hates it, Hawk knows that Wren's right. She grew up as an Outlander. She was trained to fight like one. Her father was the Commander, for sweet Terra's sake! She knows a losing battle when she sees one. So, why can't his father, who was raised by the same man, see the same thing?

Hawk goes wordlessly to the rudder. Deniel is folded over it with a spear lodged in his chest. Hawk quickly removes it and Dex comes to help, holding his hand over the wound, trying to keep the blood from seeping out. Deniel moans, not seeming to have the energy to make the same agonizing scream as when he was hit.

Knowing he's making himself a target, but not seeing much choice, Hawk sits at the rudder and pulls hard, turning the boat away from the Outlanders. A spear wooshes past him, only an inch short of his ear, and he knows he acted just in time.

"Hawk!" his father calls. "What are you doing?"

"Retreating," he shouts back.

Defeat crosses his father's face as he finally accepts what his twin sister saw first.

That this is over.

They've lost Askala.

The best they can hope for now is to not also lose their lives.

Hawk concentrates on steering the boat, aware they're losing speed. Their sail is in bad shape. They'd thought to waterproof it, but with each spear that pierced the woven fabric, the sail's become less effective. Some of the tears that the weavers had repaired have torn again like old scars opening into new wounds.

"Watch out!" screams Finn.

Hawk ducks, just as a spear that's been set on fire is thrown at the sail, catching it alight. It spreads quickly, devouring the fabric like a hungry leatherskin.

The boat instantly loses speed and Hawk loosens his grip on the rudder, knowing it will soon be useless.

The Outlanders jeer to see they've hit their target. They surge past at close distance. Too close for Hawk's liking. He'd prefer not to see the smug expressions on their ugly faces.

Corbin and Raiden are laughing, not even bothering to keep their spears at the ready.

Grace is seated in her boat, exhausted from her unexpected swim. Her gaze is locked on Ghost and he nods at her, telling her he's okay. She nods back and Hawk looks away, feeling somehow like he's intruded on a private moment meant only for them.

One boat of Outlanders drop their trousers and bend over, showing the Askalans their bare behinds as a final salute, which causes Wren to reach for her slingshot.

"Retreat means retreat," says Dex, pushing her weapon down. "No matter how tempting those targets are."

The Outlanders head into the distance and Hawk draws in a breath as their boat comes to a slow stop, and they sit, bobbing in the vast ocean.

"Can they still see us?" Hawk's dad asks.

"I don't think so," says Sam. "Why?"

"Because now it's time for Plan B." Hawk's father turns and removes an oar that Hawk hadn't even noticed was attached to the hull. He shouldn't be surprised his resourceful father would think of this. "Everyone grab an oar! We're going to take those pasty white asses by surprise!"

"You heard him!" shouts Wren, dislodging an oar of her own. "Everyone who can row, must row!"

Hawk feels a gentle tap on his shoulder.

"Move aside," says Sam. "You're better at rowing than I am. And I'm better at navigating."

Hawk shakes his head. He only has to take one look at

Deniel to know how dangerous it is to sit in this position. It would make Sam a prime target.

"Move aside," Sam says more firmly this time. "Please?"

"Hawk, we need you over here!" his father shouts. "They're saving their spears."

Hawk looks across at the Outlanders and sees that his father is right. They're no longer attacking. They're... moving forward. Not toward them, but to Askala. They haven't even bothered to kill them on their way past.

"No!" Hawk thinks of all the innocent people they left behind. "No!"

"Take me home, Hawk." Sam jostles her way into the seat beside him. "It's time to row."

And as much as it seems like a crazy idea to return to Askala and their certain deaths, Hawk knows there's not one person here who would consider any other option. Except Deniel perhaps, and he's not in any state to make a decision. And Ghost, but his opinion doesn't count given he's practically the enemy anyway.

Hawk brushes his lips against Sam's and rises from his seat. Taking an oar and leaning over the side of the boat, he digs it into the water.

The entire fleet of enemy boats is ahead of them by a distance now, having quite literally left them for dead. The fact that none of them stayed behind shows just how much of a threat they were considered. It also shows how much chance of survival the Outlanders give them.

But if being a Seeker taught Hawk anything, it was that if you don't give up then sometimes you can rise far above anything that's expected of you. Sometimes, you can even beat the odds.

Hawk rows, but it's hard at this angle, given how far away he is from the surface of the water. This vessel was designed to be powered by the wind, not brute strength.

"Mercy, we need your help," Hawk's dad says. "I know you're injured, but do you think you can row?"

"It's not that," she says, holding a folded cloth against Luca's chest. "He's bleeding too much."

"I can row." Dex leaves Deniel's lifeless body to pick up an oar. "He's gone."

"We need everyone to row," says Wren. "Come on, Mercy. The best thing you can do for Luca is get him back to Askala as soon as possible."

"Leave her be." Hawk pulls himself up from the edge of the boat with a frown. "It doesn't matter."

"Of course, it matters!" says Wren. "We're all injured. Mercy's tough."

"No, it really doesn't matter." Hawk points to the bottom of the boat, waiting for them to see what he's just noticed.

They're taking on water.

Fast.

Hawk's dad uses a word Hawk's never heard before as they all drop their oars and rush to the source of the leak.

"This cannot be happening." Mercy looks up from Luca and shakes her head. "Like, is the universe being serious right now? As if we don't have enough going on, and the boat decides to sink!"

Hawk feels a sense of dread slide over him. For once, Mercy's not being overly dramatic. This is beyond disastrous. No wonder the Outlanders hadn't rated their chances of survival.

"We can plug the hole with some of the poison," Sam calls from the rudder.

But there are leaks springing up everywhere with water seeping through the boards like it's fast becoming a sieve.

They'd thought they had more time to prepare for this day. And now it looks like they're going to pay for that lack of preparation with their lives.

Finn picks up a piece of charred sail and waves it at the Outlanders as if they might see. Or care.

"Don't waste your energy," says Wren. "They're not coming back."

"Keep rowing!" shouts Sam, still hanging onto the rudder like it's going to achieve anything. "I have an idea."

"Sammy, it's no use." Dex's eyes fill with tears as he reaches for Wren. "We're miles from land."

"I said *row!*" Sam glares at Dex and Hawk wonders if maybe she's losing her mind.

"Sam, he's right." Hawk goes to her and puts a hand on her shoulder. "Let's not waste the time we have left arguing."

"Do you remember the last time we were stranded in the ocean?" Sam takes Hawk's hand and squeezes it. "And you, Wren?"

Hawk nods, still not sure what she's getting at.

"It was right about here," Sam continues. "I'm certain of it. We're almost in the exact same spot."

"The sandbank," says Wren, launching herself away from Dex to put her oar back in the water. "Everybody row!"

Hawk's heart rate picks up as he smiles at his clever girl. It's only a glimmer of hope she's given them, but it's better than nothing.

His dad groans under the strain of trying to row such a heavy vessel and Hawk goes to the other side of the boat and digs in his oar. At least the water is a little closer now, not requiring him to lean out so far.

Everyone who's still able to row, takes an oar, including Mercy this time. They push forward with new desperation, but it's hard work and each wave that hits only adds to their problems, filling the boat with even more water.

"A leatherskin!" Sam cries, and Hawk sees that a small one's been swept into the boat.

Hawk uses his oar to pick up the squirming fish and throw it back into the sea to join its dozens of hungry siblings.

When he goes to start rowing again, he sees that everyone else has given up. They've set down their oars and are looking at each other in silence.

"We can't row this thing," Hawk's dad says. "I'm sorry. I've let you all down."

"No!" Hawk shouts the word, not wanting his dad to believe this. "This is not your fault."

The water is lapping at their thighs now, the acid already starting to sting. Mercy and Dex are holding Luca's head above water and Hawk hears him groan. He's instantly relieved to realize Luca's still alive, only having to remind himself that it's not going to be for long.

Hawk wades his way over to his father and wraps him in a hug.

"I love you, Dad." He's not sure he's ever said these words and knows he has no time to waste. "You did your best. We all did."

His father hugs him, holding him tightly as he slaps his back. He doesn't tell Hawk he loves him, too, but just like Hawk, he's never been one for a lot of words. The strength of his embrace says everything he needs it to.

"Go to Sam." His father pushes Hawk away. "Go to her."

Hawk swallows. His dad knows where his heart lies. And this just makes Hawk love him even more.

Sam is waiting, her eyes glued to Hawk and her arms outstretched.

If his legs are hurting in this water, she must be in positive agony. And it kills him that there's absolutely nothing he can do to help her.

"Let me try to pick you up," he says, slipping his arms around her.

"Don't, Hawk." She presses herself to him as the water laps at her waist. "Just kiss me."

Hawk leans down and gently kisses her, trying to ignore the sound of imminent death around them. Just for this moment he wants to pretend that he has a future with this beautiful, brave girl. That the children he'd dreamed of could still be born. That the life they'd planned could still exist.

But Sam is shivering in both pain and fear and he can't forget the reality of their situation.

The boat comes to a sudden halt and Hawk is forced apart from Sam as they're launched forward.

"What's going on?" Mercy cries out.

"The sandbank!" Wren shouts. "Hawk! Phee! Quickly, we need to drag up the boat."

"I can't see it." Hawk's father rushes to the bow and leans over.

Wren makes sure Mercy's supporting Luca's head and catapults herself over Hawk's dad straight into the ocean, landing knee deep in the water.

There's a cheer in the boat as hope soars once more.

Hawk and his father follow Wren into the sea and grip the front of the large boat, pulling with all the strength they have left.

But it's too heavy with all the water it's taken on. It remains lodged in the sand, refusing to budge.

"We need to capsize it," says Hawk. "Like we did when we took shelter. Then we can sit on the hull until the tide clears the sand."

Wren nods. "Everyone to the port side!"

The people on the boat look at each other, confused.

"The left!" Wren shouts. "Get over to your left!"

"Come on." Finn is the first to get to the port side and leans out to tilt the boat.

A sharp pain pierces Hawk's shin and he swipes under the water, feeling a slippery creature attached to his leg.

Picking up the juvenile leatherskin, he tosses it as far away as he can, wishing Raiden were still around to use as a target.

The boat leans and Hawk and his father go to the other side to help push it up. At first it feels like a hopeless mission to shift a vessel so large, until the weight shifts just enough to gather some momentum and the boat tips, trapping its passengers underneath the hull with an almighty splash.

Hawk can only hope that Luca has woken up enough by now to be able to support his own head. But he can't worry about him now. Luca has Mercy looking out for him and Hawk knows she'll do whatever it takes to keep him alive.

"We need to get them out!" Hawk shouts, shaking off another leatherskin. Hopefully, there's an air pocket big enough under there to keep the people alive.

His dad groans as they attempt to lift the enormous vessel, managing to drag it a couple of feet up onto the sandbank but unable to do much more.

It's impossible, and just as Hawk's trying to come up with a new plan, Sam appears beside him, followed by Dex. Finn is next, dragging Sam's bucket of poison sap, like it's of any use to them now.

"Mercy needs help with Luca," says Sam pointing to the bow of the boat just as Ghost emerges with Luca in tow. Mercy pops out right after them, and Ghost supports a groggy-looking Luca as he struggles to his feet.

"You might not trust me," says Ghost, seeing the surprised expression on Hawk's face. "But even some Outlanders like to pay their debts."

"I don't trust you," says Hawk. "But, thanks. Luca's one of the good guys."

"I've got him," says Mercy, forcing herself between Ghost and Luca. "You have enough injuries of your own to deal with."

Wren claps her hands. "Let's get this boat up on the sand-bank. Everyone pull together. Now!"

They tug on the boat and Hawk feels relief wash over him as it slides a couple more feet up onto the sand. Hawk helps Mercy get Luca up onto the overturned hull, and soon they're all perched on it, far from safe, but out of the water for now.

An eerie silence falls over them as everyone catches their breath and assesses how badly injured they are. Hawk notices he's not the only one to lose a chunk of skin thanks to a baby leatherskin. There are still dozens of tiny fins swarming in the water.

"There are more of them coming," says Sam, pointing.

Hawk follows her line of sight and sees more fins approaching in even greater numbers.

"Sweet Terra!" Mercy moans. "There are hundreds of them!"

"It's okay," says Wren. "When the tide clears the sand, we'll be safe."

"Wren." Sam's voice is shaky. "There's a problem with that."

"What?" Mercy asks, responding to her mother's name. "Honestly, Sam, I think we've used up our quota of bad luck for today."

"It's just that..." Sam swallows. "Never mind. I'm probably wrong."

Hawk raises a brow. Sam is rarely wrong.

"We need to know," he says. "No matter how bad it is."

"It's just that the tide isn't going out," she explains, biting down on her lip. "It's coming in."

Mercy almost loses her balance on the hull by planting her hands on her hips. "Well, that's just f—"

"Mercy!" Dex scolds.

"Dad!" Mercy glares at her father. "We have bigger things to worry about right now than my language, don't you think? Like the fact that we're all about to die."

Hawk shuffles closer to Sam and she rests her forehead on his chest. "I shouldn't have said anything."

"You had to," he soothes. "We would have realized sooner or later. This gives us time to prepare."

Finn is hanging his head in his hands and Hawk knows he's thinking of Dharma and Relic. He lets out a loud groan of despair.

"Why did you bring the bucket, Finn?" Hawk asks.

"You know why," he says, lifting his head. "We had a bucket similar to this in Fairbanks hidden under one of the tree roots just in case."

Hawk grimaces as understanding dawns on him. "Alina died a horrible death."

Finn nods. "But it was quick."

"Nobody is using that poison on themselves," growls Wren. "Do you understand me? I forbid it. I'll kick your ass if you so much as look at that bucket the wrong way. Giving up is for losers and we haven't lost yet! We fight until the very end."

Silence falls across the group.

"Wren," whispers Dex gently. "We need to accept this could be the very end."

"It isn't." Wren bites down on her lip. "What if we thought that when the lab was burning down? We'd never have found the tunnel. We'd have been charred to a crisp. We fought then and we can fight now."

"But..." Dex doesn't bother to finish whatever it was that he was going to say. He knows Wren well enough to realize he's wasting his breath.

Hawk can't help but agree with Dex. They're sitting on an upturned boat in the middle of nowhere with the tide rising, ready to be fed to a bunch of hungry sharks. And if that's not bad enough, they've just been forced to watch a bunch of savages sail past, intent on taking their home and killing who knows how many of their family members when they get there.

If that's not the very end, then Hawk's not sure what is.

"She's coming back," says Ghost, wincing as he sits up straighter and squints.

"Who?" snaps Wren.

"The Commander." Ghost says this with a mixture of awe and love. "You all underestimate her. She's coming back for us. She would never leave us to die."

"Coming back for you, maybe," Mercy mutters.

"There are two boats." Hawk rubs his eyes then regrets it as they sting.

"We're saved," breathes Finn, loosening his grip on the bucket.

Sam snuggles closer to Hawk and the life he'd wanted to have with her comes back into focus. Which goes to show that no matter how much all might seem lost, there's always hope. It seems that maybe Wren was right. Unless the Outlanders are returning to make sure they're dead...

The boats soar closer, their sails propelling them at speed, and Hawk soon sees it's not Grace returning.

It's Raiden.

Which is a whole different story.

Reminding himself of the thought he'd only just had, he tries to hang onto the hope that had taken up residence in his chest. Raiden may be the last person on this planet he'd choose to rescue them, but he's better than nobody. Even if that's only by a slim margin.

The boats drop their sails and glide forward until they beach on the disappearing sandbank.

There are three men on each boat. All with spears. All looking like they're sniffing at a rotten carcass.

"Don't get too excited," sneers Raiden. "We're here for him."

Hawk frowns, trying to work out who he's talking about.

Raiden points at Ghost. "Not sure what my father wants with him, but he sent me back. Maybe he wants to roast him as part of our victory feast. The leatherskins seemed to think he was delicious."

Ghost shakes his head. "If you want me, then you take all of us."

Hawk's jaw falls open. What is with this guy? Can they trust him, or not? So much about him makes no sense.

"Well, we might be able to make room for my future wife." Raiden licks his lips as he looks at Sam. "But that's it. One passenger on each boat."

"Not a chance!" snaps Sam.

Hawk's hand feels like it's frozen solid on her shoulder. There's no way he can watch Sam go with Raiden! But keeping her here is even worse...

"Go with him," he says in Sam's ear. "Go. You have to."

Sam shakes her head, her gaze still on Raiden. "You have room for all of us. We stick together."

Raiden points at them all, one by one. "Five men. Four women. Not a chance. Our boats were only made for four and we already have three on each. We'll take Sam and the roast dinner. That's my final offer."

Ghost crosses his arms, not budging an inch. "Your father isn't going to be happy when you fail to return with me."

Raiden flinches. It's a slight movement but enough for them to all know Ghost hit a nerve.

"Who knows what he'll do to you," Ghost continues. "A failure for a son."

"He's probably not even his son," Luca mutters.

"What did you say, Bird Boy?" Raiden puffs out his chest.

"Let him fail," says Hawk's father. "Failure is despised in the Outlands."

Hawk notices Raiden's men tighten their grip on their spears, ready to act on Raiden's orders. But for how much longer will he be able to give them orders?

"We'll take the women, then," says Raiden. "And the roast."

Sam. Wren. Mercy. Ghost.

That leaves Hawk, his father, Luca, Dex, and Finn to perish. Not exactly the deal of the century, but it's better than nothing. And at least it keeps Sam safe.

Hawk's about to accept the deal when Ghost speaks.

"No," he says. "You take us all. Or you take none of us."

"The. Boats. Can't. Hold. You. All." Raiden glares at Ghost. "Are you stupid as well as delicious?"

"Let's try it then," says Sam, giving Raiden an encouraging smile.

Hawk hates that she feels the need to do that. But he understands what she's doing. She's even prepared to be nice to this evil creep if it means saving the people she loves.

Sam slides off the side of the boat and Hawk's heart leaps to the back of his throat as he fights the urge to go after her. She's a Seeker. She knows what she's doing. He's learned time and time again not to underestimate her. Their future is in her hands right now. He must trust her.

Sam tilts her head at Raiden. "Let's see how many your boat can hold."

"Fine." Raiden harrumphs, as he nods at the men. "I'll take the women in my boat. You can see how many men fit in the other. I really don't care, just as long as my roast dinner gets a seat."

"I'm not leaving Luca," says Mercy. "He's injured. He needs me."

"Then stay here." Raiden shrugs. "Honestly, you're saying all this like I actually care!"

"We'll take Luca on our boat," says Sam. "Come on, everyone climb down. The water's rising."

Hawk helps Mercy get Luca down from the boat and clenches his fists to stop himself going to Sam.

Raiden and his men push out their boats until they're bobbing in the water and Hawk sees Wren squeeze Dex's hand before climbing aboard Raiden's boat. Mercy goes next, Luca leaning heavily on her for support.

"Not him," says Raiden. "I never said yes."

"But you have room," says Sam, rushing to Luca's other side.

Raiden rolls his eyes. "I suppose the Falcon's a bit of a girl, anyway. Besides, he'll make quite a nice trophy."

With four extra passengers, the boat sits low in the water, but it can hold them as long as the weather doesn't come in unexpectedly. It's a big improvement on balancing on top of an upturned boat. The problem is that it's clear the boat can't hold another person. Which means they're not all going to fit in the second boat. At least one of them is going to have to stay behind.

"Gimme that bucket," says Raiden, pointing to Finn. The way Finn's clutching it, it does look like it might be holding something of value.

Finn looks surprised but goes to Raiden and passes it over. The boat sinks in the water a little more as it's loaded on board. The leatherskins churn the rust-colored water around the boat, getting excited at the movement, while a few larger fins circle at a distance.

"Ouch!" Finn hollers as he pulls a small shark from his ankle.

Sam uses this distraction to hold Hawk's gaze, saying her goodbyes to him in the only way she can.

Hawk tries to let her know he trusts her as he fights the tears at the thought this could be the last time he ever sees her.

The men nod to Ghost, who ushers Dex and Finn ahead of him onto the second boat before he climbs aboard.

It lowers in the water and Hawk looks to his father, seeing that he knows what Hawk already figured out.

Only one of them can go.

"Wait!" shouts Dex, trying to get off the boat as he catches on, but Finn and Ghost hold him back.

"I'm not leaving you," Hawk says to his father. "So, you may as well go."

More leatherskins are approaching now and Hawk knows that ultimately he's not going to be able to fight them off. They want their dinner, and it looks like Hawk is it.

"You *are* leaving me," his father says. "You have your whole life ahead of you. I've lived mine."

Hawk shakes his head.

"Look at Sam," his father says. "She's your future. You're going to live an amazing life."

"I'm not leaving you," Hawk says again, his voice breaking under the strain.

One of the men stands in the boat. "We're leaving both of you in a moment if you don't hurry up."

Hawk looks back to Sam. "I'm sorry!"

She nods at him, not fighting him to change his mind, even though it's clear his decision is breaking her heart. She knows him too well to think he'd ever be able to live in place of his father.

"Hey, Hawk. I forgot to tell you something." His father gives him a wide smile. "I love you, too."

Before Hawk can figure out why he's smiling at a time like this, his father dives directly into the thick school of approaching leatherskins. There's a thrashing in the water as rust turns to scarlet. Hawk stands in mute shock as his dad disappears with nothing but a giant air bubble as evidence that he ever existed.

"Phoenix!" Wren screams, holding her hand over her mouth. "Phoenix!"

Hawk's not sure who leaps from the boat to take hold of him and force him aboard, but he thinks it might be Dex. Maybe it's Finn.

He's not sure of anything, anymore.

All he knows is his dad just sacrificed himself to save Hawk's life.

And now, more than ever, Hawk has to fight to stay alive, so he can make his sacrifice stand for something.

But how can he do that when the sharks aren't only in the ocean? They're in the very boat that's taking them home.

SAM

"To victory!" shouts Raiden, and the Outlanders in both boats cheer as they start rowing. "More food than could ever fill our bellies awaits!"

The boat gains momentum as the sail is hoisted but Sam can't tear her gaze away from Hawk. He sits in the other boat, shocked still by grief after he watched his father sacrifice himself. His gaze finds Sam and her heart constricts painfully. How she wishes she could be with him, comforting him. Trying to muster some small shred of hope.

They're returning to a defeated Askala.

Wren is still as stone as she watches the distance between herself and Dex grow. Mercy is curled around Luca, who barely roused even as he was moved, her hand pressed on his wound. His arm is coated in a thick, red sleeve of blood.

Sam can barely breathe as more emotion than she's ever felt tsunamis through her. They've lost. Not only that, the battle they tried to wage was little more than a short-lived fight. Jagger, Alina, and Deniel died for nothing. Phoenix felt he had no choice but to sacrifice himself so his son could live.

And for what? So they can watch Askala be taken?

She's never felt such anguish. Despair. Hopelessness.

And anger. Raw, burning anger at the unfairness of it all. At the waste. At what their future will look like. If they come out of this alive, every one of their tomorrows will become as desolate as the Outlands.

"Let them go ahead," Raiden instructs the two men in their boat.

Sam's pulse stutters as the men do as they're told, loosening the sail. "What for?"

Raiden turns his gaze on her, his eyes alive with something she doesn't want to name. "Come and sit with me, wife."

Wife. Repulsion churning in her gut, Sam stands on unsteady legs. Mercy's hand reaches out and grabs hers, her tense face telling Sam she doesn't have to go. Sam glances at Raiden, noting the way his body hardens when she doesn't immediately move. Knowing what he's capable of, Sam's about to take a step when his boot lashes out.

It connects with Luca's shoulder, wrenching a moan from him. Mercy gasps, her hand releasing Sam's as she wraps herself around him protectively. Beside her, Wren imperceptibly nods, telling Sam to get moving.

As she makes her way to Raiden at the front of the boat, Sam's body goes cold as she watches Hawk and the others continue ahead. She takes her place beside Raiden, pushing aside the bucket he has by his feet, trying to ignore the way his lips twist up in triumph.

"Take down the sail," Raiden orders, his voice soft, yet somehow full of anticipation.

Alarm morphs to fear, wrapping cold fingers around Sam's heart. "Won't your mother be needing you?"

"She's not my mother," growls Raiden. "I only agreed to come back for that roast dinner because my father asked me to.

Besides, I had something to gain from this, too." He trails a finger down her cheek.

Sam holds herself still as she suppresses a shudder that feels like an earthquake.

Raiden glances over his shoulder, confirming that the other boat is now yards away. They're practically alone, bobbing in the ocean, Askala so close, yet so far away. "The Commander will be happy with how this will turn out."

The threat in Raiden's words is undeniable, but Sam can't figure out what it is. She tries to shake the hold fear has on her. "I'm sure Grace is very proud of you," she assures. Stroking Raiden's ego has always helped.

Raiden's hand grips her jaw painfully, yanking hard so that she's face to face with him. "That woman," he says the word as if it's dirty, "won't be the Commander for much longer." Before Sam can ask what that means, he leans forward. "And once I've had myself a little celebration, we'll return, and I'll show you what our future is going to look like."

He leans forward, his hot, sour breath filling her nostrils. She tries to draw back but he tightens his hold, his thumb digging painfully into her cheek.

"We're going to have a lot of children, Sam." His eyes light up with a sick fire. "Children of the leaders of the Outlands and Askala. Bringing us all together, making us one. Isn't that what you wanted as a Seeker?"

Bile scorches the back of Sam's throat. Yes, Outlanders and Askalans becoming one was her dream. But not like this. Not born on a bed of blood.

Not where choice is stolen. Kindness is forgotten. Where violence reigns.

Another inch and Raiden's lips hover just above hers, ready to seal the future he just painted.

"Kill the bird boy," he states casually, as if he's not talking about murder just before he's going to force her to kiss him.

Sam draws back. "No! Luca!"

But the men are already pushing to their feet, knives in their hands. Mercy and Wren leap up, too, standing over Luca's prone form.

"Stay away from him," Mercy warns.

Raiden barely glances up, leaning forward to cover the space Sam created. "Kill them all. I have what I want."

Sam tries to pull away again, but this time, Raiden's ready. He grabs her by her shoulders, dragging her so she's against his chest. Sam struggles, desperate to get away from him. To help her friends.

"Stop fighting!" Raiden grunts, his arms tightening like vices. "One day you'll smile at me just like you smiled at that loser. You'll be glad you're mine."

Never. What she feels for Hawk is pure light compared to the sick blackness that's clawing up Sam's throat. She turns her head as Raiden's mouth seeks hers, and he painfully jerks it back.

"In time, you'll like it," Raiden mutters darkly.

One of the men grunts. "So, the bitch has a knife, huh?"

Raiden releases Sam and spins around. She looks over and sees what has him stilling and tensing.

Wren is still standing over Luca, brandishing a knife she must've hidden as she sways slightly from side to side. Behind her, Mercy's face is hard with determination. It's clear she'll do what it takes to fight for the man she loves and her mother.

Wren's hand clenches and unclenches around the knife. "I used to be one of you. I know how to kill."

The two men seem to contract, as if they're coiling. Raiden shoves Sam away and stands up. "I'm going to bet we've had a bit more practice." Two steps and he's beside his men. "Only one way to find out, I suppose."

Wren's jaw tenses. Sam's heart thuds painfully, as if her blood is too frozen to move. A mottled-gray fin slices through the water beside the boat, as if the leatherskins sensed that blood is about to be spilled again. The school of juveniles is nowhere to be seen, no doubt chased away by those larger and higher up the food chain.

The men lurch forward, and the boat tips wildly. Wren leaps, but the rocking knocks her off balance. It's all the Outlander in front of her needs. His arm whips across and knocks the knife out of her hand. It sails through the air and lands in the ocean with a *plop*. Maintaining his momentum, he follows through with a fist to her jaw.

Mercy surges forward, ready to protect her mother, but the second Outlander anticipates it. He grabs her and slams her head into his knee, releasing her to crumple over Luca. Wren screeches in rage, but the first man already has a hold of her. He clamps his arms around her, bringing his own knife to her throat.

"Stop!" shouts Sam. "I'll do whatever you want, just let them be."

Raiden spins around, holding his hand up to his men. "Wait," he barks.

He wants to hear what Sam has to offer.

"No, Sam!" says Wren. "You don't know what you're promising."

Sam keeps her gaze on Raiden. She knows exactly what she's committing to. The light leaping and twisting in Raiden's eyes tells her everything she needs to know. She draws up a smile, the process sickening her, but one she doesn't shirk from.

This is what she can do to stop more lives being lost. Lives of those she loves.

"Show me how it will be between us," she says as invitingly as she can, keeping the tremble out of her voice.

It works, because Raiden's nostrils flare as he draws in an excited breath. One stride and he's in front of her.

Sam sits back down heavily, her knees giving out, and he's

right there with her. Every cell in her body rebels at what she has to do, the denial programmed deep in her DNA.

Raiden clasps her face, gentleness an alien concept. Roughly, he jerks her forward. "I told you that you'd learn to enjoy it."

Sam doesn't fight him, waiting for his lips to descend to hers. For his body to curve around her.

"I'm sorry," she whispers.

Sam raises her hands up between them, bringing them to Raiden's face.

"I'm not," he grunts with pleasure.

Those words are all she needs. Sam's hands unclench, the film of sap she coated them with revealing like a black bloom. She slams her palms on Raiden's face, smearing the poison across his cheeks, into his open mouth, and over his eyes.

He jerks back, shoving her roughly. His own hands come to his face, frantically trying to wipe away the smears of betrayal. "What have you done?" he screams.

Sam is frozen with horror. She wishes she could say she had no choice, but that would be a lie. She could've let Raiden kill Luca, Mercy, and Wren. And it wouldn't have stopped there. When they returned to Askala, he would've killed Hawk.

And anyone else who got in his way.

So, Sam chose. She decided she couldn't let that happen. She chose to kill.

Raiden's face flashes bright red, veins protruding along his temples. His breath comes in pants as the pain builds. As the poison destroys him, cell by cell.

His hands drop away, his cheeks already seeping and peeling, his bloodshot eyes full of hatred. "I'm taking you with me."

As the realization of what he means hits her, so does Raiden. His body ploughs into Sam and he tumbles over the side of the boat, dragging her in with him.

The sea engulfs Sam as Raiden's heavy body draws her down. She struggles blindly, her eyes tightly clenched against the acidic water. But Raiden's arms are like a clamp, powered by his determination to drown her.

Sam's lungs spasm as her thrashing body starts to asphyxiate. She continues to buck and twist, even as she knows she's draining her body of oxygen. They sink, the world behind her eyelids becoming darker and darker as she's drawn away from the surface.

As consciousness starts to slip away from her, Sam clings to the images of those she fought for. Hawk. Her family. Askala. She knows she has no regrets.

Suddenly, Raiden releases her. Not only that, he's gone. Sam opens her eyes, jolting at the sting of acid, and sees his body being dragged away by a leatherskin. Another of the deadly predators ploughs into the first, its massive jaws opening as it tries to take a piece of the prey.

Terrified and steadily suffocating, Sam kicks for the surface. The boat seems so far away. The surface unreachable.

There's a flicker of movement from the corner of her eye, but Sam keeps her gaze upward, her face burning. She knows what it is. A leatherskin, maybe several. The other way she'll die if she doesn't make it to the surface.

She weakens with each kick, the water feeling thicker and thicker. It pushes her down, not willing to let her go, encasing her in a cocoon of death. Finally, she stops swimming, her oxygen-starved muscles collapsing. The surface may as well be miles away. Closing her eyes, she tries to accept the inevitable, hoping that unconsciousness will claim her before the sharks.

Something brushes her face, and she jerks back. Thrashing wildly, her hands find nothing. No massive, rough-skinned body. No open mouth trying to devour her. Her arms tangle with something, and with a jolt, Sam realizes it's rope. The moment she grips it, the hemp tightens.

And begins to pull her up.

Mercy and Wren! Sam holds with everything she has, the water rushing past her, flushing her with hope.

She keeps her eyes open, no matter how much it hurts, watching the light above come at her so fast, she wishes she could sob with relief. Only a few more seconds, and her lungs can experience the joy of air again. Above her, hands come into view, reaching over the other in rapid-fire succession.

She's only a few feet from the surface when she hears the muffled screams. Mercy and Wren's faces are blurred, but their panic is undeniable. Sam looks down, dread already clogging her throat.

A leatherskin is powering up from the deep, jaws opening in anticipation of its meal. Terror slams through her, and she instinctively draws up her knees. But the shark is coming fast. Faster than Mercy and Wren can draw her up. Sam's exhausted body will never be able to fight it off.

Wrapping the rope around her wrist, Sam screws her eyes shut. She reaches her other hand out, a futile attempt to stop the predator that sees her as little more than a fish on a hook. Her hand, with whatever traces of poison are left on it, is her only defense.

She feels the moment its jaws clamp around her wrist. Teeth as sharp as blades slice into her skin, wrenching a scream from her empty lungs. The leatherskin shakes its head, throwing her body around like seaweed, a second later spitting it out.

And then she's being hauled out of the water and into the boat. Drawing in great gulps of air, Sam curls up on the timber floor. She can hear Mercy and Wren moving and talking some where above.

"Throw those two bastards overboard," says Wren. "Their bodies will keep the leatherskins busy."

Sam doesn't hear anything else. There's a roaring in her ears. Agony. Her entire arm is on fire.

Looking down at her hand, Sam recoils. It's barely recognizable. The muscles are macerated. Nerve endings shredded. Blood is painted all over the gruesome sight. It's the worst pain she's ever experienced, yet she's strangely numbed to it. Like it's happening at a distance.

"Sam," Luca groans beside her.

She shuffles closer, tucking into his uninjured side. He slips his arm around her. "You're my hero."

The fight drains from Sam's body, and she floats in semiconsciousness. Wren kneels beside her, quickly wrapping up her shredded forearm.

"We need to get back," comes Mercy's voice, tight with worry.

The boat starts moving, but Sam is riding her own wave of pain. It ebbs and flows, distorting time and awareness. She knows there will be no relief from it when they arrive at their destination.

Askala is lost.

Sam's not sure how much time has passed, but the sound of the boat scraping over sand has her rousing.

"We're here," Wren says gently, drawing Sam up.

Leaning heavily, Sam allows Wren to lead her out of the boat and up the beach. Blinking, her blurred vision tells her they've landed away from the main colony, and that Mercy's helping Luca not far away. Sam stumbles, but quickly rights herself. Only one word is powering her now. The only reason she clings to consciousness.

Hawk.

They reach the forest, and Sam allows herself to be led, keeping her eyes closed. She doesn't want to consider what they're about to find. She can't handle any more pain.

"Sweet Terra," Wren breathes.

It's then that Sam realizes they've stopped. She squints, finding they're still in the shadows of the forest, but the beach isn't far away. Mercy and Luca are beside her, just as frozen as Wren.

Shapes slowly form and Sam sees what has a moan of anguish escaping Mercy.

The Outlanders are there with their spears and knives. Sam stares through a haze of pain, her eyes blurred by acid and tears. The people of Askala have been herded onto the beach, clinging to each other in an unidentifiable mass. Sam tries to find her parents, but her eyesight is too damaged. She thinks she sees a glimpse of Hawk's red curls, but she's not sure if it's just wishful thinking.

Her knees give out and she sinks to the sand, cradling her damaged hand. A person separates from the Outlanders, coming to stand in the center of the beach.

"Silence!" they call out and Sam recognizes Grace's voice. "Askala is now ours."

The Outlanders cheer and the sound echoes through Sam's head. They're celebrating the defeat of a peaceful people. They're rejoicing in the destruction they've wrought.

"We want no more bloodshed. Whatever huts are left once we have claimed our new homes, you may have. It is the same with the food and water. If there is enough, you won't starve. If you remain peaceful, you can keep your life."

The whimpering continues, possibly increases, as Sam's people realize what their future will look like. A life filled with hunger and fear and hopelessness.

Another body moves toward Grace and Sam recognizes the bulk and arrogance of Corbin. He stands beside his wife, taking in the Askalans.

"You do not like this offer," he states to someone in the crowd.

"It wasn't an offer," says a woman. "It's a promise of slavery."

Sam draws in a sharp breath as she recognizes her grand-mother's voice. "No, Amity," she moans.

"Bring her here," Corbin demands.

"Corbin," Grace states coldly. "We have won."

But someone drags Amity toward him. Sam blinks, her eyesight steadily clearing as it's washed by the tears streaming down her cheeks.

The Outlander shoves Amity and she stumbles, quickly drawing herself up before Corbin.

"You are everything that we've worked to rid this world of," she spits.

"Corbin—" Grace calls in alarm, her hand flying out.

His movements are short and sharp. He draws a knife out of his belt and slams it into Amity's chest. He withdraws as swiftly as he impaled it and Sam's grandmother crumples, dead before she hits the sand.

Wiping the blood from his knife on his pants, Corbin's head slowly swivels as he addresses the people of Askala. "Future deaths will not be so merciful."

"Step down!" Grace shouts, moving in front of him. "I said there will be no more bloodsh—"

The back of Corbin's hand slams across her face, sending Grace reeling and falling onto the sand. She pushes herself onto all fours. "Stop him!" she shouts to the Outlanders. "I am your Comm—"

Corbin's boot ploughs into her stomach, and a groan rips through Grace. She crumples, rolling onto her side to find Corbin standing over her.

"No one will come to help you," he sneers. "They don't want a weak woman as their leader. They didn't help you when you faked your injuries in the Newlands and they're not going to help you now."

Grace waits, as does everyone else on the beach. But no one moves. Just like when she fell in the ocean, not one Outlander comes to her rescue. Their inaction says it all.

Grace may have led them to victory, but she's now lost

everything. She wasn't savage enough to be the true leader of the Outlands.

Another swift kick, this time to the head, and Grace is unconscious. Possibly dead. Corbin turns back to the people of Askala.

"I am the Commander," he roars, brutality powering his voice. "You have two choices. Leave or die."

MERCY

"*E*nough!" Kian's voice echoes across the beach. "That is enough!"

Mercy flinches to hear the pain etched through each syllable. But she's not surprised. Kian just watched his mother killed in the most heartless way. All because she objected to these savages taking the only home she ever knew. There was no way he could stay silent.

The only thing keeping Mercy sane right now is the knowledge that after so many years of pain, Amity is finally at peace with her beloved Magnus.

Mercy spots her father in the crowd and nudges her mom as she points to him. He's looking out to the water, no doubt waiting for them to arrive in Raiden's boat and wondering why they're taking so long.

Her mom stoops and picks up a small stone, throwing it directly at the back of his head with perfect aim.

Having spent half his life with Mercy's mom, her dad rubs his head but doesn't turn around. He knows exactly who threw it and what it means. Mercy sees his shoulders relax.

His two girls are safe.

For now.

Grace groans from the sand at Corbin's feet and Hawk steps forward. Mercy has to put her hand on Sam's uninjured arm to stop her from running directly to him.

"Just wait," whispers Mercy's mom, leaning out from their position behind a clump of hibiscus plants to scan the crowd.

Sam is even paler than usual after all the blood she lost. She's clutching her injured hand to her chest and Mercy dreads to think what's underneath the old shirt that's holding it together. At least Luca is faring a little better now. He's crouched beside Mercy, looking weak but alert despite the dark circles underneath his worried eyes.

"What's Hawk doing?" Luca whispers. "He should stay back."

Hawk still has the same stunned look on his face that he had when his father dove into the school of leatherskins. But his actions tell Mercy that he's far from defeated.

Walking directly to Grace's motionless body, Hawk scoops her up off the sand and glares at Corbin.

Mercy's heart beats with both pride at her cousin's kindness and fear for his life.

"That's right," sneers Corbin. "Collect my trash, just like the garbage you are. To think I had hopes to make you one of us."

"I'll never be one of you," Hawk chokes out.

"Keep quiet, Hawk," Luca breathes. "Don't do it."

Corbin looks from Hawk to the rest of the crowd as he waves his deadly spear. "You all heard what I said. Leave or die!"

Hawk steps back, cradling Grace in his arms. Those two always had a strange kind of bond. Nothing that was ever a threat to Sam, but Grace had singled Hawk out in the Newlands, attracted to his size and strength. Which makes perfect sense now. It wasn't so much Hawk's love that she'd been seeking—it was his protection.

Grace groans again as she fights to regain consciousness and Hawk turns to walk back into the crowd. Mercy knows Hawk's not leaving. Far from it. But he's not about to tell Corbin that. She leans out from behind the shrub trying to keep him in her line of sight.

"No!" screams Sam, just as Corbin raises his right arm and lets his spear fly.

It hits Hawk in the back of the leg, and he crashes to the sand, still clutching Grace to his chest.

Sam breaks away from their small group and runs toward him. She stumbles before she can reach him, this time out of sheer exhaustion rather than any clumsiness, and Mercy chases after her, catching her just before she hits the ground.

"He's okay," Mercy hisses, trying to keep them both low. "He didn't kill him. He's alive."

"Oh, look who it is!" Corbin turns to them and sniggers. "It's the clever one. And the Falcon's wench. Where's my son? Celebrating in one of your huts? I'm sure you two were able to help him with that."

"Don't tell him what happened," Mercy whispers, knowing how tempting it must be for Sam to wipe that smirk from Corbin's face with the news of his son's death.

"You told Hawk to leave." Sam gets to her feet and hugs her hand to her chest. "And when he did, you threw your spear. You have no honor."

Corbin shrugs as one of his men goes to Hawk and wrenches the spear from his leg.

Hawk grimaces, but he doesn't scream. He doesn't so much as grunt. But his anger is palpable.

The goon returns the spear to Corbin who wipes it on his trousers, screwing up his face like Hawk's blood is an inconvenience.

"He was going the wrong way," says Corbin. "Not my fault."

"Where did you want him to go?" asks Sam, even though Mercy is tugging on her arm, begging her to stay quiet. "Where do you want any of us to go?"

"You can swim," says Corbin, nudging the goon beside him as he laughs. "You can fly. I don't really care, just as long as you get the hell off my island."

Hawk struggles to his feet, lifting Grace with him. He takes another step away from Corbin, limping badly.

Hawk looks at Sam, his eyes brimming with unspoken words. Grace needs the infirmary. So does Hawk. And Sam. And Luca. Probably half of Askala after being rounded up by the Corbin's men. And he wants them to walk out into the ocean?

Not. A. Chance.

Corbin raises his spear again, aiming at Hawk.

"No!" Mercy and Sam cry out, despite being unable to stop it.

Kian leaps forward this time, landing on the spear mid-air and bringing it down before it can do more harm.

"Give that back!" Corbin roars. "How dare you!"

Kian scrambles to his feet, clutching the spear, not pointing it at Corbin, but making no move to return it.

Corbin's men rush at Kian, grabbing him by his arms and dragging him before their Commander. Kian tries to fight them off, but he's outnumbered and it's no use. The spear is torn from his hands and returned to Corbin.

"Dad," Sam yelps.

Mercy puts an arm around her, fearing what they're about to witness, and hoping that Sam's strong enough to cope with it.

Luca stumbles from the trees, just as distressed as Sam to see his father's life at risk. Mercy's heart constricts at the sight of him. Was it really only last night that she'd slept in his arms as they'd whispered to each other of their plans for the future? What she wouldn't give to turn back time and be held by him once more.

Nova also steps out onto the sand and Mercy wonders just how many Askalans are watching from the trees.

Kian is forced to his knees, the goons gripping his hair and forcing him to look at Corbin.

"This is the Commander now," one of them says. "You're not the leader anymore."

"I never was," Kian chokes out. "Every single person here leads Askala. We all take responsibility for the future of our land."

"Well, isn't that sweet?" laughs Corbin. "And foolish. No wonder you were so hopeless in your attack out on that over-sized boat. If you can even call it an attack."

Mercy can hold her anger no longer. It bubbles over until she feels like she's going to burst. Perhaps she already has. And part of it is because Corbin's right. Fighting isn't in their blood. That was why they'd tried to avoid hand-to-hand combat. And their attempt at fighting from a distance had been no better. They simply don't stand a chance.

Unless... An idea lights in Mercy's mind as she scans the frightened faces of those who surround her. Or perhaps it's not so much an idea as it is a feeling. A belief. Some kind of spark that illuminates the only possible path her people have left.

They won't win this war with violence. The only way they can succeed is by using the weapons they know best.

Love.

Solidarity.

Kindness.

And the very virtue that Mercy herself was named after...

"We are peaceful people," Mercy shouts, breaking away from Sam and walking toward Corbin with blood thrumming in her veins. "We fight for the land, but we do it with our hearts and minds, not our fists. We will never leave Askala. If you want to kill us, then you'll need to kill every last one of us."

Mercy raises her shaking hands above her head as she stands beside Kian. Nova positions herself on Kian's other side and does the same.

"I will not fight you," Mercy says. "None of us will fight you. If you wish to kill us then you'll need to look us in the eye while you do it knowing that it didn't have to be like this."

There's a movement behind her and Mercy turns to see the people of Askala crowding in, all with their hands raised. More people step from the trees and walk down to the beach, including a limping Hawk. Sam and Luca stand directly behind Mercy. Just having Luca so close brings her strength. Hawk joins them, and now the four of them are together once more.

"We have no weapons," says Mercy as the people form a ring around the Outlanders. "All we've ever done is live in peace. All we ever want to do is live in peace. We can move Askala forward, together, if you choose to live in peace, too. There's plenty for everyone here. Join us, don't fight us."

"Like Jagger?" says one of the Outlanders, shaking his head. "You pushed him in the water and fed him to the sharks."

"The man who pushed him wasn't one of us." Mercy glances around, looking for Ghost. But he's nowhere to be seen, which is more than a little convenient given the difficulty he seems to have in choosing a side.

"Don't fall for their cunning words," Corbin says to his men as he glances around at the circle of peace he's been enveloped in. "They outnumber us, but each one of us is worth five of them in a fight."

"Except, we're not fighting you, Corbin," Mercy reminds him. "When you look at our faces as you kill us, I want you to think of your sisters, your brothers, your parents, your children... We're no different to any person you've ever loved. You may be Outlanders. We may be Askalans. But we are *all* people. And we wish you no harm."

Mercy swallows, hoping her words are hitting home with at least some of Corbin's men. She knows he's a lost cause, his heart far too cold to ever be melted by reason. But some of his goons flinched at the mention of their families. It's one thing to kill a man in battle, but it's a whole other thing to slay an unarmed person who stands before you with their hands in the air. She's not sure where her plan came from but the entire thing hinges on these men having retained a shred of the humanity they were born with. Which she admits now, is a bit of a risk…

The people of Askala stand firm with their hands in the air and terror in their eyes as they wait. They're trusting Mercy and she feels ill at the thought of it. She has no idea if her plan will work. All she knows is that it's the best hope they have.

"You heard her," growls Corbin. "Kill them all!"

His men raise their spears, flexing their muscles and grunting as they work themselves into the kind of frenzy they'll need to commit the horrors being asked of them.

Sweet Terra. Has she just led them all to a bloodbath?

There's a disturbance just behind the ring of Askalans and Mercy looks away from Corbin, trying to see what's going on. She lets out a small cry when Tarquin breaks through the crowd. She's covered in dirt and her hair is matted into rats' tails, but she has the same determined look as always. She puts her hands in the air and stands beside Mercy.

"No," Mercy sobs, trying to push her back into the crowd. "Stay hidden."

Relic breaks through the circle next, his white hair reflecting the setting sun as he takes up place beside Mercy.

Mercy shakes her head to see this isn't as bad as it gets. All of Askala's children push their way forward.

There's Hawk's sister, Dove, leading her four younger sisters with pride burning in her eyes. Even little Lark has her chubby arms in the air. Mercy swallows to think these girls have just lost their father, then reminds herself that may not be the worst of what might be taken from them tonight. Horror is a black weight in her gut.

"No," breathes Hawk from behind her. "Go back!"

Dozens of brave children form an inner ring to the circle, all standing there in a pose of peaceful defiance. If Mercy could see them from above, it would be like a flower with a large ring of petals on the outside, interlacing in circles until they reach the smaller, more delicate petals in the center.

"They're children," hisses one of Corbin's goons. "I'm not killing no kid. That one there's younger than my own boy."

Hope ignites in Mercy's chest.

Tarquin steps up to Corbin and jams a finger in his chest. "When I was little, I wanted to be fierce."

Mercy inches closer, her heart tearing in two. Tarquin is *still* little.

"But not now," says Tarquin. "Now that I've seen Askala, all I want is to be kind. To have a future. I want to learn how to fix up the land that we all broke. I want to learn how to read. If you kill me now, I'm never gonna learn how to read. And I promised Alyx that I would."

Corbin rolls his eyes. "Your sister was a—"

"Strong, intimidating woman," Tarquin finishes.

Mercy smiles at her correct pronunciation. Alyx would be so proud in so many ways of this incredible girl she raised.

"My son enjoyed killing your sister," Corbin sneers, bending down so his face is close to Tarquin's. "Just like I'm going to enjoy killing you."

"Your son is dead," Sam says from behind them, unable to resist a moment longer. Mercy can't say she blames her after that last comment. "And so is your daughter."

Corbin staggers back as if Sam punched him in the gut. "You're lying."

"We took Charity in and treated her like she was one of our own," says Sam, her voice laced with pain. "And she repaid us by murdering us, including my own brother who never hurt anyone in his life."

"His name was Seb," Luca adds. "He was just a little boy like any of these children here, and she killed him like he meant nothing. She made the wrong choice. You all have the chance now to choose something different."

"What did you do to my son?" Corbin asks, making it clear he has no interest in either Seb, or what became of Charity.

"Raiden tried to kill us," says Mercy, not wanting Sam to admit he died at her hands. "But he fell into the ocean. We couldn't save him."

"Finish them," says Corbin, his nostrils flaring and his eyes wide. "Finish them now!"

The people hold firm with their hands in the air, staring at the men who've been commanded to take their lives.

Lark whimpers and Dove pulls her to her side with one hand, keeping her other quivering hand above her head. Mercy's never seen anything so brave in all her life.

Corbin's men spread out and walk toward the people, but not one of them makes the first move.

"Kill them!" Corbin screeches. "I said kill them, you idiots!"

There's another pause as the men stand frozen in their duty.

"You're not our Commander," the tall man holding Kian says through gritted teeth. "Grace is our Commander and she told us she wants no more bloodshed."

"I am your Commander," Corbin shouts. "And I want you to kill them! Do it now!"

The men look to each other then back at the innocent people before them.

One by one, each man drops his weapon to the ground and puts his hands in the air.

"We answer to Commander Grace," the tall man says.

Mercy lets out a long breath that's cut short by a blood-thirsty scream coming from Corbin.

And suddenly, she's not sure if this is truly over, or if it's only just begun.

LUCA

The moment Corbin moves, so does Luca. He ploughs past his father and mother, ignoring the agony that screams down his arm. Mercy's gasp echoes in his ears as she jolts into action, too.

There's no doubt in Luca's mind where Corbin is going to strike. He'll go for someone vulnerable. Someone young. Someone who can be an example of what he's asking the Outlanders to do.

He'll go for Tarquin.

Tarquin must realize it, too, because she goes to streak away. Except Corbin's too fast. And too furious.

He grabs Tarquin by her matted hair and jerks. Tarquin yelps in pain, her hands coming up to grip Corbin's. Tears sting her eyes as he pulls her against his body, bringing his spear across her throat. One sharp yank backward and Tarquin's neck is painfully stretched as her face bulges.

Uncaring of the consequences, Luca tenses every muscle, ready to plough into Corbin. He knows with only one working arm, he can't stop this monster. But he can buy Tarquin some time, maybe her freedom, and that's all that matters.

Corbin's gaze flares as he registers Luca coming at him. He arcs his spear out wide—something Luca wasn't expecting because it leaves Tarquin free to dart away—and slams it across Luca's injured shoulder.

He crumples, pain exploding through his mind and ricocheting down every nerve. His legs collapse, no longer under his control. Through sheer force of will, he twists as he ploughs into the sand, keeping his gaze desperately on Tarquin.

Maybe this was enough. Corbin no longer has hold of her.

Everything slows. Luca's breathing stops. Time dissolves as the future becomes the present, moment by agonizing moment.

Mercy's rushing forward, her arms outstretched as she tries to get to a terrified Tarquin. Sam stumbles, Hawk catching her before she can fall. Luca's parents are each holding frightened, teary children.

And throughout this whole time, Corbin's spear has continued its arc as if Luca's strike never happened. Like he was simply batting an annoying insect out of the way. Because Corbin's winding up for a far deadlier target.

Tarquin.

The spear slices through the air with a *whoosh* as everyone around Corbin leaps to get out of the way. It arcs high, a clock striking midnight, then begins its lethal descent.

Corbin twists as he brings it down and across. A silent sob catches in Luca's throat as he realizes Tarquin won't get away in time. That the spear is swinging at her head.

Mercy screams. Luca's heart is already shattering.

There's a flurry of movement and Luca wonders if he blinked as he loses sight of Tarquin.

"No!" he cries hoarsely. It was if seeing her meant he was keeping her safe somehow. That impossibly, he could stop this.

Crack. The spear splinters into two as it hits flesh.

It takes breathless moments before Luca's pain-riddled brain finally realizes what happened. Ghost is standing before Corbin, becoming a shield for Tarquin. The spear just snapped across his upper arm.

Moving so fast, Luca sees little more than a blur, one of Ghost's hands slams into Corbin's chest as his other grabs the half-spear Corbin was still holding.

Corbin sails backward and crashes into the sand. He's barely gouged into the soft grains when he's scrabbling to get back up. Every Outlander knows there's no more vulnerable position than being on your back.

But the pointed tip of a spear appears at his throat and he stills. His eyes track upward to find Ghost standing over him.

Luca pushes himself to his feet, finding Mercy by his side before he's upright. She slips under his arm, Tarquin plastering herself to his other side. Then Sam and Hawk are there, Luca's parents not far behind.

By silent agreement, they all turn toward Corbin.

"He's mine," Ghost states flatly, unmoving as he stands over his prize.

Everyone stills, including the wider circles of Outlanders and Askalans. The primal hate in Ghost's words was undeniable.

Corbin's eyes dart left and right. "Kill him," he mutters through heaving breaths.

No one moves. Including the spear pointed at his exposed throat.

"Kill him!" Corbin shouts hoarsely. "I am your Commander!"

But in the same way that the Outlanders didn't try to save Grace, they fail to come to Corbin's rescue.

It appears their loyalties lie with neither of them. Or perhaps whichever one suits them at the time.

"Quiet," Ghost growls.

Corbin freezes. He's no longer facing an injured man. What's more, he's not facing an Askalan. There's a harshness, a ruthlessness, in Ghost that's born within every Outlander.

The crowd parts to Luca's left, and Grace hobbles through the circle of Askalans, then the ring of Outlanders. Her gaze is nowhere but Ghost. His spine seems to take on another level of alert, as if every vertebra just came to attention, as she moves toward him. Although he never takes his eyes off Corbin, Ghost knows Grace is approaching him.

She comes to stand beside him and they both stare at Corbin. Luca wonders if they're aware their breathing just fell into sync.

Corbin's eyes widen as Ghost and Grace stand above him, side by side. "You! I thought you were—"

The tip jabs into the dip below his Adam's apple, a drop of blood appearing. Corbin's eyes flash with a strange mix of disbelief, fear, and fury.

"Enough," says Ghost.

"You've taken too much as it is," adds Grace.

Luca's mind whirls with pain and confusion. There's something passing between these three that he doesn't understand. That he doubts anyone here understands.

Grace lays a hand on Ghost's arm. "This is what we were supposed to end," she says quietly.

In one fluid motion, Ghost nods his agreement then impales the half-spear through Corbin's neck.

Corbin falls back, gurgling and gasping through his blood-filled throat. His body writhes and twitches for long seconds, then goes as still as every person watching the awful death throes. Corbin's body collapses, losing the fight for air and life, and splays on the sand.

Killed by his own broken spear and jagged hatred.

Shocked silence blankets Askala. Luca's arms tighten around Mercy and Tarquin. What happens now? Is it possible this is all over?

Grace's hand slips into Ghost's and their fingers entwine, clenching tightly. They turn slowly to face Luca and the others.

Grace's gaze connects with Kian's. "We surrender and are at your mercy."

A grumble rolls through the Outlanders as they shift uneasily. This isn't what they expected to result from their inaction.

But Luca's father shakes his head. "I am not Askala's leader. And it is the Seekers' forgiveness that you should be asking for."

Luca draws in a sharp breath as Grace and Ghost turn to them. Mercy's hand tightens around his waist while Sam straightens. Hawk draws them both forward so they're standing beside Luca and Mercy.

Grace's lips tip up. "Your courage was always impressive. But it was your hearts that changed everything."

She's right. It was the connections they forged and the love they found.

Ghost nods once, humble but proud all at the same time. Luca realizes it was their bond, the love that no one knew existed, that shaped this outcome just as much as the Seekers.

Mercy glances up at Luca, and although he has no idea what she's about to say, he tells her without words to go ahead. Whatever it is, it'll come from a place of beauty. Her heart.

She looks around at the silent, waiting crowd. "Today, the unexpected happened. Something that seemed impossible." Her blood-streaked, dirt-stained face smiles and softens. "We all won. We're all here, together, forging our future."

Yep. Luca knew she'd ace it.

Hawk nods agreement. "With unity and friendship."

Luca's chest swells with pride. Of course the man of few words would say it so beautifully.

"You are welcome to stay," Sam calls out in a thready but determined voice. "As equals."

"Or you may leave in peace," Luca adds, knowing choices are about to be made.

Everywhere, people turn to look at each other. Outlanders.

Askalans. Every mind trying to picture the tomorrows that were just born.

And then, in the very unison the Seekers just described, a roar of victory explodes across the beach. Fists thrust into the air as the sound rises into the twilight sky, filling it with joy. People jump and dance and hug. For a brief moment, there's no easy distinction between Outlander and Askalan. The lines blur as the same expression of hope lights up their features.

Luca watches, astounded and deeply proud, as several Askalans embrace shocked and suspicious Outlanders. They start to usher them back to the village. At the edge of the crowd, several other Outlanders make their way back to the water and the boats. They'd rather return to the Newlands and the life they've built there.

Beside Luca, Hawk and Sam are already cocooned in their own bubble of celebration and love. Hawk holds her tenderly as he favors his good leg, her damaged hand between their curved bodies, unaware they're portraying everything the future holds.

Just like Sam, there are still wounds to be healed. And yet, they have each other, which means anything is possible.

Luca turns to Mercy. His shoulder aches. His arm has gone numb. They barely survived the battle for the life that now lies before them.

Mercy smiles and slips in close, her hands gently looping around his neck. "It seems we have a future to forge," she says softly.

Luca can barely breathe. His heart, no, his very soul, is bursting with more happiness than any one guy can hold. What long list of tomorrows does he want to build with this beautiful, brave woman?

His head tips down, his lips seeking hers. He pauses a breath away, wanting to savor this moment. "I have a feeling it's going to be everything I never dreamed would be possible."

One where the Falcon and the Peregrine will soar.

Together.

FIVE YEARS LATER

HAWK

*H*awk stands in the middle of the vegetable patch and draws in the fresh air. He's never felt more at peace anywhere than he does right here.

He digs this soil with his own hands.

He plants the seeds.

He lugs water from the wells.

He prunes, he nurtures, he harvests.

And with his efforts, he feeds an entire community.

There's a giggle to his left and Hawk turns to see Lark hiding behind a corn stalk.

Pretending he doesn't see her, he scratches his head.

"Oh, no," he says in a loud voice. "I think there's a giant rabbit trying to eat my corn."

His little sister squeals in delight to see Hawk joining in on her favorite game.

"Let me see." Hawk walks over to the corn stalk, aware of the limp he acquired when Corbin put a spear through his leg. The muscle has never quite recovered. He doubts it ever will. But there's no way he can complain given how much worse Sam fared in the battle for Askala.

Lark leans out from behind the corn stalk and twitches her nose like a rabbit.

"There it is!" cries Hawk. "A giant rabbit!"

Lark takes off and Hawk chases after her, letting her get a few yards away before he scoops her up and swings her high in the air, tossing her over his shoulder.

"Excellent," he says. "Rabbit soup for dinner tonight. I can't wait to find Lark to tell her about it. She loves rabbit soup."

Lark pummels her fists on his back. "Don't cook me! Please, don't cook me!"

"That's strange." Hawk spins around in a circle three times, the motion making Lark laugh uncontrollably. "I swear I thought I heard Lark. Where is she? She must've smelled rabbit soup."

Lark wriggles on his shoulder. "I'm right here!"

Hawk swings his sister forward and catches her, cradling her to his chest as he plants an overly sloppy kiss on her cheek.

She wipes her face even though she's clearly chuffed with the attention.

Hawk's heart aches to remember how his dad used to fuss over his sisters like this. And to think he'd always believed his father favored his sisters, when it was Hawk who he ultimately gave up his life for. Hawk hadn't had time to say any words of goodbye to his dad, but if he had, he'd have promised him that he'd care for his sisters and mother. That he'd do his best to fill the gaping hole left in their lives. An impossible task, really, but he's determined to try.

"Why don't you go and find Starling and Robin," Hawk suggests, as he sets Lark down.

"Because Sam's reading to them." Lark rolls her eyes. "Reading's boring."

"Reading's how we learn new things." Pride swells in Hawk's chest at how seriously Sam's taken on the task of ensuring his sisters grow up knowing as much as they possibly can about the world they live in.

"My brain's full today." Lark huffs dramatically, reminding Hawk of Mercy.

Hawk ruffles Lark's hair. "Then go and find Swan, or maybe Dove."

"They're being boring, too." Lark pouts. "Mom's teaching them how to weave."

"Excellent," says Hawk. "Because if you're not busy, then I could really use your help with weeding the herb garden."

Lark's eyes widen and she takes off before Hawk can stop her.

"Cheeky rabbit!" he calls after her.

Hawk heads over to the herb garden and surveys the plantings. It's not nearly as impressive as the garden in the Oasis with the fertile soil from the enormous fire when the old ship burned down.

But he's not in Askala. He hasn't lived there for years.

The Newlands is his home now.

A twig breaks behind him and Hawk turns around, expecting to see Lark sneaking back.

His heart skips a beat when he sees who it is, and he wonders if Sam will always have that kind of physical effect on him.

Probably, he decides as she goes to him and wraps her arms around his waist.

"I missed you," Sam says, even though they just saw each other that morning.

"I missed you, too." He leans down expectantly.

Sam draws up her arms to his chest as she kisses him. One with a perfectly formed hand, and the other taken by the leatherskin. Hawk's told her a thousand times that she's even more beautiful to him now, but he worries she doesn't believe him. When he looks at her injury, he sees strength and bravery. And there's nothing more beautiful than that.

"I've been reading to your sisters," she says, breaking away. "Robin asked some great questions today. She's very bright."

"Hmmm." Hawk is barely listening as he kisses her again. Each kiss is like the first with her. He'll never get used to the joy of being able to hold her so close.

"Grace left this morning," says Sam, pulling back slightly, seeming distracted. "She said to say goodbye."

Hawk nods. Although not their official leader, Grace shares her time between both Askala and the Newlands, helping to ensure peace remains between the people. The Outlands has proven a little more difficult to tame, but little by little progress is being made.

"Did Ghost go with her?" Hawk asks, his eyes still trained on Sam's lips.

"Of course," Sam giggles. "They're worse than us."

"I remember the first time I set foot in the Newlands." Hawk brings a hand up to Sam's face and strokes her cheek with his thumb. "I was certain I was supposed to live here. Then as Seekers it all fell apart and I thought I was wrong."

"But you weren't wrong," says Sam. "This is exactly where you're meant to be. Where *we're* meant to be."

Hawk nods as he holds Sam close. There had been some challenges when they first settled here, but nothing like when Corbin had been alive. With Grace's help, Hawk and Sam had been able to do all the things they'd tried and failed to do as Seekers, eventually able to bring the rest of Hawk's family here to live, along with a few other Askalans keen for a fresh start.

Without Corbin interfering, it hadn't taken too long for the Newlanders to see the sense in what Hawk and Sam were doing here. Once the vegetable gardens, water wells and pod breeding facility were set up, nobody in the Newlands had to go hungry anymore. The fire in the Round House had been extinguished and the trees allowed to regenerate, providing a home for the rich fauna that makes the Newlands home.

A raven swoops down, landing on the ground just in front of Hawk.

"Another note from Tarquin?" asks Sam, raising an eyebrow.

Ever since Mercy taught Tarquin to read, she's sent a steady stream of ravens to the Newlands, keen to show off her new talent. All signed as the Peregrine, of course. Usually, the notes are addressed to Dove even though Tarquin had sworn she'd rather be friends with boys. Maybe she's grown tired of kicking Relic in the nuts.

"I don't think this one has a note," says Hawk, studying the bird. "It's here for my corn."

"Shoo!" Hawk lets go of Sam to wave his hands at the giant black bird, sending it flying back into the sky.

"That really is the worst scarecrow I've ever seen in my life," laughs Sam as she points to the giant silver statue of Ronan in the middle of the vegetable patch.

"Hey, not all my ideas can be genius." Hawk smiles at the statue of his grandfather that he'd insisted on dragging out here to scare off the birds. Four more ravens are perched on the effigy, one on Ronan's head and the others on his shoulders. Birds' droppings coat the surface, and Hawk often imagines his grandfather's fist shaking at him from the clouds at this show of disrespect.

He'd hate it.

And after all the havoc he wreaked on Askala, that just makes Hawk love this scarecrow even more.

"Why don't we take the rest of the day off?" Sam asks.

Hawk tilts his head. It's not like Sam to want to take a break. She's barely stopped since the day they arrived here.

"What did you have in mind?" He tries to kiss her again.

"Plenty of time for that later." She presses a fingertip to his lips, her promise sending delicious shivers down his spine. "I have a surprise planned for you."

"I really don't like surprises," Hawk says, which is entirely true ever since the Outlanders turned up on their shores well before they were expected.

"Maybe I'll change your mind." Sam steps up on her toes and gives Hawk the kiss he'd been wanting. It's a slow, delicious kiss and he already knows that no matter how long it lasts, it will leave him wanting more.

Maybe she will change his mind about surprises. If anyone can change Hawk's mind about anything, it will be Sam.

No longer his best friend, but his future.

The only girl he's ever loved.

"Okay," he says. "Surprise me."

SAM

*S*am leads Hawk out of the gardens and back to the village. Some people nod and smile as they pass, others are absorbed in their tasks. Building. Growing. Harvesting.

Drawing in a deep breath, Sam tries to calm her fluttering heart. Hawk will like her news. She's sure of it...

They reach the center of the village where the Round House used to be and find Gust's parents busy working on the Community Circle. Liger and Skye straighten as they approach, both wiping sweat from their brows.

"Wow," says Hawk. "It's really coming along."

Liger nods solemnly. Sam's not sure he's smiled much since losing his only sons, Bryan and Gust. "Our boys wanted to make a mark on this world, this is our way of making sure our family does just that."

A woodworker, he's made good progress on a large circular table for the center and chairs for members to sit on. Each piece has been carefully crafted.

Sam's chest aches and warms at the same time. "Gust and

Bryan would be proud." She turns to Skye. "I love how you used *Gaillardias* and *Begoniaceae* to honor their names."

Skye, on the other hand, is a natural at gardening. She was the one who pointed out the ash from the fire that was forever burning in the Round House would provide fertile soil for flowers and shrubs.

She flushes. "Once established, it will make for a very striking display."

"It will be a beautiful place to conduct our community meetings," Sam agrees. A wonderful, living display of the beauty that can bloom after so much pain.

Skye's eyes mist over as Liger slips an arm around her shoulder. They return to their work, intent on making this 'mark' in the Newlands as beautiful as the love they have for their sons. Hawk takes Sam's hand again and they continue on, walking a little closer together. They both know how fulfilling their life is, but neither of them will be forgetting the price that was paid.

Sam glances down at where her left hand should be. The damage from the leatherskin attack had been too vast and too significant to save it. Amputation at the wrist had been the only option. Now, five years down the track, it no longer hurts to look at it. Once she realized she would make the same choice again—kill Raiden to save those she loved—she accepted her new body and the decisions that led to its evolution.

Just like she accepted that the line between Outlander and Askalan had always been a blurry one. She chose to kill, just like many of the people she now lives with.

"You're beautiful," Hawk murmurs huskily.

She looks up, realizing he noticed her looking at her stump. Love fills her, overflowing until it saturates every cell. She knows Hawk is telling her the truth—he loved her differences even before she lost her hand.

She stops to press a lingering kiss on his lips. "I love you, too." Joy bubbles through her veins. "I can't wait to tell you your surprise."

Hawk's lips twist with mock frustration. "I'm getting a little impatient myself."

Sam giggles, almost blurting it out there and then. But a new sound reaches her ears, and her eyes widen. "No," she breathes, her eyes instantly scanning the trees around them.

"What?" Hawk spins around, trying to see what she's looking for. "Is it that raven again?"

Sam shakes her head. "Although, Ronan is as good a scarecrow as he was a Commander." She points to a small, yellow bird high in some branches nearby. Its thready, lisping call trills through the trees again. "It's a wood warbler, from the *Parulidae* family. It's the first one I've sighted!"

"Nice," says Hawk, impressed.

"They're called the butterflies of the bird world," Sam says excitedly. "They feed on insects, which means the ecosystem here has matured enough to support them."

Biodiversity is blooming in the Newlands, as if it's proportionate to the love and contentment that grows within Sam every day.

Hawk chews on his lip. "Are you going to rush off and make a note in those journals of yours?"

Sam schools her face in mock innocence. "Only in the one that records the fauna of the Newlands. You don't mind, do you?"

For a second, he looks like he just swallowed the wood warbler. "Ah, sure. I can wait."

Sam giggles then rolls her eyes. "Then you don't realize how special this surprise is."

Before Hawk can answer, she darts away. "Keep up or you'll miss out!"

"Hey!" he calls, jolting after her.

Sam's laughter joins the songs of the birds above them as she runs. Hawk quickly catches up, but never quite seems to grab her, just like they did when they were children. A couple of Outlanders look at them as they dash past, unsure whether they should smile. They're still getting used to seeing happiness being so openly expressed.

The run is short as Sam reaches her destination, panting as she touches the wall like it was a game of tag. Laughing, Hawk stops beside her, then realizes where they are.

"It's in the apothecary?" he asks, his voice tinged with curiosity. Maybe a hint of relief. He's probably assuming she wants to share her latest herb mix. Although she has found just the right ratio of gooseberry to clove to treat an upset stomach, that's not why they're here.

Sam grins. "It will be."

Hawk's brows scrunch with confusion but she draws him in before he can ask any more questions.

Inside, the timber walls are lined with orderly shelves. On each are neat rows of jars and urns, all clearly labeled with their contents. Sam draws in a deep breath, enjoying the sense of equanimity she always feels when she's in here.

Her small apothecary hut was built by Luca and Hawk. Watching them had been quite fascinating. They'd grumbled and grouched at each other, and yet within half a day, they'd passed tools without the other having to ask for them. They'd taken their breaks together. And they'd grudgingly acknowledged the work the other had done as they'd stood back to survey it.

And the whole time, Hawk had learned all the skills his father would've passed onto him if he'd lived. Luca's years of being Phoenix's shadow means his craftsmanship will live on in his son. And Luca had...well, Luca had belonged. He had Mercy there, touching and brushing any chance she got, along with friends and family. Sam had smiled until she tried to help and was firmly told by both protective males not to over exert herself.

It was that condescending statement that sparked the idea for what Sam's about to show Hawk.

She turns to the table on their left and withdraws a basket from beneath it. Hawk watches her, his handsome face intent— possibly a little cautious—as she withdraws the contents.

Realizing she's suddenly nervous, Sam quickly slips on her invention. The material slides over her stump and she tightens the straps that hold it in place. Choosing the hook attachment, she clicks it into place.

Holding it up, she smiles nervously. "There were five proto- types before I got it right." She holds up several other wooden gadgets. "The attachments are interchangeable, depending on what I need to do. Ghost carved them for me."

Hawk looks at her prosthetic creation with wide eyes. "You made yourself a hand?"

"Well, it's not quite a hand, but it's close."

He blinks. "Have you shown Dex?"

Sam shakes her head. "It was the apparatus he used so he could shoot the bow and arrow that gave me the idea. Next time we visit Askala, I'll show him. He may be happy to continue just as he is."

Dex was her inspiration that life could continue despite the loss of her appendage.

"Anyone else who has a similar challenge might be inter- ested, though," she adds. Sam wasn't the only one to sustain injuries in the battle for Askala.

"But now Dex has a choice." Hawk grins. "You're a genius, Sam!"

He throws his arms around her, squeezing tightly. His embrace pushes her laugh out on a huff.

Pulling back, he marvels at her invention. "Show me every- thing. What will you be able to do now?"

"Ah, well…" Sam flushes. "That wasn't my surprise."

"It wasn't?"

Shaking her head, nervousness hits Sam all over again, except this time, it's more like a tsunami. She swallows, her mouth suddenly dry.

Hawk frowns, as attuned to her as ever. "Sam?"

Drawing in a breath, she places her hands on his shoulders. "You know how we decided we were going to wait to have children? Because we wanted to focus on establishing the community here?"

Once they'd agreed, Sam had created a special mix of herbs to stop her monthly cycle.

Stilling, Hawk's gaze sharpens. "Yes."

"Well…"

Sweet Terra. She was so sure this was going to be good news. But they never discussed this…

He grips her shoulders. "You think it's time we tried for a baby?"

Sam swallows again. "It's too late for that."

"What?"

The excitement falls from Hawk's face and Sam rushes to reassure him.

"We can't try for a child. I—"

Hawk steps back, unable to hide the disappointment in the same way he did when she pretended she wasn't going to reveal her surprise.

"Oh. Well, I'm sure we'll be able to…" His voice fades away, leaving nothing but anguish hanging in the sweet smelling air.

Sam jams her hands in her hair. She's really messing this up.

"No, what I'm trying to say is, the contraception failed. I'm pregnant."

Hawk gapes. "You're…pregnant?" he whispers.

Sam's hands drop to her sides as she nods. "Yes. I'm pregnant."

This time, when Hawk grabs her, he lifts her high and spins her around. They twirl and whirl as he whoops and she laughs, their joy a flurry around them.

Hawk slows, his face bathed with equal parts shock and delight. "But, how?"

"Mother Nature overruled us," Sam says with a shrug. "It seems it was time."

"This is the best surprise, ever," Hawk says with so much feeling, laughter bubbles through Sam all over again.

"A beautiful child," she whispers with awe. "With your red curls."

"And your bright mind."

"And your gentle soul," Sam shoots right back.

Hawk's gaze simultaneously brightens and softens. "And your quiet courage and unfailing faith and fierce determination." He draws in a sharp, happy breath. "If it's a boy, we'll call him Phoenix."

"Yes! If it's a girl"—Sam angles her head in thought, wondering if she should mention she's sure it's going to be a girl —"we'll call her Cormorant."

Hawk blinks and stills. Sam waits with her breath held. The name fits beautifully with his family's tradition of using bird names. If she didn't know him better, she'd think he didn't like it.

Shaking his head, he laughs and picks her up to spin her again. Sam's about to join him in his joy when she grips his shoulders as a wave of turbulent nausea whirls through her gut.

Hawk stops, suddenly serious. "You're feeling sick, aren't you? Do you need to sit down? Here, let me get you a chair."

He tries to move, but Sam just holds tighter, glad she has the hook attachment on her prosthetic. "One of the attachments I made is shaped like a club. It's in case you, or anyone else, gets too overprotective..."

Hawk jerks to a stop as a grin that could reach all the way to

Askala spreads across his handsome features. He wraps his arms around her again and rests his forehead on hers.

"I wish I had the words to tell you how happy I'm feeling right now..." he says softly. Almost achingly.

Sam clasps his face. "You don't need to, Hawk. Everything we have says it all."

The family they've built in the Newlands, or Newskala as Sam likes to think of it.

The deep connections that reach all the way to Askala.

The love that's so strong, it's a living, breathing bond between them.

And now, in the precious family that they're building.

"I love you, Sam," Hawk breathes.

Caressing the face so full of tenderness, it takes Sam's breath away, she pushes up until her lips are a hair's breadth away from his.

"I love you, too, Hawk. Just like I'll love our daughter."

Little baby Cormorant.

MERCY

*M*ercy looks up from the pod barrel as Luca walks into the breeding center, her heart swelling with love.

"How did you know I needed to see that face?" she asks, beckoning him to come closer.

He goes to her and gives her a tender kiss. She presses up on her toes in an attempt to turn the kiss into something a little more risqué, but Luca pulls back and rubs his nose against hers.

"How's our baby?" he asks, pressing his palms against her swollen belly.

"Never mind the baby!" Mercy throws out her hands. "I feel like a polar grizzly has taken up residence inside me. I swear this is the most enormous baby on the face of the earth. She's huge!"

"She?" Luca tilts his head. "You said *he* the last time you were pregnant, and Hope is definitely not a boy."

Mercy smiles at the thought of their daughter who likes to wear flowers in her hair and twirl around in circles, making her dress fly out like she's a fairy. Mercy's mom has been doing her best to turn Hope into more of a tomboy, but so far this seems to be having the opposite effect, much to Mercy's dad's amusement.

"I'm used to saying *she*." Mercy gives Luca a tired grin. "I'll just be happy to get this baby out, no matter what it is."

"Even if it's a polar grizzly?" Luca pulls his face into an expression of mock horror.

Mercy laughs. "You know what I mean. I'm too busy to have to waddle around like this. It's slowing me down."

"But I like you like this." Luca trails his fingertips down Mercy's cheek. "It makes it so much more difficult for you to run away from me."

"Since when have I ever tried to run away from you?" Mercy steps up on her toes again and this time Luca kisses her with the kind of passion that got her into this situation in the first place.

"Warning! Children present!" cries Tarquin from the doorway. "Time to stop being gross."

"I thought you were looking after Hope." Luca breaks away from Mercy and puts out his hand to Tarquin.

She skips over and tucks herself under Luca's arm like she was born to fit right there.

"Hope's having a tea party with Relic and Annabel," she says, fiddling with the blue diamond that she never removes from around her neck.

"You didn't feel like any tea?" asks Mercy. "That was my favorite game as a child."

"Tea parties are for girls." Tarquin rolls her eyes. "And Relic."

Mercy and Luca look at each other and laugh, wondering what exactly Tarquin thinks she is.

"I came to help with the pods." Tarquin picks up one of the nets and starts expertly scooping out the excess phytoplankton floating on top of the tanks.

Kian taught Mercy everything he knows about pods and now it's Tarquin's turn to learn. She's proven to be an invaluable help. Between Kian, Mercy and Tarquin, Askala's breeding center is a hive of activity. So much so that they were able to transfer some of their equipment to the Newlands to help Sam and Hawk get started.

"Shouldn't you be working on our house?" Tarquin lifts a brow at Luca. "Because I'm not sharing my room with another sister. Or a brother. Actually, maybe a brother would be okay."

Luca lets out a breath. "I was just taking a rest, Miss Bossy Boots."

"Good." Tarquin rewards him with a smile. "Because there's still a lot of work to do."

"It's almost finished," says Mercy. "Be patient."

What started as the little shack where Mercy and Luca used to sneak away during the night has now become their home. Luca extended and transformed it beautifully as their family grew to include Tarquin and Hope. And now he's working on it again to make room for their new addition—who had better hurry up and arrive before Mercy explodes!

Mercy makes a mental note to ask Sam about those herbs she takes to stop her cycles. There's no way she wants to end up like Hawk's mom with seventeen thousand daughters hanging onto her skirt. There's also no way she'll ever be able to keep her hands off Luca to stop that from happening. She needs some magic herbs. Stat.

"Don't forget we have the leaders' meeting soon," she reminds Luca.

"Oh." He slaps his forehead. "I did forget. Sorry, Tarquin, your new bedroom will have to wait."

Tarquin drops the net on the floor, leaving a puddle of phytoplankton at her feet. "What did you just say?"

Luca grins. "I said *your* bedroom. You didn't think I was building it for the baby, did you?"

"But…" Tarquin blinks back tears. "But the baby is your real baby and I'm just—"

"Our daughter," Mercy finishes. "Just as much as Hope is. Or any other child we might have."

"Do you really mean that?" Tarquin's voice breaks.

Luca goes to Tarquin and wraps her in a hug. "Of course, we mean that. And do you want to know what makes you extra special?"

"What?" A smile creeps across Tarquin's lips.

"We chose you," he says. "Just like Nova and Kian chose me."

Mercy nods, even though she's well aware that Tarquin chose them. But she wouldn't have it any other way.

"I'm going to love my new bedroom." Tarquin wriggles away to get back to her work with the pods. "Thanks, Luca."

"My pleasure." Luca looks at Mercy and smiles.

She nods, as proud of him right now as she's always been. He's not only the hottest guy she's ever seen, he's also the best dad.

"What's a cormorant?" Tarquin asks.

"They're a large bird that lives near the ocean," says Mercy, remembering Sam pointing one out in a book she used to read her as a child. For some reason, Sam was always fascinated by them. She often said they were her favorite bird. "Why do you ask?"

"Do you think it's a good name for a baby girl?" Tarquin has a strange expression on her face. The sort she uses when she's trying to keep a secret, which is definitely not one of Tarquin's talents.

"It's...different," says Mercy, carefully. "Has someone in Askala called their daughter Cormorant?"

Tarquin shakes her head, concentrating intently on the tank of pods she's moved to. "I just wondered. That's all."

Mercy looks to Luca who shrugs. Deciding not to push the issue, she lets it go for now. Whatever it is that Tarquin wants to tell them, she'll do it in her own time.

"We'd better get to this meeting," says Luca. "Are you going to come, Tarquin?"

She shakes her head, that strange expression creeping back on her face. "I need to reply to Dove. I got a raven from her this morning."

"Everything okay in the Newlands?" Mercy asks, refusing to call it Newskala, like Sam has taken to doing. She sure has some strange ideas sometimes.

Tarquin nods. "It's all good in the hood."

Luca chuckles as he pulls Mercy close. "We'll find out later," he whispers in her ear.

"Stay out of trouble," says Mercy, ruffling Tarquin's hair as they turn to leave. "I don't like leaving you here on your own."

"I'm not a baby!" Tarquin scowls. "Besides, Annabel said she was going to come here when she was done drinking tea. She wants to learn how to measure temperatures."

"Great." Mercy's pleased to hear this. Annabel has been a marvelous help, always so keen to get involved in everything they do. It's hard to remember a time when she didn't live here, she's become so much a part of the fabric of Askala.

The walk to the Oasis gardens is slower than Mercy would like with this giant baby pressing against her ribs, but she does her best to keep up a decent pace.

"Hey, slow down." Luca takes her hand. "It doesn't matter if we're a little late."

"I'm okay," she tells him, trying not to puff.

"Mercy, the days of trying to prove yourself are long gone." He tugs on her hand. "Just slow down. You do too much."

She lets out a sigh, knowing he's right. She used to worry she'd never find her place in Askala. But it turns out she needn't have been concerned. Her life has turned out quite the opposite. With her work at the breeding center as well as looking after Hope and Tarquin, she barely has a moment left to think. She's also been spending more and more time with the other leaders so she can learn from them. It seems that since she delivered that speech on the beach to Corbin, she's somewhat respected around here. People actually ask her for advice, which is totally weird. She's just making life up as she goes like anyone else.

The leaders' meeting is just about to start when they arrive. Kian no longer speaks first at the meetings. Sometimes he doesn't speak at all, as if determined to prove he's no more the leader than anyone else.

"Oh, good you're here," says Nova. She has a sparkle in her eye and Mercy wonders if everyone around here has a secret today. "We were waiting for you."

Mercy opens her mouth to ask if anyone has happened to notice that she has a baby the size of Jupiter inside her, when Luca jumps in.

"It was my fault," he says. "I forgot. We got here as soon as we could."

"Not to worry," says Kian. "Sit down. We have news to share."

Luca puts a gentle hand on Mercy's back as she does her best to perch on a stool that seems to have been designed for only one butt cheek.

Mercy's dad raises an eyebrow at her from the other side of the table. She nods at him to let him know she's okay.

"We received a raven this morning," says Nova, unable to wait another moment before starting the meeting.

"Is this the one from Dove to Tarquin?" Luca asks.

Nova shakes her head. "No, a different one. From Sam and Hawk."

"Just tell them," laughs Kian. "You've been waiting all morning."

"The Newlands is going to have its first Askalan baby." Nova clasps Kian's hand and beams at the group gathered around the table. "More to the point, Sam and Hawk are going to have their first baby. She's pregnant!"

Mercy's eyes widen. So much for Sam's special herbs to stop her cycles! It looks like Mercy's destined to have seventeen thousand daughters after all.

"That's wonderful news," says Luca, beaming. "My first niece or nephew."

"Kian and I will be making a short trip to the Newlands to check on her health," says Nova. "We'll leave this afternoon."

"I wonder what they'll call the baby," says Mercy's mom. "I mean, if Hawk will follow tradition and use a bird's name."

"Sparrow or Teal are both nice choices," says Nova, unable to wipe the smile from her face. "But I guess that's up to them."

Mercy suppresses a giggle as she puts together the pieces of what Tarquin was trying not to tell them in the breeding center.

Cormorant.

Sam's favorite bird.

Dove must have told Tarquin in the note she sent her that's what Sam plans to call the baby if it's a girl. Only Sam could come up with a name like that!

"What's so funny?" Kian asks, leaning forward.

"Oh, nothing," says Mercy, deciding it's best they hear the name from Sam herself.

Besides, what does it matter anyway? It's only a name and this baby represents so much more than that.

This child will grow up as a symbol of what can happen when two rival factions decide to make peace instead of declaring war. How the land can be healed along with the hearts of the people who depend on it for survival.

And that's exactly why every person around this table is smiling.

They did it.

Askala is safe once more and the lungs of the Earth continue to breathe.

Mercy looks to Luca as a familiar cramp grips her center.

"Nova," she squeaks. "Before you go to Sam, I think I might need your help."

"What's wrong?" Luca slides off his stool and squats in front of Mercy, gripping her hands.

"Our baby's coming." Mercy's eyes fill with tears as she prepares for what lies ahead. Her own little symbol of what's possible when two people love each other so much they don't let anything stand in the way.

Luca breaks into a wide grin. "I love you, Mercy."

She swats him over the head. "I love you, too. But if you ever do this to me again, I'm going to kill you."

"Are you sure about that?" He reaches up and tucks a lock of her hair behind her ear.

"I've never been more sure about anything in my whole entire life." She rubs her belly as another cramp takes hold.

Luca gives her one of those megawatt smiles that she knows he saves only for her and she groans, trying not to get hypnotized by that face of his.

Yep, she's a lost cause.

Seventeen thousand daughters, here she comes…

LUCA

There are few things that truly scare Luca. Dizzying heights used to be welcome. Impossible tasks were a challenge he sought out. It's why the Falcon was born. Luca lived like he had nothing to lose.

But, now, everything's changed.

And the woman inside the hut, screaming like she's being cleaved in two, is responsible for all that.

"Luca!" she hollers. "Why would you do this to me?"

He winces. "Did you want me to come in? I could rub your back?"

"Stay the hell away from me! Never touch me again!"

Luca resigns himself to pace again. Hope's birth was the same. Mercy demanding him by her side. Mercy kicking him out a few moments later. And each time, he did as he was told. Luca's never seen anything as tortuous as childbirth, and if the woman he loves wants him in and out like a puppet on a string, then so be it.

"Mommy's screaming really loud."

Luca's head snaps up to find his daughter coming down the path. Her dark hair is braided with flowers entwined through the strands, her top and skirt immaculate in ways Luca's clothing never was. She's holding a bunch of scraggly daisies as she skips toward him, acting like the hollers from within the hut aren't shaking the leaves above them.

"You're supposed to be with Aunty—"

"She told me she was going to pick flowers for when the baby came," Grace says wryly, appearing from the trees. "And she didn't come back."

Hope smiles as she flutters her lashes at Grace. "I forgot to tell you I wanted to bring the flowers straight here."

Luca chuckles. His daughter might look and act like a princess, but she's just as cunning and clever as the Falcon and Peregrine ever were.

Grace plants her hands on her hips, but her own smile is dancing along her lips. "That must've slipped your mind." She holds her hand out, face soft with patient exasperation. "Come on, you know we'll get called when the baby is born."

Even Mercy agreed it might be best for Hope to stay away while she gave birth...as loudly as she does.

But Hope wraps her arms around Luca's leg. "I want to be here. With Daddy."

Daddy.

Luca never imagined it was a label he'd be gifted with. Nor did he realize what the word would do each time he hears it, wrapping around his heart and squeezing it tight.

Hope looks up at him, eyes round and pleading. He sighs, acknowledging he's never been good at saying no to her mother when she looks at him like that.

"She can stay with me."

Grace glances at the wall of the hut as if she wonders how it's still standing. "It might be scary, Hope."

Hope puffs out her chest. "I'm a fierce woman," she announces. "Just like Mommy and Tarquin."

Grace raises an amused brow as she glances at Luca. "I think she might be fine. Let me know when my next nephew or niece is born." With a shake of her head, she heads back down the path.

"Love you, Aunty Grace!" Hope calls after her.

Technically, she's Hope's great aunt. Because Luca's mother was Grace's older sister.

The memory of the day he finally found out the truth is branded brightly in Luca's mind. It had been the day after the battle. Askalans and Outlanders were walking around a little dazed, both grateful that more blood hadn't been shed, yet grieving for those who'd lost their lives.

Grace had approached Luca, Ghost beside her. Luca had tensed at the tight expression on her face, and Mercy must've sensed something too, because she'd clasped his hand as she'd moved in closer to him.

"We...just wanted to thank you," Grace had started haltingly. "We see now that we did so much wrong."

But Luca had stopped her, not wanting to go over the painful memories. "You did what was right in the end, and that's what matters."

Grace's eyes had flashed at being interrupted, a flicker of the Commander still alive in her. "Which is why I wanted to tell you the truth."

Luca had stilled. There was only one truth left for him to learn.

Ghost had nodded. "We knew your mother and father."

Luca was glad Mercy was there, holding his hand, because his knees had gone weak. "Tell me," he'd whispered.

Grace had glanced at Ghost before drawing in a deep breath. "Grace was my older sister. She fell in love with a warrior from another village."

"The man who taught me how to carve," Ghost had added. "He died a warrior's death trying to make sure you were okay. He was very proud of you."

"My sister also died not long after giving birth to you." Grace shrugged with a sad smile. "It wasn't until years later that I found out she'd left you to be raised in Fairbanks. She knew it was your best chance of survival."

Luca had stood there, stunned, breath coming in shallow gulps.

Her eyes had become moist. "Your parents loved you, Luca. It broke their hearts to leave you, but it turns out it was the greatest gift they could've given you."

Mercy's brow had scrunched a little. "Why did you take your sister's name?"

Grace had looked away. "I was determined to live the life she couldn't. I took on her name to honor her."

"Daddy, is Mommy okay?"

Hope's worried voice brings Luca back to the present. The fact that his own mother died shortly after childbirth is weighing heavily on his mind, but he can't let his daughter see that. He squats down and she tucks herself between his legs.

He tugs one of her braids. "Actually, your mom screamed louder when she was giving birth to you."

Which is the truth. Even though their hut is slightly away from the village, Luca's father came to check if everything was okay,...twice.

Hope's eyes widen. "She's screaming louder than Kozue did when she was giving birth."

Luca nods.

"And Dharma."

"Having a baby hurts a lot, but like you said, Mommy is one fierce woman."

Hope chews her lip as she considers this. Suddenly, her face brightens. "Well, she did help save Askala."

"She really did."

Right after she saved Luca—by teaching him the power that comes from purpose. From love.

Another scream assaults their ears and Luca hides his wince. "It's almost over," he murmurs, unsure whether he's comforting himself or his daughter.

"Luca!" Mercy wails. "I need you!"

Luca shoots to his feet, torn as to what to do with Hope. He'll need to ask her to stay out here. If his panicked brain had the space to think, he'd try to send her on an errand.

But before he can talk, Hope rushes to the door. "Quick, Daddy! My flowers will help."

She holds up the wilted bunch of daisies, her face anxious. Not knowing if he's doing the right thing, Luca enters, not having the heart to say no.

Inside, Mercy is red-faced and panting as she lays on the bed. Wren is kneeling in front of her drawn up legs, while Luca's mom is wringing a cloth in a bowl of water at a nearby table.

Hope skips to her mother and sits on the pillow beside her head. "Here Mommy, I'll fix your hair." Without waiting for an answer, she gently combs back the damp strands, preparing to weave flowers through them.

Mercy's face unwinds a notch. "Thank you, sweetie."

Luca stumbles to his knees beside them, taking Mercy's hand. "You're doing so good."

Her breath coming in gasps, Mercy turns her sweat-soaked face toward him. "It hurts, Luca!"

"I know, honey," he soothes, hating the feeling of helplessness. "I'm here."

"Push," says Wren.

Mercy scowls at her mother. "I did the last five times you told me to!"

"Push again," Wren encourages.

Mercy's whole body contracts as she has no choice but to do exactly that. Luca feels the tightly wound tension in the muscles of her arm as she strains, sees the cords in every joint jump out in sharp relief.

The seconds seem to draw out interminably. Mercy's face scrunches tighter and tighter as her skin flushes red. Luca's frozen with anticipation and pulse-stopping fear.

Wren gasps and a second later, a new wail fills the hut. A sweet, fragile sound that signals the entrance of a new life into the world.

Wren quickly passes the slick bundle to Mercy, who takes her child with trembling arms. She draws the baby closer, the pain of a second ago already forgotten.

"A boy," she breathes in wonder. "Luca, we have a son."

Luca's lost the ability to move. He stares at the miracle, a thick shock of dark hair plastered to his skull, as the baby contentedly falls silent. "He's beautiful."

"Tarquin wanted a little brother!" Hope chirps with joy, throwing the remaining flowers high in the air.

As the daisies rain down, the baby nuzzles Mercy and she melts another few degrees. "He really is beautiful." She looks up at Luca. "I have an idea for a name."

Luca waits. Right now, his dazzled brain can't even remember which ones they decided on. He stills as he realizes she's talking as if this name was never on that list...

Mercy's arms tighten around their son, her eyes blazing with happiness. "Falcon."

Luca can already hear Hawk's chuckle, but it doesn't bother him. One, Hawk might be having a daughter named Cormorant yet, which affords Luca his own chuckle. And two, they stopped being rivals long ago. In fact, Luca likes the idea that the name Falcon links their two families even more strongly.

Actually...

"I love it."

Mercy's exhausted features mold into a sweet, soft smile. She strokes their son's dark hair. "Me, too." She lifts her arms. "Here."

Tenderly, his heart aching it's so full of love, Luca takes his son. Falcon. Skin crinkled and red, he blinks up at Luca, his dark eyes solemn as he stretches. A tiny hand clamps around his father's finger.

Luca's smile feels like it just reached straight down to his soul.

Falcon's mouth begins to work, and Luca quickly recognizes the sign for what it is. He passes his son back to Mercy. "He's getting hungry."

As Mercy sets about nursing their child, cooing contentedly, a movement in the doorway catches Luca's attention.

Tarquin is standing at the door, unsure whether she can enter. Wordlessly, Luca opens his arms, and she rushes forward. She tucks in beside Hope, and they all gaze down at the newest addition to their family. Soft breaths and whispered words of wonder fill the hut.

Luca's conscious of Wren and his mom hovering, their hands clasped to their chests. Dex will be here soon, as will Luca's father. And Thea and Avis. Each a concentric circle of love around them.

But it won't stop there. Beyond that, will be the community of Askala, now far more diverse than it's ever been. And over the ocean, are Sam and Hawk and their budding family, along with the Outlanders and Askalans who now call the Newlands home.

Each and every one of them the center of their own circle.

Luca's never felt so connected. So whole. So...happy.

He's never wanted to stay still as much as he does in this one single moment. And all the others that will come after it.

He presses a kiss to Mercy's flushed cheek. "You're amazing."

She leans her head against his shoulder, sighing with contentment. "It takes two to make something this incredible."

Wrapping his arms around Mercy and Tarquin and Hope and Falcon, Luca has to tell himself not to squeeze too tight. "Do you know what would make it really awesome?"

Mercy looks at him, her eyes brimming with a glorious mix of love, humor, and suspicion. "What?"

Luca grins. "Twins."

THE END
Ready for the next installment in The Thaw Chronicles?
Check out Book 9, TOURNAMENTS OF THAW, now!
http://mybook.to/TournamentsThaw

BOOK NINE - TOURNAMENTS OF THAW

Four teens. Seven tournaments. One survivor.

The Outlands are a deadly place to grow up. In a world devastated by global warming, resources are scarce. Humanity and kindness are even scarcer. The struggle to survive is a deadly war. And a bitter one.

Because great riches lie just over the waters. There's one place that has everything the Outlanders could ever want.

Askala.

But to seize power, they'll need to unite the factions. And choose a leader. Only the strongest will succeed. The one person who can do what needs to be done—attack Askala and share in their riches.

The Tournaments are announced. Deadly games where there can be only one winner.

No one expects siblings to enter...let alone two sets of twins. Lexis and Raze. Born to rule, trained to win. Winter and Gray. Born to poverty, expected to lose.

In a world where survival comes first, there's no room for mercy. Loyalty. Or love. And yet four teens are going to have to choose what matters most.

Let the Tournaments of Thaw begin.

Lovers of Divergent and The Hunger Games will be blown away by this latest epic dystopian adventure brought to you by USA Today best-seller Tamar Sloan and award-winner Heidi Catherine, authors of the smash hit series, The Thaw Chronicles.

Grab your copy now!
http://mybook.to/TournamentsThaw

WANT TO STAY IN TOUCH?

If you'd like to be the first for to hear all the news from Tamar and Heidi, be sure to sign up to our newsletter. Subscribers receive bonus content, early cover reveals and sneaky snippets of upcoming books. We'd love you to join us!

SIGN UP HERE:

https://sendfox.com/tamarandheidi

ABOUT THE AUTHORS

Tamar Sloan hasn't decided whether she's a psychologist who loves writing, or a writer with a lifelong fascination with psychology. She must have been someone pretty awesome in a previous life (past life regression indicated a Care Bear), because she gets to do both. When not reading, writing or working with teens, Tamar can be found with her husband and two children enjoying country life in their small slice of the Australian bush.

Heidi Catherine loves the way her books give her the opportunity to escape into worlds vastly different to her own life in the burbs. While she quite enjoys killing her characters (especially the awful ones), she promises she's far better behaved in real life. Other than writing and reading, Heidi's current obsessions include watching far too much reality TV with the excuse that it's research for her books.

MORE SERIES TO FALL IN LOVE WITH...

ALSO BY TAMAR SLOAN AND HEIDI CATHERINE

The Sovereign Code

Elemental Games

ALSO BY TAMAR SLOAN

Keepers of the Grail

Keepers of the Light

Keepers of the Chalice

Keepers of Excalibur

Zodiac Guardians

Descendants of the Gods

Prime Prophecy

ALSO BY HEIDI CATHERINE

The Kingdoms of Evernow

The Soulweaver